The Impossible Mission

Mission

(Book 3)

Ilona Hawkins

TSL Publications

First published in Great Britain in 2021
By TSL Publications, Rickmansworth

ISBN / 978-1-914245-12-1

Cover image by Jonathan Kandolo

Author's Note

I have used the known planets as a backdrop to my story. Please bear in mind that this is a work of fiction and therefore not really an indication of the atmosphere, etc of each planet.

CHAPTER 1

Craig Carter was asleep in his spacecraft after having just completed a particularly tiring mission for his boss, Commander Simms, and he was presently on course for Earth.

Suddenly his dreams were interrupted by a vision, which formed in his mind.

"Craig Carter, I need your help!" The voice begged. "You don't know me, but I'm one of Tanus' subjects. She's in terrible trouble and has requested that I contact you on her behalf. She's in the clutches of Andocia, whom you have already met, and she was captured by a subtle plot. It was her wish that you search for her, but it will be a trying and dangerous time for you. Tanus was very reluctant to ask this of you, but you are her last hope and she doesn't know where else to turn. If you decide not to do this though, my mistress will not hold it against you. However, if you decide to help us, she will be eternally grateful to you. I've been asked to allow you to think about this on the way back to Earth. I will contact you again when you have landed safely and spoken this over with your boss. It won't be an easy mission, but you must persevere. To help you on your journey, you'll find a ring of solid gold, with a white stone set into it beside your bed when you wake up. It has magical properties and you must take very good care of it. Good luck, Craig Carter ..."

The voice faded away and Craig slept on. When he awoke his gaze fell on the ring, which dazzled him as the glow from his ship's lights reflected in it.

"So, it wasn't my imagination; I really did see that strange man! I remember Andocia, but she has stayed out of my life so far, thank goodness. Now however, someone wants me to cross swords with her once more."

Craig stared at the ring but he made no move to take it. Instead he stood up and paced around the cockpit of his spacecraft, deep in thought.

"I don't know what I should do! I know that Tanus helped both me and Constance when we were Andocia's prisoners, but I doubt if I'll be able to go against someone as powerful as that woman. I feel bad for Tanus, but if she managed to get captured by Andocia, I cannot see how I'll be able to stand against her. Tanus must be really desperate to want my help."

Slowly, hesitantly, Craig's hand hovered over the ring and then he slipped it on to his finger where it fitted snugly. The explorer looked at it thoughtfully for a few minutes. "I wonder what sort of powers this ring possesses."

Carter's thoughts were interrupted by the ringing of his mobile device.

"Come in, lazybones – time to rise and shine!"

His heart leapt at the sound of the voice, because it belonged to his beloved Constance, and he smiled at her. "I'm awake, darling."

"How did the mission go?"

"Okay I suppose. I had quite a battle, but fortunately it all turned out well in the end. He killed himself, because he couldn't stand the humiliation, but I'll fill you in on all the details later. I should land on Earth within the next few hours or so."

"Hurry home, for I've missed you," she pouted. "I'll see you later, dearest."

Craig switched off the device and stared once again at the ring on his finger. "How will you help me to find Tanus I wonder?"

The craft touched down safely in the control centre and Craig climbed out. Several of his friends and associates greeted him and he returned their greetings. Constance came and kissed him, then they went to Commander Simms' office, where Craig told them about the mission.

"Poor Craig, you always land up with the most difficult cases!" remarked Constance sympathetically.

"That's very unfortunate, Craig, but at least you survive," interjected the Commander. "You gave us some scary moments out there! Who would've thought that such a straightforward case could become so hazardous?"

Constance squeezed her boyfriend's hand and smiled. "Well, all that matters to me right now is that you're home safe and sound."

Craig smiled at his girlfriend and turned back to his boss. "Sir, do you have any more cases lined up for me in the near future?"

"I don't have anything for you that I know of, why?"

Carter paced up and down, frowning. "Sir, I really need some advice! While I was travelling home, I received a desperate plea for help from one of Tanus' followers. He told me that Andocia had captured her and she asked him to get in touch with me. I'm not sure why she wanted me, but at the same time I don't feel very confident that I'm the right person to do this. Andocia is very powerful and what chance will I stand against her?"

Commander Simms rubbed his jaw thoughtfully. "It certainly sounds like an impossible mission Craig, but Tanus must have formed her own opinion of you. Don't you find it flattering that she has so much faith in you?"

The space explorer shrugged his shoulders and sighed. "Well yes, but I cannot help wondering if it is just desperation on her part. How can I accomplish such a mammoth task when I am just one solitary human being?"

Simms patted his employee on his shoulder. "Craig, if you think about it, you already have achieved the impossible. Remember when Andocia took over control of Earth; you managed to stop her diabolical plan and sent her packing."

"I know that Sir, but I had help from very willing and dedicated people. I didn't do that alone."

"I realize that, son, but you are a pretty amazing person," replied Simms emphatically. "However, it is your decision to make. I certainly don't relish sending you out to do this because it is a great risk, but I have faith in you, so you have to make the call."

Craig took Constance's hand and smiled tentatively at her. "What do you think Constance? Should I do this or not?"

His girlfriend shrugged her shoulders. "I also don't like the idea of you willingly putting yourself in harm's way. You know what Andocia is capable of, as do I. You could very well be killed."

Carter showed them his ring which sparkled in the sunlight. "This ring was given to me by the man I spoke to. He told me that it could help me in some way, but he didn't elaborate."

"What does it do?" asked the Commander interestedly.

"I don't really know, but it obviously has some powers, so I'll only know when I test it out, I suppose."

Simms put his arm companionably around his employee's shoulders and smiled. "I think that you and Constance should go and enjoy each other's company for a bit. Don't decide just yet what should be done. Discuss it with one another and then let me know what you decide. When does this man want to know what your decision is?"

"He said that he would give me a day or so to settle down and think about it. I'll probably have to give him my answer by tomorrow evening the latest."

"All right Craig, you and Constance may leave now. I'm sure that you lovebirds would like to be alone for a time."

"Thank you, Sir," said Craig as he put his arm around his girlfriend's shoulders and they left.

Once they were in a secluded spot, Craig discussed the vision at great length.

"What do you think about this strange message, Constance?"

"It's really odd, but it must be genuine. Why do you suppose Tanus was asking for your help?" she asked curiously.

"I'm not sure, but the person I spoke to never elaborated," her boyfriend replied.

"Well Tanus did help us on several occasions when Andocia tried to kill us. She put Andocia and all her followers to sleep once, thus enabling us to escape from her spacecraft."

"I know and my indecision is making me feel guilty somehow. I do have the feeling that I should try to help her in any way that I can, because without her, Andocia will have free reign to do whatever she wants in both universes and we won't have Tanus to help us if she is out of the picture, but there are still some doubts creeping in. Constance, if you had been asked to help Tanus instead of me, would you have agreed to do so?"

Miss Gregg shrugged her shoulders. "I don't know, but I have to admit that I feel the same way about the situation as you do. If I could help Tanus in any way, I would certainly like to try."

"Exactly, and if she is in trouble, then maybe I should risk my life for her because she saved ours. I know we never spent much time with her, but I felt − I don't know − some kind of a connection I suppose. I know that she represents good, and we could use all the friends we can get in our line of work anyway. This ring must have been given to me so that I can somehow stop Andocia from causing me some grievous harm."

"I hope so, but do you realize what you'll be up against?! Andocia is a force to be reckoned with and you could come off second best, even with the ring."

"I thought about that, darling, but I have the feeling that I must try to help her nevertheless. I'm positive that someone will explain to me how the ring works. Does this mean that you think I should undertake this mission?"

Constance nodded her head. "Call me crazy, but yes, I think you owe it to Tanus. I just hope that everything will work out. I've become quite attached to you and I don't want to hear any bad news regarding this mission, so make sure you do the very best you can − and come back home to me alive and in one piece."

Craig held his girlfriend close, taking comfort in her presence. "I love you so much my darling. I promise I will do everything in my power to fulfil that request. For now, let's enjoy ourselves though, for we have so little time left before I leave once more. Once Tanus' follower contacts me, I will have to go."

They went out and had a wonderful time, but on the way back, Constance was very quiet and Craig put his hand on her knee. "It will be okay, I promise you. I'll come back to you, because without you, my life has no meaning."

"I know, but I'm going to miss you. Keep in contact with me every day!"

Craig smiled and put his arms around his girlfriend and their lips met in a tender kiss.

"Oh Constance, I'll do the best I can. I'm not sure how the signal will be in the Golden Way, but hopefully our technicians will be able to boost it so we can stay in touch. I love you so much and it hurts me to be away from you too, but we both have jobs to do. For tonight though, let's forget about work and just enjoy one another's company."

CHAPTER 2

That night, Craig was sitting in his living room when his mobile device rang. He accepted the call and the man he had spoken to before was visible on the screen.

"Craig Carter, I'm contacting you as I promised I would. Will you help us find and rescue our mistress from Andocia's clutches? I apologize for being so blunt, but time is now of the essence. If you don't wish to help us then we will make other arrangements."

Carter looked at the screen of his device and a prompt appeared on it. The word "hologram" flashed and he pressed it. Immediately the image of the man filled the room and he looked as though he was standing there with Craig. The young man smiled at the image facing him. "I've decided to help you. My boss has given me his blessing and I will leave tomorrow morning and rendezvous with you wherever you want me to."

Relief was evident on the man's face and he bowed low. "Thank you, Mr Carter! You don't know how much we appreciate this. I understand what this means to you and we will be forever grateful to you and Earth."

"It will be an honour," Craig replied. "Now can you please tell me what I can use the ring for."

"The ring can be used to activate a force field around you. When you are in trouble, the shield will protect you from danger, but don't use it for long periods at a time or its powers will be depleted, leaving you defenceless. Use it in combination with your mind – in other words, think about what you need and it will materialize until its usefulness has passed, but be selective and think carefully. I feel it is only fair to warn you that Andocia can only be stopped for a few seconds, so bear that in mind. On no account must that ring be taken off your finger. Only certain of your foes will be able to accomplish this. There isn't a time limit for this rescue, but it would be in your own interests and that of both universes, if you could do this speedily, otherwise Andocia will succeed in taking over both universes. The 'hologram' function you have enabled works similar to your vidscreens that are standard issue on all known spacecrafts, so you can use it at any time if you need to contact us."

"I understand," Craig replied.

The man smiled. "We will always be grateful to you for this leap of faith. You hardly know us, yet you are prepared to help our mistress. I hope all goes well with you. Good luck to you, Craig Carter."

"Thanks, I have the feeling I'm going to need all the help I can get."

He watched the hologram wave and then vanish.

∕ ∕ ∕

The next day, Craig set off for the Space Control Centre and prepared his craft for the journey. Constance was there to see him off and she waved as the craft rose into the air and vanished from sight.

"God bless you my darling Craig. Andocia isn't one to be trifled with. She blinded you once and she could do something worse if you fall into her grasp again. Look after yourself and think of me often, just as I'll be thinking of you."

With a final glance at the blue sky, the woman turned around and left the observation section.

Carter soared off into the darkness, his lights cutting into the inky blackness showing the way.

"I wonder, should I start my search in the Golden Way or should I make enquiries in our own universe? No, I must contact the Saturnians first and see what they advise. They are the most intelligent race in our universe."

Craig pressed a button and soon he was looking at Karnd. "Hello Karnd, how are things on Saturn today?" he asked brightly.

"We have no reason to complain, thank you. It's always a

pleasure talking to you, Craig. What can I do for you?"

"I have a problem and I need some advice."

"What do you need to know?"

"I've been asked to help someone who means a lot to me, but she's been captured by Andocia and I want to try, but I'm not sure where I should begin my enquiries. You see, the Golden Way is the obvious choice, but I'm not sure it's the safest, because Andocia has spies everywhere and she's sure to know when I put in an appearance, and bang will go my sneak attack!"

"I understand completely, but you still need to begin in the Golden Way, because it is Andocia's territory. I do have a suggestion though, but you'll have to go to Sonambro. Sonambro has perfected an ingenious machine that changes the shape of people. Perhaps he can give you some kind of disguise so she won't recognize you, and therefore not bother with you."

Carter thanked him and set course for Sonambra.

On arrival, he was treated for radiation and then he and Sonambro were able to talk.

"Sonambro, Karnd of Saturn suggested I come and see you, because I have a favour to ask. I have to rescue someone who is in Andocia's clutches and he told me you have a machine that can change a person's shape. I dare not go to the Golden Way in my normal form, for Andocia will recognize me and I don't want that to happen."

"Naturally, it makes sense. I'm sure we can make a plan for you, but eat first and then we'll set about doing it."

"Er, Sonambro is the process reversible?" asked Craig tentatively.

"Yes of course it is!" he replied reassuringly.

He duly ate with them and then they went to the laboratory. There Sonambro produced a syringe.

"Do not be alarmed Cragus, but in order to compete the disguise, I have to feed your DNA sample into my computers. I also need to weigh you and get a few answers before we can do the experiment. May I proceed?"

Carter shrugged his shoulders. "I guess so. This really is reversible?" he asked nervously.

"I guarantee it!" replied the sun creature.

Craig allowed the sun being to inject him and remove a small blood sample. He watched fascinated as Sonambro placed some blood onto a slide which he then placed in another tray. The tray disappeared inside the computer and soon Carter was watching in fascination as his genetic makeup appeared on screen. Afterwards the computer gave various sketches of how Craig's face would look once it had been altered. The explorer was then asked to pick some faces that he liked and the instruction was given to the computer. The explorer was told to go and sit it the guest lounge for a while.

A few hours later, Carter returned to the laboratory. The machinery whirred into life and hummed contentedly, while Sonambro adjusted dials and levers, and pressed various keys on the keyboard in front of him, nodding approvingly to himself. When he was done, he held a device in his hand and beckoned Craig to come closer. "As you can see, this is an exact copy of the emblem that appears on your spacesuits."

He held it over the existing badge and it fitted onto it as though it had been glued on. When Craig looked in a mirror, he couldn't tell the difference.

"Okay, that is excellent!" Sonambro smiled. "Now watch what happens when I press the emblem."

Immediately Craig's face appeared to change shape.

"Good grief, is that really me?! How different I look."

He ran his hand over the strange face that was reflected in the mirror. His face was lined and wrinkled and he had a large Roman nose. His mouth was much smaller and his eyebrows were bushier. Craig's shoulders were broader and more muscular, while his fingers were long and thin, but the ring clung to him nevertheless. His legs were thicker and very muscular. "You've made me look older."

Sonambro was delighted with the result. "That's exactly as I intended you to look. It's virtually impossible for Andocia to recognize you now. I programmed all the images you liked into this emblem. All you need to do is press the emblem several times. Each time you press it, you will be able to change your disguise. There are six different disguises programmed into it. Basically, this device is a hologram. In fact, your features haven't really changed, but by activating this, your body appears different. Just don't go near any electromagnetic devices or they will make the device malfunction. I have also manufactured a similar device for your ship. I took the liberty of having a button placed on the controls of your craft. For the finishing touch, I'll change the shape of your ship and the markings thereon, but the controls will remain the same. I have checked our archives and found various designs of spaceships over the years. Again, I have given you a few choices of the older models. This device can only be used in the short term or it will deplete the fuel cells of your spacecraft. You must only use this when you need to make a quick escape. It would also be prudent if you try to do away with your American accent when you are using one of the disguises that are programmed into your emblem device."

"I'll do that," said Craig in a typical Australian accent.

Sonambro clapped his hands in glee. "That's excellent! I like that accent. What's your name?"

"Name's Buddy Blow, but you can call me Bud," he drawled.

Sonambro laughed. "Good to meet you Bud. Good luck on your mission."

The sun creature followed him to his ship and aimed a portable device at it. As Carter watched, the ship changed shape and became elongated.

"But it looks just like the old models we had in the 20th century!"

"Correct, with one vital difference of course; it is faster than the older models."

Craig grinned at the sun creature. "Thank you very much! This will definitely help me."

Sonambro smiled and waved until the craft was out of sight. When Craig was in deep space once more, he deactivated the button on his console and the ship returned to its normal shape. He then pressed the device on his chest and he too returned to his normal shape.

*   *   *

Craig made for the Golden Way, but he began to have doubts.

"This mission is almost impossible. I hope I'm doing the right thing."

Not long after the Golden Way had been discovered, Earth's scientists had started looking for the entrances to the blue universe. With the help of Tanus, Saturn, and their friend Sonambro, they were able to obtain the relevant information.

Craig's ship entered one of the jump vortexes that catapulted him into the Golden Way and he stared at the blue sky in trepidation.

"Well it won't be long before Andocia finds out that I'm here. I just hope my disguise will fool her into thinking that I'm just a curious traveller."

The space explorer made for the yellow planet and touched down on their landing strip. The inhabitants stared curiously at him, and then they greeted him pleasantly.

"Craig Carter, it's good to see you again, but why do you look so different?"

Carter gawked at the being. "How did you know that it was me?"

"It's hard to explain really – it has something to do with your ... essence I suppose. Why are you in disguise anyway?"

"I was asked to rescue Tanus and if Andocia recognizes me, then she'll probably kill me. This was just a safety precaution. Call me Bud, and I'm an Australian."

The creature shook its head sadly. "Oh Craig, you are such a fool! Do you really think that you'll be able to get away with it! Andocia's powers are awesome and I am just a humble being, yet I recognized you immediately. She can read your mind and no matter what you look like, she'll know it's you. You have to get away from here quickly, because Andocia is at this moment visiting our planet."

Not wishing to have a confrontation so soon, and cursing his bad timing, Craig decided to leave and hurriedly climbed back into his ship. He blasted off just as Andocia appeared, and the last thing he saw was the evil woman questioning the Meltoni-an, just before he went into time lapse and disappeared from view. The space explorer flew until he was a safe distance away and then he contacted the Sonambrians. Sonambro was very surprised to hear from him.

"What happened Cragus? Is something wrong?"

Craig sighed miserably. "The disguise failed. I went to Melton and it was just unfortunate that Andocia was visiting them. They recognized me just as soon as I got off the ship and I was advised to change back to my own form. Luckily I got away before Andocia saw me."

"I'm sorry it didn't work, Cragus, but I suppose it is understandable, because I can only change your body, not your mind. What are you going to do now, my friend?"

"I don't know. I cannot return your devices to you for time is now of the essence. I will have to return them to you when I pass your way next time. Will that be okay?"

Sonambro smiled at his friend. "You can keep them Cragus. Consider them a gift. You may not be able to fool Andocia, but they can still serve you well as a disguise in a desperate situation. What will you do now?"

He shrugged his shoulders and sighed. "Well I'll just have to remain in the Golden Way and hope for the best. I don't know if Andocia will be waiting for me or not, but I hope she isn't."

Sonambro watched on his vidscreen as the ship rose upwards into the sky and he stared worriedly at it. "May it go well for you, Cragus. You are a brave man."

Craig flew around and scanned the sky, but there was no sign of Andocia and he breathed a sigh of relief. Just to be safe though, he made a wide detour of Melton. As he cruised in the universe, not sure where to begin his search, his transmitter beeped and he switched it on, and came face to face with Andocia. Even though he wasn't in the same room as her, he felt his body tensing up.

"Greetings, Carter; what brings you to my part of the world?"

"I came to visit some of my friends – I do have some friends here you know."

"I'm aware of that, but you came here earlier in another form, why?"

"I was asked to take part in an experiment and I just came to get an opinion from the Meltonians, but they weren't fooled by my disguise at all. Andocia, why did you hurt that creature? I saw what you did to him as I lifted off."

"I don't like insubordination and he refused to tell me who was in the spacecraft, but I found out though. He was anxious to tell me anything when I hurt him," she gloated.

Carter stared at this woman he hated so much and knew without a doubt, that the Meltonian had told her of his mission. His mouth was dry as he posed the next question. "What else did he tell you, Andocia?"

"Funny you should mention that, but I believe you know the answer. You have come to try and rescue Tanus, but you're wasting your time. I realize you are a shrewd adversary and I must admit that I enjoyed our little get together last time, but you got lucky. Tanus helped you to escape or you would be dead by now. Here's some friendly advice Carter. Tanus must be really desperate to ask for your assistance, but you can't win and you know it. Go back home and don't cross my path again. If you are entertaining any ideas of trying to thwart me, I *will* kill you. Tanus has many friends a great deal more powerful than you and they failed, so how can a mere mortal even consider doing something so impossible? You may continue on your tour unmolested, but stay away from me."

Craig was despondent and stared unseeingly into the blue universe. "She's right! I need to have my head examined just for agreeing to do this. I have no idea where her planet is, so how can I even find where she has imprisoned Tanus? Knowing Andocia, she'll have Tanus imprisoned in some horrible place, surrounded by deadly creatures that follow her."

He paced up and down for a while, when an idea struck him.

"I'll go and visit the planet that saved me from Andocia before, when she blinded me. I know they're grotesque, but they have kind hearts. Andocia made them her slaves as punishment, and I would really like to thank them for forcing me to go to Saturn for help, when all I wanted to do was kill myself. Perhaps they can tell me more about Andocia's planet and give me some idea where to look for Tanus."

CHAPTER 3

He went to the area in which he judged them to be and hovered around, but he couldn't find anywhere to land, so he contacted them. They answered, but there was no picture.

"Greetings Craig Carter; what can we do for you?"

"I was wondering if you could clear a space for me to land."

On the planet, the grotesque creatures looked at one another in amazement.

"He wants to land, even though he knows we are ugly. What should we tell him?"

Another being shook his head. "Tell him he can't land. He'll be most unsettled by the sight of us."

Before they could reply, Craig cut in. "I don't care how grotesque you are. You people saved my life once and I would like to meet my rescuers face to face."

The being sighed and spoke heavily. "Very well, but be warned, we look worse than you could ever imagine. Do you still want to take the risk?"

"Yes, I do," he replied emphatically.

"Very well then, look to your right and we'll clear the landing strip."

As he looked, the vegetation parted and he headed for the clearing. When he landed, he opened the hatch and stepped down. Several beings were standing some distance from him and began to approach tentatively. Even though he steeled himself for the sight, it still took him by surprise and he recoiled in horror. They looked like refugees from a very bad horror movie. While it was apparent that they had once resembled human beings, their features were now grossly distorted. Craig could see they had two legs and two arms and also two eyes in their heads, but the beings reminded him of someone caught in a terrible fire. He could make out their features, but their bodies were very thin and seemed brittle, almost as if they would crumble into dust if touched. Both sides of their bodies were uneven and some of them walked crookedly. They all had tiny wisps of hair clinging to their scalps, but the hair was thin and scraggly. They looked at him and were embarrassed. "See, we warned you about us, yet you still came."

Carter recovered his composure and smiled at them. "Forgive me for that – I did receive quite a shock, but it's over now. I still owe you so much and I would like to thank those who helped me. Could you show me where to go?"

The creatures took him to some buildings where he was introduced to those who had helped him. He thanked them effusively. "I couldn't let this moment pass by, because I wanted to let you know how grateful I am for the help and kindness you showed me. You took a complete stranger in and helped him, risking Andocia's fury, and then you still refused to let me commit suicide and I'm grateful to you. I was very depressed when I landed here before, but thankfully I've recovered. Actually, I came here to return the favour, for I know that Andocia has made you her slaves because of it. In return for my help, I would like you to share some information with me, regarding the possible whereabouts of Tanus. Before I continue though, I would like to know why you have such strange forms. How did it happen? Was there some kind of poisonous fallout?"

One of the beings smiled mirthlessly. "You could say that I suppose. Let me begin at the beginning. We may as well get comfortable and then I'll tell you our story."

The grotesque but kindly being took him to a secluded spot where several chairs and tables stood. He gestured to his friend to sit down and then signalled to a waiter who came over and stared nervously at the new arrival. However, his nervousness soon passed when the being introduced Craig to him. The man was taken aback by the space explorer's kindness when he stood up and shook the gnarled hand firmly. They exchanged a few pleasantries and then the kindly doctor asked the waiter to bring them something to drink. When their drinks arrived, he began the story.

"A long time ago we lived in peace and serenity. We were beautiful once and this place was like a paradise. Everything grew without much help and anything we planted always flourished. Nothing died once it was placed in the soil. We are not immortal though but our people had a lifespan of two hundred of your Earth years. We grew and multiplied as was the custom, and had many offspring. For the most we were healthy, but we had our share of diseases, for which our doctors were always fortunate enough to find cures. We lived an idyllic life and I suppose we grew complacent and lazy. No one really bothered to wage war against us and we lived in harmony with the rest of the Golden Way.

"Then one fateful day, Andocia arrived on our planet. Many of our kind were scientists, much like the Saturnians in your universe. Because we were a peace-loving community, we never turned our talents to the making of weapons, although we had the skills to do this. Andocia wanted us to manufacture weapons for her and we refused. She became most insistent and still we steadfastly refused to accede to her demands.

"She first threatened us, but we didn't pay any attention, thinking she would grow tired of nagging and leave us alone. We were not aware of her great powers at that time. When she realized we would not do her bidding, she killed a few of us. Naturally this distressed us, but we still remained headstrong. Our top scientists were again ordered to manufacture weapons and they refused.

"Andocia blew up a few of our laboratories, but even that couldn't convince us to do what she wanted. After a while, she left our planet, vowing vengeance on us all. The months went by with no sign of her and gradually we began to relax, thinking she had given up the notion of harming us.

"A few more months passed and seven months after our refusal to help her, our weather patterns began to change. Our summers were usually warm, but not excruciatingly hot, and our winters were just a little cooler. Suddenly the sun seemed to burn with more intensity and we began to get sunburned. We took measures to keep our skin cooler, but the sun grew even hotter, until finally everything began to melt! Our buildings collapsed and our possessions took the strain, as did we.

"Many of us died that year and our spacecrafts were rendered useless because the metal parts began to fuse together. Our beautiful gardens shrivelled up as our water evaporated. By that time, half our population had died.

"Andocia arrived amidst all this carnage and gloated. She confessed she had unleashed a poisonous substance on our planet that would continue doing its deadly work as long as she still had stock. She wanted us to become extinct! That woman left us to die, but although we had sustained irrevocable damage, we were determined to teach her a lesson.

"Those of us who were strong enough, manufactured a spacecraft made of several layers of titanium that could withstand drastic temperature changes and we went in search of Andocia. We found her planet and managed to destroy the evil machine that she had unleashed on us. All her deadly noxious gasses were destroyed, but many brave beings died in the attempt. It was not in vain though for we managed to break her stranglehold on us. Afterwards she left us alone, but we lost everything that mattered to us. We no longer lived in a paradise and now the food we eat is chemically manufactured, because nothing can grow on our planet due to the poison she unleashed on us. We are also sterile because of this. When we all grow old, there will be no one left to live on this planet and it will become a desolate wasteland."

Craig was horrified. "Andocia did all this? Just because you wouldn't do what she wanted?"

"Yes," replied the being sorrowfully.

Carter shook his head. "Oh boy, I need to have my head examined! Here I am promising to help someone I don't know very well, just because one of her followers asked me to. If Tanus and Andocia are enemies and I step in to help, what will become of me?"

The kindly being smiled crookedly at him. "You must do what you feel is right. What does your heart tell you to do?"

The space explorer paced thoughtfully. "My heart is telling me to do everything I can to help Tanus, but my head disagrees. I'm not terribly excited to cross paths with Andocia again, but she had no right to do what she did to your planet and its people. She tried to take over Earth and I stopped her, along with many of my friends, so I can sympathize with you. Now of course she has targeted your planet again, just because you helped me. I don't understand the logic behind that!"

"Well I certainly do," the being replied. "Andocia isn't a very good loser and you also taught her a lesson. When she couldn't finish what she had started with you, she lost face with her enemies. She couldn't find you, so she rounded on us instead and made us her slaves."

Craig sighed heavily. "I'm so sorry! I had no idea what she was capable of. I feel responsible for your situation."

The being put its withered hand on Craig's shoulder. "You are not responsible for Andocia's actions, please understand this. It's not in our nature to hold a grudge against you, or anyone else for that matter. How could you know that you would land up here? You were blind when it happened, so there was a reason for your arrival. We simply did the best we could under the circumstances."

Craig in turn held the scarred hand and squeezed it reassuringly. "I have no words to thank you for what you did for me, so let me at least show you. Let me help you regain your freedom at least."

"You have a deal, Craig, but in helping us, you'll incur Andocia's wrath again," the being warned.

"I'm expecting that, but I suppose a confrontation will be inevitable. I must say that I'm not looking forward to it at all though, but I always try to repay generosity, and Tanus has helped to save my life on more than one occasion as well."

"We are grateful to you, Craig."

"Nonsense, I always help my friends. Please could you camouflage my ship in some way, otherwise Andocia's followers will see it and then the element of surprise will be lost. When do they come here?"

"Usually in the early morning, and they make us work for most of the day. When we get visitors, they stop and all appears to be normal."

Carter hid in the dense bushes and waited for the trident ships to land. He watched as the women followers got out and began to round up the inhabitants of Bartha. Several shuffled along too slowly for one girl's liking and she took out a whip and lashed them across their backs. Immediately Craig showed himself and they stared at the solitary human.

"Hey you!" He called to the woman who had hit the creatures, "do you take pleasure in hurting innocent beings?"

One woman turned around and snarled viciously. "Who do you think you are?"

"My name is Craig Carter of the planet Earth. Your mistress and I are acquainted."

They looked at one another and recognition dawned. "Why, he's that pesky Earthling who thwarted our plans to take over his planet!"

Craig smiled. "In the flesh. Now why don't you leave them alone and find some other target who can at least fight back?"

The women smiled cruelly. "In that case, you'll have to do."

"Be my guest," he invited.

Several women advanced and Craig pointed the ring at them, causing them to bang into an unseen barrier that he had erected around himself. Then he removed it and the woman holding the whip charged forward. Craig ducked and caught the whip in his hand, and then tugged and she lost her grip on the weapon. The space explorer grabbed it by the handle and whipped her once across her back, causing her to cry out in pain and anger.

"Try some of your own medicine for a change," he replied, as he flung the whip contemptuously onto the ground and, completely humiliated, she stalked off.

They formed a ring around him and raised their weapons. He shook his head warningly. "Don't do it! I have no conscience about hurting all of you. Why don't you go home and leave these beings alone? They have suffered enough!"

The group advanced and Carter raised his hand. Immediately the women screamed furiously as they were all lifted up and slammed mercilessly down on the hard ground. They fell in a tangle of arms and legs and the explorer watched impassively as they untangled their limbs. One woman stood up and shook her fist angrily at him. "You haven't heard the last of this, Craig Carter. Andocia will decide what should be done about you."

"I doubt it," he replied, "but tell her if you want to."

The women climbed back into their ship and blasted off. Carter stroked the ring fondly. *"If it wasn't for this ring, I would soon lose heart. This ring gives me courage as well as protection,"* he thought gratefully.

The beings swarmed around him and shook his hand vigorously. "Thank you for doing that – at least for today they won't come back, so we'll be able to have a rest. Although we are very grateful, Andocia will come after you and your death will be painful."

Craig shook his head. "I doubt it. I don't know Andocia very well, but I think that she'll give her followers a good talking to."

CHAPTER 4

The women returned to Andocia and told her about Craig.

"Mistress that Earthling, Craig Carter deserves to be taught a lesson. We were getting the Barthians together so that they could begin their work, when he hit me with my own whip. Didn't you make them slaves because they helped him before?"

"Yes, I did, but what do you expect me to do? You were stupid enough to let him outsmart you, so you deserve the humiliation. He is a cunning adversary, but not immortal, and you are all well trained, so go back and teach him a lesson. Don't expect me to clean up after you," she replied crossly.

"But Andocia ..." her follower whined.

"Enough! Leave me alone and deal with him yourself," she ordered as she turned to leave.

Another woman stepped forward. "Mistress, there's something else. When we tried to overpower him, we ran into an invisible barrier, something like the one you possess."

"*What!* But that's impossible! I saw no such evidence in our dealings before," remarked Andocia incredulously.

"It's true though," remarked another girl. "When we could move forward, then he grabbed the whip."

"Now that is very interesting," mused the evil woman. "I have to put him in some situation where he'll be forced to use this power and then when he reveals it, I'll deal with him accordingly. I think that this is a job for his enemy, Tyrus."

Andocia went to contact Tyrus and she chuckled wickedly.

"Tyrus is willing to help us, but we have to lure Carter back to his own universe, for those creatures can't breathe in the Golden Way."

While Craig was still on Bartha, a message was put through to him. "Please Mr Carter, help me! I need you to come to Pahos in your own universe. I have been badly injured and I'm dying slowly, but before I go, I must give you something important. I tried to contact some other ships close by, but my transmitter has malfunctioned and only works long distance. Hurry ... please ... hurry!"

Carter was visibly disturbed by the message and made preparations to leave, promising the Barthians that he would return and finish what he started, once he had rescued the unfortunate being on Pahos.

⚡ ⚡ ⚡

He arrived on the star and looked around, but all that greeted him was silence and a chill ran up his spine. Craig berated himself for his stupidity. "I shouldn't have come here in such a hurry. Something about that voice struck me as phony, but I gave the being the benefit of the doubt. I think it would be wise of me to return to my ship and get off here as soon as possible. This is obviously a trap! Sometimes I'm my own worst enemy!"

He strode purposefully towards his ship, but when he got nearer, Tyrus blocked his way. Craig backed away slowly, keeping some distance from his enemy.

Tyrus grinned evilly. "Hello Mr Carter! It has been a while.

Don't you think it is time we got re-acquainted? We have so much to talk about!"

The explorer cursed his stupidity on his hasty decision and put more distance between them.

"I have nothing to say to you Tyrus," he snapped angrily. "I should have known that something was wrong when I got that phony distress call! I'm getting out of here!"

Unbeknown to him an invisible trident ship was hovering nearby and the occupants were watching the two figures on their scanners.

Craig didn't bother to waste time, he took to his heels and ran, hoping to outwit Tyrus and backtrack to his craft, but the silver creature simply laughed and teleported himself until he was in front of the explorer. Craig ran back towards his craft, but a hidden root tripped him up and he fell heavily. He landed on his hands and twisted onto his back, just as Tyrus bent over and extended his arms to attack him. Carter pointed his right hand at his enemy and Tyrus squirmed in amazement, for he grabbed only fresh air. At this point, the trident ship landed and Andocia walked over to the two figures.

"So, it's true!" she exclaimed triumphantly.

The unexpected confrontation distracted Craig and the barrier vanished, but in that split second, Tyrus grabbed him around both wrists and hauled him to his feet.

"*Andocia, what are you doing here?*" exclaimed the startled explorer.

"In case you haven't realized it by now, this was a set-up. I sent that transmission to Bartha and you fell for it as I thought you would. Tyrus was kind enough to help me trap you."

"What was the point of this elaborate setup anyway?" he asked curiously. "I've been in the Golden Way for a while already. If you wanted me so badly, why didn't you capture me there?"

"I had my reasons. My followers mentioned that you had obtained some sort of power and I needed to make you use it, so that I could take it away from you. No humans possess any powers, so it has to be a device. What is it?"

Craig stubbornly stood his ground. "Why should I tell you anything?"

"Tyrus, would you do the honours?" Andocia asked, turning to the silver creature.

"With extreme pleasure!" He said as he let some electricity flow into Craig's body, raising him a few centimetres off the ground.

"I ... won't tell you!" he repeated desperately.

"Do it again, Tyrus!" commanded Andocia.

The power coursed through his body and he screamed in agony. When the silver being stopped again, Craig sucked in a lungful of air.

"Tell me about this power!" she demanded.

"No! If I tell you, I will lose the only advantage I have."

"I don't see any advantage from where I'm standing," Andocia replied snidely. "Why are you refusing to tell me what I want to know?"

"I can't! I made a promise. The consequences would be too terrible to contemplate if I told you."

Tyrus looked pleadingly at Andocia. "May I electrocute him again? He can't hold out forever against me. Eventually he will give you the answer you want."

Andocia shook her head. "It is very tempting, but he is stubborn and your method might just render him unconscious if you continue."

Andocia regarded Craig quizzically for a moment, then turned to the creature. "Very well, I'll just have to find another way to persuade Mr Carter. Release him Tyrus and thank you for your help. You may return to your own planet now."

The creature threw Craig onto the ground and vanished. Carter massaged his aching wrists.

Andocia ignored the man and turned to her followers. "Come let's return to the Golden Way. When Carter comes to his senses, he can think about the words he uttered. We'll take his ship with us and let's see how he survives on this barren star. In one day, Carter, we'll return to pick you up, and by that time you may consider telling me where this power comes from. If you do so, your life will be spared."

Craig watched despondently as Andocia's ship vanished, pulling his along in a tractor beam. His last link with the rest of the world had disappeared.

"How do I get myself into these situations?" he admonished himself. "It gets very cold up here and there is nothing available for me to build a shelter. I've failed already and this mission has hardly begun."

Just then, Craig's mobile device rang. Puzzled as no signal could reach him from his universe as it was too far, he accepted the call. He recognized the caller as the man who had come to him in his dreams, asking him to help Tanus. The man smiled at him. "All is not lost, Craig Carter. The ring possesses the power to transport you to any planet you wish to go, without a craft, but you had better have a good explanation for Andocia when she tracks you down. This will only work once though, otherwise you will deplete the power of the ring. Good luck Carter – you've done well so far." Craig blinked and the man vanished, then he looked at the ring reflectively.

"Okay, take me to Bartha!" he said.

The ring emitted a white glow and Craig was conscious of a breeze in his face. He closed his eyes and when he opened them again, he found himself back on Bartha and he shivered. "Wow that felt very weird! I don't know if I would like to try that again any time soon."

He looked up and a Barthian stared at him in surprise.

"Craig, you're back, but how come we didn't see you arrive?"

"It's a long story, but I had help. Andocia left me stranded on Pahos, and I managed to escape, but she has my ship. It'll take her hours to get back here. We need to come up with some sort of a plan to rid you of her followers once and for all. Could you organize some kind of riot maybe?"

"It sounds like a good plan, but unfortunately she confiscated all our weapons, so we have nothing to fight with."

"Where did she put them?"

"In the river of danger. No one will dare set foot in it, because evil and dangerous creatures live there. We are doomed!"

gulped the creature.

"No, you aren't! Tell me where this river is and I'll try to get them for you."

"No, Craig, we appreciate your help to now, but we don't want you to kill yourself on our account!"

"But I want to help!" the explorer replied. "I'm doing this for me just as much as for you. When Andocia finds out that I've escaped, she'll come after me too, and I'd like to be able to defend myself."

The creature relented and nodded his head. "Very well, I'll draw you a map, but you'll have to take one of our skimmer crafts."

"No problem – just show me how to operate it and I'll do my best," he replied reassuringly.

"Well the levers are simple to operate. If you want to turn left, push the left lever down and if you wish to go right press the right lever. To keep in a straight line, just press the middle lever."

Carter waved and set off on his task. Soon he came to the river and stared at it in disgust. "Ugh, I bet it smells as bad as it looks!"

He landed on the swampy ground and the air was stagnant and smelt foul. He put a special breathing apparatus on his mouth and nose and plunged in to begin his search. The ring was once again used to place the barrier around him and he was very grateful, especially when a very large and ugly swamp creature tried to catch him for dinner. He thought about a harpoon and instantly one appeared and speared the creature, killing it instantly. Immediately there was a blood frenzy as all the other creatures smelt the dead thing and surged forward to feast off it. In the ensuing chaos, he passed unmolested through them all and soon found the weapons. Using a net that the Barthians had lent him, he gathered them all and using his mind he made a large shovel appear. It scooped up all the weapons and deposited them on the river bank, then he swam to the surface, and loaded these into the ship. He went back to his friends and returned their weapons.

"Craig, we are indebted to you."

"It was no trouble. I wanted to help you, so now I'm returning the favour. You helped me before, now we are even."

"What are you going to do?" asked the Barthian.

"I'll have to impose on your hospitality a while longer if you don't mind, as I'm unable to leave your planet without my ship. Tomorrow, Andocia's followers will return to taunt you, and what a surprise they'll get. I intend to stow away on their ship, because they will probably return to Andocia's planet and I want to recover my spacecraft."

CHAPTER 5

The next day, Andocia's followers returned and ordered the Barthians to begin working, but they created a diversion, enabling Craig to climb into the trident ship unnoticed. He found a little storage room and quietly closed the door. He could hear a noise outside and knew the Barthians had begun retaliating against their tormentors. It wasn't long before the women returned to their ship and blasted off, not knowing that they had another passenger on board. From his vantage point, he heard them discussing the incident amongst themselves.

"How did they get their weapons back?"

"I've been wondering the same thing, but it's obvious someone helped them. If I didn't know better, I'd say that Carter helped them, but he's imprisoned on Pahos, so it couldn't be him. Andocia should be rendezvousing with us soon, and then we'll see if the Earthling is still so stubborn."

"Yes," remarked another, "but do you think he'll tell Andocia about his power now?"

"Most probably, but if he's still stubborn, our mistress will deal with him. He's a fool to have tried to cross Andocia in the first place and if it were I personally, I'd eliminate him at the earliest opportunity. He spells trouble with a capital 'T'. I really think Tanus has lost her mind! Imagine asking a mortal to help rescue her, when others more powerful have been crushed. He'll never defeat Andocia, no matter how hard he tries."

Andocia joined her soldiers and they flew to Pahos. The ship landed on the hard ground and she ordered her followers to spread out and search for Craig. The planet was not very big and half an hour later, they had searched the entire planet, but there was no sign of him. Andocia was furious.

"It's impossible! There was no way he could escape." She stood with her hands on her hips, glaring at the barren landscape.

One of her soldiers spoke nervously to Andocia. "Is it possible that someone friendly spotted him and he was rescued?"

Andocia shook her head. "It is certainly a possibility, but this isn't a busy section of the galaxy. However that man's luck is uncanny! I suppose that is what must have happened. We are wasting our time here!"

The evil woman strode crossly to her spaceship, followed by her soldiers, and the ship lifted off, leaving a whirlwind of dust in its wake.

↓ ↓ ↓

The trident ship came to rest on a strange planet and Carter waited for them all to disembark before creeping stealthily out of the enemy ship. Then he made his way cautiously to the hangar, where he found his ship. A quick search revealed no one was lying in wait for him and he climbed thankfully into his own craft and blasted off. From a safe distance, he scanned the planet but to his dismay, there were not many buildings on it. He activated the heat scan, which picked up a few beings in the buildings, but there was no sign of any cell and he had to conclude that this was another of Andocia's hideouts and not her planet at all. He sighed and the ship rose until it was just a speck on the horizon, but Craig was concerned as he had heard Andocia ranting while he was secure in his hiding place on her ship. A sixth sense made him concentrate on his worst enemy and he watched as Andocia took out her mobile device and began to text furiously.

Craig centred his scanner on her and enlarged the picture so that he could read the words that she had typed:

Carter has become a nuisance now and I'm tired of this game of cat and mouse. Issue an all points alert for any sign of him. Four of my best warriors are to go to Earth in secret and capture his woman,

Constance Gregg. She is to be imprisoned in the castle, but Craig Carter is to be detained if seen. Issue an order to all the inhabitants of the Golden Way to hold him for us if he shows his face. Failure to comply with these orders will result in immediate destruction for the guilty planets.

Craig was dumbfounded. "Oh no, I must warn Constance to get away! Mission Control will see that she goes to some other planet where she can be guarded."

He pressed a key and immediately was in contact with the Space Control Centre, where he was put through to Commander Simms. "Sir, there's trouble brewing! I've just intercepted a message that endangers Constance's life. Andocia is sending some of her followers to kidnap Constance and she mustn't succeed. Please send her to another planet, where she can be guarded. If I weren't in the Golden Way now, I'd come and fetch her myself. Sir, I must try to rescue Tanus – more so now than ever before."

"All right Craig, I'll do my best. Please be careful!"

As Simms disconnected, Constance knocked on his door and he took hold of her hands. "My dear, I've just been speaking to Craig and he fears for your safety. He and Andocia have clashed again and she wants to kidnap you. He suggested you leave Earth now and hide on one of the planets in space."

"I see, but which one?" she asked worriedly.

"I thought about Sonambra, for it's not so easily accessible and they should be able to guard you well enough. Hurry, grab a few things and get out of here."

Later on, Simms watched nervously as Constance blasted off.

↙ ↙ ↙

When she reached Sonambra, she explained the situation and Sonambro took her to a room.

"We'll do what we can for you of course, but I fear Andocia. She is a deadly foe. However, she won't know where you have gone, so it should save precious time. Perhaps Cragus will succeed in rescuing Tanus before Andocia finds out your whereabouts."

"That's what we're counting on. Craig must do everything he can to rescue Tanus, because without her help, both universes will be in trouble," remarked Constance worriedly. "If they manage to capture me, it'll put Craig in a very bad position."

Sonambro nodded his head in agreement. "Would he give himself up to Andocia if she had you, do you think?"

"I don't really know, but I sincerely hope not! I don't want to take that chance though."

Constance spent most of her time talking to the Sonambrians and was never left unguarded at any time. They were kind and considerate to her, but despite all their security precautions, she felt uneasy and couldn't relax.

Two days passed and suddenly Sonambro hurried to her room. "Constance, there's a trident ship hovering above us! I don't know how many ships have been sent to find you, but I think it would be wise if you made a hasty departure. Come with me – there's a secret exit you can use! Andocia's followers cannot really harm us because we are energy beings, but I'm not sure if we can stop them from taking you. We have no idea what their weapons could do."

They set off at a run and he led her to a door, which opened quietly.

"Constance, I wish you the best of luck and I'm sorry we couldn't do more for you. Hurry please!"

Obediently she went through the door and it closed once again. Constance looked at it and could no longer see it, for it formed part of the landscape. She set off at a run and reached the hangar, where she flattened herself against a wall. The trident ship was parked near her craft and she cursed her bad luck. Several women were milling about, holding nasty looking weapons, so she stood further back in the shadows and waited for a suitable opportunity to escape. As she watched, the women began to move away, leaving only two to guard her ship.

Constance kept to the shadows and managed to come up behind her craft. Her laser was set on stun and she fired at the two women, bringing them down instantly. The door whined as it opened and she jumped aboard even before the steps had opened fully. She was in two minds whether she should just blast off, or wait until it was safe, and finally decided on the latter. Miss Gregg crept up to the observation deck of her craft and watched as the women milled about. They questioned all the beings and shook them furiously, but no one was volunteering any information. Eventually, to her horror, several women arrived in the docking area, holding a struggling Sonambro. While some women held him, others aimed their weapons and fired at him and Constance winced as each flash scored a direct hit. She knew that it would only take one of those blasts to kill her outright, but Sonambra was an energy being, and she wondered idly how long it would take for Sonambro to start feeling the effects of the blasts.

Constance watched, her hands frozen on the controls, when suddenly Sonambro began to weaken and sway on his feet. Even from that distance she could see the pain reflected in his face. Her mind kept telling her that it was now or never, but her heart told a different story. Sonambro had always been kind to her, Craig and any other Earthlings who had visited him, and she knew, deep down, she couldn't allow this to continue. At the same time, Craig had warned her to get away from the red beings and she knew that if they managed to capture her, it would be very unfortunate. The woman bit her lip and fired up her engines. As she blasted off, she smiled despite the situation, for the look of amazement on Andocia's warriors was one of total confusion.

"I'm truly sorry Sonambro," she thought, *"but I have to do this. I cannot fall into Andocia's clutches under any circumstances."*

Back on the sun planet, Sonambro watched her go and he allowed himself a smile of satisfaction. *"You go and don't stop for anything! I wish you the best of luck Constance."*

When the women saw their quarry had escaped, they ignored the sun being and jumped to their feet.

"Don't just stand around like idiots!" admonished their leader. *"Get up there and capture her!"*

The women ran for their ship and soon lifted off into space, in hot pursuit of Constance.

The woman space explorer urged maximum thrust from her

craft and she sped away, not even sure where to go. All she was interested in was putting as much distance between her and the trident ship as she could. Constance knew that the trident ships were faster and were able to sneak up on her without her realizing it.

About half an hour later, her vidscreen beeped and one of Andocia's followers glared at her. "Come on Miss Gregg, give this up! I find chasing you very tiresome. You may have got a small head start but it won't help you — we have a fix on your position. You cannot outrun us."

"Come and get me then!" she challenged, before ending the communication. Constance wanted to put her ship into time lapse but it used too much fuel that way, so she decided to wait until the trident ship was within striking distance. She would use this in an emergency only. As Miss Gregg sped through space, she scanned nearby planets and stars, hoping to hide on one of them, but everyone she saw would leave her at a serious disadvantage, so she continued fleeing.

A planet appeared on her screen and as it was in deep shadow Constance decided to hide on it in the hope that she could disappear from her pursuers. She landed and hid in a thicket of trees, where she cut her engine. Not long afterwards the trident ship flew overhead and disappeared from sight. Constance peered out from the trees but there was no sign of them.

However, the ship reappeared above the trees and hovered for a while. Miss Gregg was unaware that she had been holding her breath and she exhaled noisily when she saw the ship disappear once more. After half an hour, she decided with a measure of relief that the women warriors had finally given up and decided to continue cruising through space. While examining a map of the universe on the ship's computer, the explorer saw there was an American space station about two hours away and decided to take refuge there. The woman turned her craft in a complete circle and scanned the emptiness of space around her, but there was no sign of the trident ship. Relieved, she continued on her journey.

Miss Gregg hadn't gone very far when the trident ship loomed up close to her and she swerved hastily to avoid a collision.

"Are you totally insane?" she screamed at them. *"You could have killed me!"*

The leader of the warrior women smiled malevolently at her. "I knew exactly what I was doing my dear and there was plenty of clearance. Now be a good girl and surrender!"

"Go to hell!" Constance spat furiously. She typed in a code and immediately guns appeared in the front of her ship. "Now you give up this silly notion. I'm not coming with you, not now, not ever. If you don't leave, I *will* fire on you," she threatened.

The woman looked at Miss Gregg in mock horror. "No, please don't shoot us!" she simpered.

Constance gulped as guns from the trident ship were trained on her. "Oooh guess what," Andocia's follower remarked mockingly, "ours are bigger than yours. Let's play shall we!"

The American spaceship rocked as a laser beam shot across the observation window, narrowly missing her. She pressed a button on her console and the computer responded immediately. *<Force field activated!>* it stated. Constance then began getting her weapons online. Even before she had loosed off a single shot, beams were crisscrossing her ship. She abandoned the idea of trying to shoot at them, and decided it would be better to run away than to try and fight them. Constance turned tail and ran for her life with the larger ship in hot pursuit. Several laser beams slammed into her and she knew that if it continued for any length of time, she would be left defenceless.

Knowing the trident ship would soon overpower her, Constance put her ship into time lapse and disappeared from view. Her intention was to get to the space station and ask for help. Although they were neutral to all, the space stations did have some impressive weaponry that could hold off any threat.

CHAPTER 6

Miss Gregg was almost at the space station when she came out of time lapse. At that exact moment, the trident ship moved in behind her and trained weapons on the rear end of her ship. Her vidscreen came to life and once again she was looking at the woman soldier. "You took your time dear. We've been waiting for you."

Constance was dismayed when she saw how vulnerable she was. Her guns were not armed, but theirs were. The computer confirmed this. <*Enemy ship is closing in. They are locked on and weapons are primed to fire on us. Must I take evasive action?*>

"Not yet! They are too close," she cautioned.

The red being spoke again. "Miss Gregg, you cannot outrun our guns. I'll give you a choice though. Either you surrender, or I will fire at your space station and many beings are going to lose their lives. If Andocia didn't want you alive, you would have been destroyed long ago. I'm running out of patience. Make up your mind!"

"Don't you dare fire on the space station," Constance snapped. "In our galaxy the space stations are neutral and are a haven to both friend and foe."

"Make your choice Miss Gregg, or else I'm going to destroy this space station and then cripple your ship, but either way, Andocia will triumph," the woman snapped commandingly.

Constance looked frantically around her, but there was no way to escape. She clenched her fists in anger, but knew it was hopeless. She pressed an emergency switch on her computer console and it delivered the following message in coded form. "*Constance Gregg: captured by Andocia.*" It also transmitted her co-ordinates. She then opened a channel and spoke to the pilot of the trident ship. "All right you win!" she sighed. "Don't fire. I surrender."

"That is very sensible my dear. Turn around and bring your

ship inside. I'll open the hatch for you."

Miss Gregg began turning her spaceship around until she faced the enemy one. A huge panel slid aside and reluctantly she made for it. The woman flew in and the hatch closed. She was told where to land and did so. Her ship was instantly surrounded by many women warriors brandishing deadly laser rifles.

All eyes turned to her as she moved towards the group with her hands in the air. Constance was ordered to surrender her weapon and did so, putting it gently on the floor and then kicking it over to Andocia's followers.

When they reached the Golden Way once more, Andocia materialized in the trident ship where Constance was being held and went to see her. "So, we meet again Miss Gregg! You are going to suffer and so is your precious boyfriend."

Constance didn't answer and Andocia continued. "We are going to my palace far away. There you may converse with Tanus, who has begun to lose hope of ever being rescued. Carter is a resourceful man, but he will never be able to free Tanus. As things stand, he doesn't even know where my planet is situated, and even if he knew, there are many obstacles that'll be in his way. Even supposing he finds her he will find she is bound with special chains that no one can break. When I've contacted your precious boyfriend and given him the news, he'll see things my way, or else you'll suffer the consequences."

"Let's just assume that you're right, Andocia – what's going to happen to Craig when you catch him?" Constance asked tentatively.

"I haven't really decided yet, but whatever I plan to do, you can be assured that I'll enjoy every minute of it!"

Constance said nothing. She looked morosely out of the window and watched the planets speeding by. Most of them were a blur as the trident ship passed by and Constance understood just how much faster the trident ships were compared to NASA's crafts. Three of Andocia's female warriors stood to attention and waited for their mistress to speak. Andocia put her hand on Constance's arm and she jerked away as though she had been stung. Her enemy glared at her, then turned to the warriors waiting patiently for their orders.

"Take Miss Gregg to her suite and see that she's comfortable."

One of the women gestured with her weapon and Constance went with them. A lift took them down another two floors and the female warriors escorted her down a narrow passageway. Several doors were visible on both sides of the passage and the lighting was dim. The carpet looked old and worn and the place reminded her of a cheap hotel. One of the women took out a keycard and inserted it in a lock. Miss Gregg was ordered into the room. The furniture consisted of a single bed and chest of drawers. A television set stood on top of the chest and there were a number of data discs in a wicker basket. Another door led to a small bathroom. A small window was set into the wall between the bed and chest of drawers. There was also an armchair in one corner and beside it stood a small metal table which was bolted to the floor. An electronic reading device lay on the table.

Someone brought Constance's suitcase inside and the women left. The door locked securely behind them. When she was alone, Constance went to the window and opened the curtains. Not surprisingly the window was barred and the glass looked thick enough to be laser proof. The window looked out onto another passageway. Despite the modest accommodation, the young explorer was pleasantly surprised. She had expected to be imprisoned in a tiny room containing an iron cot. She set about examining the entertainment left for her. The data discs contained many diverse movies to watch and the electronic reader also had some interesting books loaded on it. She wondered if Andocia would send for her, or whether she would be left to her own devices until they reached Andocia's planet.

That evening as she sat in the chair, she was startled by a metallic noise and jumped up nervously. A portion of the door slid open and a tray of food appeared. The panel shut firmly again and she took the tray off the shelf and examined its contents. She was surprised, for while the food was not of the gourmet variety, it smelt surprisingly good. The stew was delicious and she realized just how hungry she was. All the crockery and cutlery were plastic, including the tray.

The days sped by and Andocia never sent for her even once. She didn't mind though as she knew that things would be different on the evil woman's planet. Constance was filled with trepidation and she wondered what Andocia had in store for her. She kept busy and tried not to dwell too much on what would happen in the future. Constance lost count of the days that they travelled through space, but it didn't seem a very long time. She estimated it had taken about five days to reach their destination.

The trident ship landed and four women came to fetch her. She was taken out of the ship and put in a hovercraft containing several other heavily armed women warriors. They stared at her and she met their gaze unflinchingly. As they drew near to the palace, Constance stared miserably at the fortress. There were guards everywhere, and ugly statues stood like silent sentinels along the walls. The walls were dark and made of stone. A drawbridge lay across the moat and as the party crossed over to the iron gates, Constance could see large scaly creatures swimming around. She shuddered as she thought of what their diet probably consisted of. The iron gate lifted up vertically and as the party entered the castle grounds, Miss Gregg paused for a moment and stared at the huge building. It was impressive in size, but not looks. The woman continued walking and ignored the curious stares of the onlookers. Her back was straight and she held her head high.

Flanked by a large contingent of armed guards, Constance found herself in a large entrance hall. She saw several staircases which led to the floor above. They were very huge and imposing, but the wood was stained in black varnish. The stairs were also constructed of wood and the carpeting was an ox blood colour. A number of paintings hung on the walls depicting obscure people and scenes. None of the people in the frames were smiling. Several huge chandeliers hung from the ceiling. In contrast to the dull and dreary furniture, the lights seemed to overcompensate for the gloom. All the décor was black and red, but while the furniture looked comfortable and expensive, it added to the gloom of the room. Even the carpeting looked out of place. There were other colours in the scheme, but they looked dull and uninteresting, giving the impression that she had just walked into a mausoleum.

At that moment Andocia came into the room. Everyone bowed reverently, except Constance, who stared coolly at her captor. The woman made a dismissive gesture with her hands and Constance's guards bowed and moved away.

"Follow me," she ordered.

Constance did as she was told. They went into a smaller living room where some of Andocia's helpers were arranging platters of snacks and something to drink on a nearby table. Miss Gregg sat down on a chair opposite her hostess and placed her hands in her lap.

Andocia crossed one shapely leg over the other and smiled at her guest. "Welcome to the red planet my dear. Over the next few days we are going to get to know one another very well – or maybe I should re-phrase that; I'll know a great deal more about you than even your mother does. I have a number of questions before I show you to your room though. Let us first have something to eat and drink before we begin. I'm being polite to you now, but tomorrow will be a different story entirely."

Constance looked around the room and saw that even though the guards had left her alone, they were not far away. Constance had lost her appetite, but she nibbled at the food, not really tasting any of it.

After they had eaten, the helper began putting the items back on the tray. Andocia turned to her "guest". "Well Constance, what do you think of my castle so far?"

Miss Gregg looked levelly at her captor. "For a start, if I were you, I would fire my decorator. She is absolutely hopeless. This place looks like a funeral parlour!"

A few cups clattered on the tray and Andocia glared at her helper. "Watch it! That's my best china!"

The woman ducked her head. "Sorry mistress!" she mumbled, and then scooted away quickly.

Andocia glared at her captive. "What's wrong with my décor?"

"You asked my opinion so I gave it. I'm just being honest. I'm not an interior decorator, but it's depressing."

"All right, let's get down to business, shall we?" The evil woman remarked. "I want to know what's happening with Craig. Is he still determined to free Tanus?"

Constance shrugged her shoulders. "I don't know what's happening. I haven't spoken to him in a while. I know he wants to help her, but he doesn't even know where your planet is! Whatever his plans are, he hasn't shared them with me."

"In other words, he isn't rushing to rescue you either. I imagine he knows I have you by now."

"He probably does, but unless he locates this planet, I won't be seeing him anytime soon."

A gleam appeared in Andocia's eyes. "Ah! I can help with that problem. Maybe I should just get in touch with him and give him the co-ordinates. Then he can charge up and rescue you, his fair damsel in distress."

"Didn't you warn him not to attempt to rescue Tanus? Do you honestly think he is going to give himself up to you without a plan? Is Tanus even imprisoned here?"

Andocia smiled cruelly. "She's here, but she won't be going anywhere soon."

"I would like to see her, if I may?" Constance asked.

"Why should I let you see her? You are also my prisoner in case you have forgotten!"

Constance looked down at her hands and sighed. "I'm just making a request that's all. She's my friend and I wanted to talk to her."

Andocia smiled evilly. "Maybe it will be a good idea for you to visit with her for a while. If you are thinking of some way to rescue her yourself, you'll soon forget that silly notion."

Andocia motioned to the guards and they came closer. "Take Miss Gregg to Tanus and lock her up in the cell as well. I have other matters that require my attention."

The guards surrounded the young explorer and then proceeded to a lift which took them down another two levels. A narrow passageway faced them and they walked down until they reached the end of the corridor. One of the guards stood in front of a keypad and typed in a code and the heavy steel door creaked open. They walked down another passageway similar to the one they had just left, and again they came to a door. A security guard punched in a code again and the heavily barred door swung open.

Another corridor faced them, but this time the guards moved to a cell at the end of the passageway and again keyed in a code. One of the security guards then waved Constance inside and the door clanged shut.

The cell was dark and Miss Gregg waited until her eyes adjusted to the gloomy interior. She looked around the small cell and noticed a small barred window at the far end. The sun shone on the stone floor, illuminating the dark stone. To the right of the window stood a bed and a light glowed dimly over it. Something white lay on the bed and she hurried over to the prone figure. "Tanus, is that you?" she asked tentatively.

The figure sat up. "Constance! What are you doing here?"

The young woman put her arms around Tanus and hugged her. "It's good to see you! I would've liked it to have been under better circumstances, but I'll take what I can get right now."

Tanus's arms encircled her and only then did the young woman see the shackles on her wrists. Constance stroked the bound wrists tenderly. "I'm so sorry you're in this predicament! Andocia is such an evil *bitch!*"

The woman in white put her hand on Constance's forehead and rubbed it gently. She spoke quietly to the distressed woman. "It's going to be okay I promise you! I know you are frightened, but you have to keep a clear head."

Tanus's touch calmed her and Miss Gregg sat down next to her friend. "I'm so sorry for the outburst. It's hard trying to keep a brave front in the face of your enemies."

Her friend smiled sympathetically. "I know how you feel, but why has Andocia captured you? It doesn't make any sense!"

Constance shrugged. "I don't know how her mind works. It has been puzzling me as well. According to Craig, Andocia contacted him and warned him not to come here and rescue you. If she didn't want him to, why give him an incentive to do so?"

Tanus stood up and paced the floor. Her face was a mask of pain and misery as she thought of the strange circumstances. She bit her lip and wondered how to break the news to Constance gently.

Tanus returned to the bed and took Constance's hand in hers. "My dear, I think I know what's happening here and it worries me."

"What is it? Tell me please," she pleaded.

"I think the two events are not even connected. Andocia captured you because it's you she wants. It has nothing to do with Craig's mission. You aren't going to be used as bait to lure him here."

"I don't understand! Why would she tell him I am her prisoner, if she doesn't have an ulterior motive?"

Tanus sighed heavily. "How does Craig know you are here? I presume he does, but how did he find out? Did she contact him?"

Constance wrung her hands together. "Yes ... no ... I don't know! Oh, wait a minute; I sent out a distress signal when Andocia's followers caught up with me near the American Space station. I might have mentioned it then."

"Aha, so that's how he found out. Commander Simms probably told him when he got the distress call."

"That makes sense I guess."

Tanus began pacing the floor miserably. "This is not good at all. Tell me Constance, is Craig coming to rescue me?"

"Yes, I believe he's going to come. The last time we spoke though he said he couldn't locate this planet. Everyone he spoke to didn't know where it is."

"Very few people know where Andocia lives, but some of the planets in the blue universe could help him. He just doesn't know which ones. Look Constance you have to do me a favour! Please, when you speak to Andocia, ask her to contact Craig. I want you to tell him not to come here and rescue me! I made a huge mistake asking him to help me, but I was so desperate! He's very resourceful, but he'll die if he tries. I cannot have that on my conscience. Andocia has a trophy case containing the heads of all my friends who have tried to rescue me. They were all very good at their jobs, but they sacrificed themselves for nothing! Please tell Craig to stay away!"

"All right Tanus. I understand. I'll pass your message on."

They were interrupted by a sound at the door and Tanus hurriedly sat down on the bed, pulling Constance down with her. The guards aimed their weapons at the two women.

"Visiting time is over, Miss Gregg."

The young woman held tightly to her friend's hand. "Can't I stay with Tanus please?"

"No, you can't. Come with us now!"

Tanus released the woman's hand. "Go with them! I'll be fine."

Reluctantly she got up. Just as the door closed behind Tanus, Constance heard a voice in her head. *"Go quietly with them my dear. Do as Andocia says and don't question her. You have great inner strength! Draw on it when you are afraid. May all be well with you."*

"Thank you for your advice my friend. Hopefully I can visit you again soon," Constance replied telepathically.

She was marched back upstairs and taken to a room on the third floor. It was similar to the one she had occupied on Andocia's trident ship, only a little larger. The entertainment was also very much the same as that on the ship. The bathroom was plain, but everything functioned properly. Most of all she was relieved that her captors hadn't put any kind of restraints on her. She moved to the barred window and looked out. Night was falling, but she could still see the expanse of grass far below her. Flowers grew around what looked like a small pond and somehow it comforted her that some beauty existed on the red planet. Later she got ready for bed but she didn't think she would sleep very much.

Constance was woken up by the door opening and to her surprise she realized it was morning. She had managed to sleep after all. A dark-haired woman, a few years younger than her, came in with a tray of food. She placed it on a table. "Good morning Miss Gregg. You have an hour to eat your breakfast and get ready. Andocia will expect you to be prompt. She hates tardiness."

"Thank you, miss …?"

The younger woman smiled but said nothing. She closed the door and locked it.

Constance tucked into her food and despite the butterflies in her stomach, she found she was quite hungry.

Miss Gregg was ready before the guards came to fetch her. They took her to another section of the castle where Andocia was waiting.

"Good morning my dear. I hope you slept well. We have a lot to do today so we had better get started immediately."

"Wait Andocia. Have you heard any news about Craig perhaps?"

"Nothing at all, but I'm not interested right now. Come along, time is wasting."

Constance followed her captor reluctantly.

CHAPTER 7

In the Golden Way, Craig was still searching for Andocia's planet. He was concerned about Constance, but he didn't want to land on any planet, just in case they captured him, as Andocia had ordered. He pulled up a chart of the blue universe on his computer and expanded it to cover the entire cockpit of his ship. As Earth and the rest of the planets in his universe were still not very clued up about this new universe, the details were sketchy at best. The explorer typed in a request asking for the nearest unexplored planet that had a breathable atmosphere and was inhabited. The computer showed a planet not too far away and he made for it. As he hovered in space, out of range of any spy satellites, he scanned the planet. There were buildings here and also what looked like a sort of tavern where many beings were sitting around tables.

Craig decided to take a chance and land on the planet. He hoped that someone there would know the location of Andocia's planet. While he was still out of range of any possible scanners, he pressed the holographic device on his chest a few times until he found the disguise that he wanted. When he looked in the mirror, he couldn't recognize himself at all. His hair was now dark brown and his eyes were also brown. He had the same body shape, although this one was thinner, but firm.

Then he pressed the key on the controls of his spaceship and it began to take the shape of an earlier model. Once he was satisfied and the transformation was complete, he flew closer until he could see his ship had been spotted. The control tower on the planet hailed him. "Greetings stranger, please identify yourself. This is the planet Meltron."

Carter opened a channel and spoke in a Texas drawl. "Howdy there Meltron. My name is Dwayne Wilkes. I'm from planet Earth."

"Kindly state the nature of your business here. Is it for business or pleasure?"

The explorer chuckled. "Maybe a bit of both."

"Very well then, welcome to our planet. You will see a diagram on your computer screen. Please follow the directions to the landing bays."

"Thank you kindly. I'll see you soon."

The directions appeared on his screen and he followed them until he came to the landing bay as instructed. Once Carter had landed, he entered a building and walked up to the reception desk, where he was surprised to see a human woman sitting on a chair. He stared at her and then smiled in a friendly manner.

"You are a sight for sore eyes darlin'. What would a fellow human being be doing here in this galaxy, seeing as it has only been discovered recently?"

She shrugged. "I had no job on Earth and very little prospects. My boyfriend heard about this place and here I am. It's a living."

"Tell me honey, where can I get something to eat? I'm hungry."

The woman pointed down the passage. "Go through that set of double doors and then turn right. There is a restaurant a little further on."

"Thanks, darlin'. I was wondering, seeing as I'm on a schedule, is there anyone I can talk to about some possible business ventures?"

The woman smiled. "Sure! My boyfriend is there in the restaurant. He might have something to offer you. Tell him I sent you.

His name is Spike."

Carter thanked her and made for the restaurant. When he opened the door, he was greeted by the sounds of many beings talking, but they were doing so in hushed tones. He wandered up to the bar and looked around. A barman appeared as if by magic and spoke in a voice that seemed to echo and Craig realized that he was a robot, but the fact didn't surprise him.

"What can I get for you mister?"

Unsure of what the drinks were made of he asked for a bottled water. While he waited for the barman to bring it over, he looked around the bar, which was dimly lit and very crowded.

The barman brought his water and Craig took it. While he was sipping it, he spotted a man sitting in a corner booth laughing with some beings that Craig didn't recognize. The man's hair was bright red and it was gelled up with a piece of hair near his forehead that looked like a spike – hence the name. Craig got up from his seat and went over to the man.

"Hi mister!" he greeted him. "You must be Spike."

He extended his hand but the man stared at him and scowled. "Do I know you mister?"

"No sir, you don't, but your girlfriend outside said that I should come and see you."

For a moment the man looked blank and then he smiled. "Oh, you mean Melody!"

Carter nodded and the man shook his hand. "So tell me, what can I do for you Mr …?"

"Wilkes – Dwayne Wilkes. Pleased to meet you."

Spike nodded. "Same here. You looking for business or pleasure?"

Dwayne smiled. "Pleasure sounds good but unfortunately I'm on a schedule so business it will have to be."

Spike crossed his arms over his chest. "What sort of business are you wanting to get into?"

"Well I'm a delivery guy essentially. I used to work at NASA some years ago. I was a technician who fixed up the spacecrafts. Anyway, I got bored and decided to branch out for myself, so as a farewell gift they gave me an old spacecraft to keep. I fixed it up and now I go around delivering stuff to planets that need it."

Spike's eyebrows rose and Dwayne saw that the man was interested. "What 'stuff' do you deliver and to where?"

Dwayne shrugged his shoulders carelessly. "You know – stuff; anything that needs to be delivered, to anywhere. Supply and demand – you understand."

Spike scowled but his eyes were mischievous. "Hey mister, are we talking illegal contraband – stuff like that?"

Dwayne put up his hands. "Hey, not so loud!" he said, looking around to see if anyone had heard. "Like I said, anything that needs to be delivered – I'm not choosy so long as the bills get paid. I got me a bitch of an ex-wife who's always on my case and she's got expensive tastes."

"Yeah, I can relate to that!" Spike replied.

"So, can you help me?" Dwayne asked.

Spike smiled. "Maybe I can. Do you have certain areas that you deliver to, or is anywhere okay?"

"No, anywhere is fine, but like I said I'm on a schedule right now. I just finished a delivery now and I have another one to pick up in a few days. Give me your contact details and I'll call you when I'm available. We can organize something then. Is that okay?"

"Sure," Spike replied, handing over a gold embossed business card.

Dwayne pocketed the card, but before he left, he turned to Spike.

"I'm also looking to expand my business to the Golden Way as well. I know there are lots of planets here that we know nothing about, but one in particular interests me. I heard about a planet that has lots of sexy women living there. Their boss/leader – whatever is something else or so I've been told. I heard that the boss lady's name is Andocee – or something like that. I would sure like to do business with her. Do you know where her planet is?"

Spike paled at the mention of Andocia. "Oh man, that is one sexy lady, but you don't want to mess with her! I heard she's bad news!"

Dwayne smiled. "Yeah? But I'm curious. Do you know where her planet is though? I just want to have a peek."

Spike looked around but no one was paying any attention to them. He leaned over and whispered in Craig's ear. "Write this down somewhere buddy!"

Dwayne took his mobile device out of his pocket and put it down on the counter. Spike rattled off a few numbers and he saved them on the device. He nodded his thanks and returned it to his pocket. Then Craig drank the rest of his water. He stayed a few minutes longer, then shook Spike's hand once again. "Thanks for the chat. I'll definitely contact you as soon as I have a gap in my schedule. I better go now before I miss my deadline."

Spike shook his hand again. "It was a pleasure meeting you. I hope I'll see you soon."

Craig smiled and waved to them as he left the bar.

He returned to his ship and blasted off. When he was out of reach of their scanners, he changed back to his normal self and continued on his journey.

"Well that was a stroke of good luck! Spike is an interesting character. Even in this universe, there are opportunistic people out there who just want to make some easy credits."

The space explorer took out his device and typed the co-ordinates of Andocia's planet into his computer. Afterwards he went to prepare something to eat. He was sitting at the console thinking of a plan of action when a huge white bird appeared in his sights. It spoke telepathically. *"Craig Carter, I'm a friend – please let me in. I serve the mighty Tanus and I'm sure that we can help one another."*

Carter did so and the bird flew inside and shrunk to waist height.

"Who are you?" he asked curiously.

"My name is Tarmin and I'm Tanus's friend. I see you are using the ring and that's good, but you can drop the barrier, for I mean you no harm. In fact, my life is in terrible danger, more so than yours."

"Why is that?" he wanted to know.

"Let me explain the situation and perhaps then you'll understand. When Andocia came to my mistress' planet and captured her I fled, hoping to rally some kind of an attack, but Andocia pursued me and unleashed her deadly power and I dropped senseless to the ground. It was fortunate she was in such a hurry, because she never came back to see if I was dead. When I recovered my senses, the trident ship and all its occupants had vanished of course, along with Tanus. I've been searching for you, because my mistress seemed to have great faith in your abilities. Her people told me she had managed to get a message out, requesting that you help her."

Craig nodded in the affirmative. "Yes, she did request my help, but I've had trouble finding the location of Andocia's planet, so I've wasted a great deal of time ..."

The bird interrupted and hopped up and down excitedly. "That's where I come in; I know where Andocia's castle is.

"That's great, but I also know where to find it. Someone gave me the co-ordinates just a few hours ago. My ship is already programmed to go to her planet ..."

He was interrupted by the vidscreen as it beeped and the bird shrunk still further and went to hide behind a handy piece of equipment.

"Craig Carter, answer me!"

The white bird peeped out from behind the chair.

"It's Andocia, you'd better answer her, but don't mention me!"

Carter pressed a button and Andocia was staring at him. "Oh good, there you are. I have some news for you."

"What would that be exactly?" he asked tersely.

"I think you know! I've managed to kidnap Constance and I want you to surrender to me. Failure to do so will result in your girlfriend suffering needless pain."

Carter shrugged his shoulders and stared balefully at the woman he hated and feared above anything else. He kept his face impassive, even though he was as tense as a coiled spring. "I don't like you very much Andocia, but I believe you. Constance managed to send off a distress signal before she was captured and Commander Simms informed me. I had really hoped Constance would get away from your followers, but it wasn't to be. However, I'm sorry, but I can't give myself up to you, especially not now; there's just too much at stake! Correct me if I'm wrong, but didn't you threaten me regarding Tanus. I was warned not to try and rescue her. Why the change in plans?"

"I still don't want you to come and rescue Tanus. I'm ordering you to come to my planet voluntarily."

"I need a good reason to do this. Why should I risk my life to visit you?"

"Not even for your precious woman's life?" she asked incredulously.

"No, not even for her, I'm sorry," he replied regretfully.

"Your love is very shallow, Carter. She's going to suffer, that I promise."

"Andocia, I love Constance very much, but I cannot keep on putting myself in danger because you are trying to use her to get back at me. In fact, we both discussed this a while ago and decided that neither of us would put ourselves in harm's way to rescue the other. Both Constance and I know the risks we take out here in space but we have our jobs to do."

Andocia smiled slyly. "You are lying! You promised to come and rescue Tanus and you never go back on a promise! It's one of the things about you that I admire a great deal, even though I consider it a weakness of yours. I just thought I could save you the trouble, so I invited you to come to me voluntarily."

Craig shook his head regretfully. "Andocia, you're quite correct – I try to help my friends, even if it means putting myself in danger, but I have to decline. I've thought of nothing else but rescuing Tanus these last few weeks, but I have decided not to go through with it. I made a promise, but I can't keep it! I'm just a human being, not a superhero and I know I will be hopelessly outnumbered and outclassed, and probably killed." Craig wiped his eyes wearily and turned back to the screen. "Andocia, give Tanus a message for me. Tell her I'm sorry but I have to decline her request. Will you give Constance a message as well. Tell her I love her and I hope she understands. Promise me you'll pass the messages on. I don't want either of them to have any false hopes."

Andocia stared incredulously at the man she was talking to. "You are really serious aren't you! I never thought the great Craig Carter was a quitter! Don't worry, I'll definitely tell them what you said. I guess I'll be seeing you around sometime."

"Don't count on it," he replied.

Andocia's face disappeared from the screen as she disconnected, and Tarmin grew until she was shoulder height to the explorer. She was stunned by what she had heard. "What was that all about?" she demanded. "I thought we were going to Andocia's planet to rescue my mistress and your girlfriend. Why the change of heart?"

Craig grinned at the bird. "Did you believe me?"

"Well of course I did," she huffed.

"Then Andocia probably believed me as well."

"What ...? Wait a minute! You were *lying!*"

"I was lying!" he confirmed.

Tarmin punched him in the arm. "I believed you! My heart nearly stopped beating!"

"Ouch! You pack quite a punch Tarmin!"

"Serves you right! Don't do that again," she complained.

Craig's face crumpled in misery. "I may have fooled Andocia, but I fear for Constance's life. She may just kill her out of spite."

Impulsively, the bird placed a wing around his shoulders.

"You did well Craig. It must have taken every ounce of courage you own to do that and I'm proud of you, as Tanus would be."

"Tarmin, do you suppose she'll really hurt Constance, or was it just a giant bluff?"

Tarmin shook her head regretfully. "No Craig, if Andocia says she'll suffer, then she will. Just try to be brave. I know this won't comfort you but I know Andocia much better than you do. Whatever her purpose in capturing Constance was, I really don't think it has anything to do with your mission. Tanus and I discussed this subject before Andocia kidnapped her, and we came to the same conclusion. Constance is very special in her own way and she too has done remarkable things. Maybe Andocia is just curious. You know she has a preference for women warriors and your girlfriend is very competitive. Maybe she is just conducting some tests."

"Using her as a guinea pig you mean!" Craig snapped.

"It's a possibility, but I'm not sure what she wants with Constance. We need to come up with some kind of plan and hopefully we can rescue her and Tanus before anything bad happens."

"How long will it take to get to the red planet?"

"We have two days to plan a strategy," Tarmin stated.

Carter put his head in his hands. "I hope Constance will understand. Damn it how I despise that woman!" he exploded. "Why did I ever have to meet her?"

"I suppose it was inevitable Craig. The way space exploration is expanding in the universes, it is shrinking the galaxies. As technology improves more, other beings learn that many planets exist, with very varied life forms on them. I'm sure your girlfriend will understand why you made that decision. I suggest you put your craft onto automatic pilot and sleep for a while. When you are refreshed, you'll be able to think more clearly."

"What are you going to do?" he asked curiously.

"I'll sleep in here and make any necessary course corrections if that's okay with you."

Craig nodded and then went to lie down on his bed. He fell asleep almost immediately and Tarmin watched him as he slept.

"You are an exceptionally brave man, Craig Carter. My mistress is a good judge of character, and I really hope you can save her, for stronger beings than you have tried to rescue her and been slain. Several of them are now in Andocia's trophy case," thought Tarmin as she repressed a shudder. *"The ring will help to a small extent, but Andocia's powers are awesome."*

Craig awoke eight hours later and came to see what was happening in the flight section. Tarmin stood up and greeted him with a gentle peck on the cheek. "Good morning Craig, did you sleep well?"

"Yes, thank you. How much further is it to Andocia's planet?"

"Oh, still another day at least," replied the bird.

"Okay, then we have to use this time wisely. Between us we must come up with some kind of strategy to rescue our loved ones. I'll do everything I can, but I cannot do this alone. Can you contact Tanus's friends on her planet and enlist their help?"

The bird hopped from one leg to the other. "They'll do anything for Tanus! She's very good to those who support her! I'll contact them immediately."

Tarmin contacted the white planet and spoke to the head of the army. He was introduced to Craig and pledged his allegiance to the cause. He asked to be excused for a moment while he called several of the elite soldiers in the army to join the discussion. While they were waiting, the man who had first contacted Craig, asking for his help in rescuing his mistress, came online. He was beaming from ear to ear. "It's wonderful to see you again Mr Carter! I'm so happy that this is finally going to happen. Hopefully Tanus will be freed soon. Thank you once again for your bravery. I'm not a soldier unfortunately. I'm the technical guy. Anything you need, let me know and I'll see that you get it."

"Thank you. I appreciate it! When I have finished discussing our strategy with the soldiers, we'll give you a list."

The man left and several men took their places in front of their vidscreens.

"Okay Mr Carter, let's talk strategy," the leader ordered.

The time passed quickly and soon it was dark once more. Tarmin ordered Craig to get some rest before the big day. He went obediently to bed, but sleep evaded him. He managed to close his eyes for a few hours though and all too soon it was morning. In another two hours they would descend on the red planet.

CHAPTER 8

Craig stared at the red planet and a shiver went up his spine. Seeing the expression on his face, Tarmin gently brushed his arm with one of her wings.

"Look Craig, this isn't going to be easy. If you want to pull out now, Tanus will understand. We have discussed many tactical manoeuvres and I'm sure our soldiers can manage without you."

Carter shook his head decisively. "No Tarmin I have to go through with this. I'm personally involved now anyway, because Andocia made it personal by kidnapping my friends, so there's more than one life at stake. If I don't make it, I'll have tried at least, but if I don't try, my conscience will bother me for the rest of my life."

"Then you must do so Craig and the very best of luck to you."

"All right, let's keep out of range of the scanners. I want to do a thermal search on the castle and maybe that way we will know what areas to avoid."

Craig trained his scanners on the front of the castle and zoomed in on the large structure.

"Wow this place is *huge!* It looks more like a city than a single home."

"Well Tanus always said that Andocia liked to keep her staff close by. This obviously proves it."

Carter scanned the front of the castle. "There's no way I'm going to approach from the front! Andocia will be onto me in a nanosecond."

Tarmin agreed. "Well according to Tanus, Andocia has always been a drama queen," the bird replied drily. "Did you notice the moat, Craig?"

"Yes, I did. What type of creatures inhabit that water I wonder?"

Tarmin shook her feathers and preened one wing. "I don't think you really want to know."

"Have you ever been on her planet before?"

"No, this is as close as I have dared to go."

The space explorer hovered a while longer and scanned the levels in the castle.

"I count six levels Tarmin. What about you?"

The bird paused and counted. "That's right, but I'm willing to bet that there are more levels below ground. If I were to guess,

Tanus is probably incarcerated underground."

Carter shuddered again. "I have to agree with you. Where do you suppose she's holding Constance?"

"I have no idea, but I'm sure they are far away from one another. You have no doubt noticed that you can link telepathically with Tanus and myself, yet you are not really telepathic yourself, and nor is Constance."

"I have noticed that, but I'm not sure why."

The bird bent her head down and pecked him gently on the top of his head. "You are linked with Tanus and me because we are your friends and she has permitted this. Andocia can communicate with you because of what she tried to do to you when you both met."

Craig shuddered at the memory.

"If the Saturnians hadn't saved me, I would have been her willing slave, but they helped me."

"Yes, they did, but even though Andocia cannot blind you again, she still has power over you, just as she has with most species. By delving into your brain, she opened a channel in your mind, linking the two of you together. She must think you are very exceptional, or she would not have done this. I doubt if the Saturnians even knew about it. Even if they did, they would never have managed to close this channel. Unfortunately, you will have to deal with it for the rest of your life."

"What about Constance? Can Andocia communicate telepathically with her?"

"Probably. Tanus mentioned something about Andocia having done tests on her cerebral cortex as well. She must have put in some connection there, but that was her choice and I don't need to tell you how powerful her mind is. She even scares me! I am also telepathic as you now know. Anyway, the reason I think that your girlfriend and Tanus are far apart, is because they cannot link with one another from a long distance. It's one of Andocia's tactics. Both are kept guessing. That devilish woman probably has some type of shielding on the walls surrounding the dungeons."

Craig nodded in agreement.

"I'm going to fly around to the back and see if there is another way in. How much time do we have before Tanus's army will rendezvous with us?"

"Another half an hour at least. We have plenty of time to do a recon."

Carter came to the rear end of the complex and scanned the castle again. He scanned every floor but beings were everywhere and no place really stood out. Several staircases led to different areas of the castle and he found many empty rooms, but nothing out of the ordinary. He paid careful attention to one of the kitchens on the ground floor, but he could find no doorways leading to anything underground.

Then he flew further away from the castle. The grounds were huge and seemed to go on forever. He noticed many cages which housed strange and exotic animals.

"Well I have a good idea where we should start our search, but I don't like going inside without knowing what's waiting for us."

Tarmin placed a wing on his shoulder. "It doesn't matter! We have very sophisticated equipment that should help us to locate the prisoners. It's all quiet at the moment, so they aren't expecting trouble. Andocia must have believed you. Let's find a place to land where we can wait for the army."

Craig found the perfect spot quite a distance away. The area was full of large trees that obscured the view from above. He hovered just above the grass and then moved into the forest of trees. He cut the engine and they waited.

It wasn't long before Craig's mobile device rang.

"Okay Mr Carter, we have arrived. Give us your location please."

Craig explained where they were and soon afterwards, a number of small troop carriers appeared and joined them. The General shook his hand. "Good to meet you in the flesh Mr Carter. So, are you ready for 'operation rescue'?"

"As ready as I'll ever be!" he exclaimed. "Please, call me Craig."

"Excellent!" He turned to the troops gathered around them. "Right, this is a good place to set up base. Tanus's mother ship is currently on a nearby uninhabited planet and we'll be in constant contact with them. They will be our eyes and ears. We have a number of medical staff up there to take care of the casualties. Every one of these troop carriers will be held in readiness to ferry people to the mother ship. The pilots have medical training and will stay here to guard the ships."

He indicated to a pile of weapons stacked in a box. "Take your pick of whatever weapons you require. Our technical staff are busy downloading a satnav guide to your cellphones and other devices. We don't know what we'll be facing once we enter that fortress and this app will help you to find your way. Put your devices on vibrate mode now. We don't want them ringing and giving away our positions."

A soldier came up to him holding a box which he set down in front of the leader. "Okay, here are your comm units. Put them on just before we leave."

The general then pointed to another box. Some of the soldiers took out circular devices that suctioned onto walls. He spent a few more minutes explaining the tactics and when he was satisfied that everyone knew what their orders were, he smiled at them. "Good luck everyone! Let's do this!"

There was a murmur of agreement and the highly trained men and women began to fan out.

Craig put his hand on Tarmin's wing. "Tarmin, take my ship and fly it to the mother ship. I won't need it now anyway, because Constance's ship is still here and we can use that one. I'll come and get it when this is over."

"Okay Craig, I'll do that. Just a word of advice before you go! Don't forget to use the ring to its maximum capacity and keep your wits about you. One of Andocia's many talents is the gift of illusion. Things aren't always what they seem, so watch out."

"I'll be careful, I promise."

The bird nodded and smiled nervously. "Good luck! I'll see you later."

CHAPTER 9

The young man hurried to catch up with the soldiers as they crept stealthily through the bushes. When they were still a distance from the castle, a voice spoke in Craig's ear. "Hey everyone, watch your step! We just found a trip wire."

The general's voice came online. "Be careful ladies and gents! Be vigilant! If we disturb these wires, we'll lose the element of surprise."

The castle came into view and they began to split up. Craig watched as some of the soldiers sneaked up to the walls of the castle and, by using the suction devices, they began to climb the steep rock face. He went to a door which led to a cellar, and opened it cautiously. Six soldiers accompanied him.

The place was dark and he shone a torch around the small space. A door led upwards, but someone laid a cautionary hand on his arm. The satnav device on their phones showed it to be inhabited by a number of people. The men and women walked around knocking gently on the walls. One portion of the wall sounded hollow and someone pointed to their cellphone. Craig nodded when it showed there was a hidden doorway. One of the soldiers took out a knife and inserted the blade into a crack and the door swung open. They went through, closing it quietly behind them.

A long passageway stretched out before them and they began to walk. They shone their torches into the gloomy interior, but no doors could be seen. The group continued up the passageway and when they had reached what looked like a blank wall, they found another door. This one was locked with a keypad bolted onto it. One of the women took out a small device and placed it near the lock. There was a puff of smoke and the lock disintegrated. A soldier peeked around the door, but the room was empty. She indicated that they must follow her and continued on their way.

Yet another corridor lay before them and Craig looked at the display on his device. "It looks as though the cells are somewhere to the left of our position," he whispered.

They nodded in agreement and began looking for another door. Halfway down the passage they found another one, but when they consulted their phones again, it showed that this door led away from the cells. There was a quick discussion and most of the soldiers decided to go that way anyway. Craig was not convinced.

"There has to be another door hidden somewhere. This place is huge and we will never find our way to the cells if we deviate from the route."

One of the men looked at his watch. "Time is of the essence people! We have to make a decision soon."

The soldiers walked to the door and began to place a device on the lock but Craig hesitated. "Just give me two minutes to look for another door. If I don't find one then we can go that way."

"Okay, just hurry!"

Carter went back to the previous door and began knocking on the opposite wall. He had barely taken ten steps, when he felt a crack and shone his torch on it. "Here it is, I found it!"

It was then that things went horribly wrong!

The first door was opened suddenly and several of Andocia's soldiers burst in, firing as they did so. Tanus's soldiers were taken by surprise and they died where they stood. Everything seemed to be happening in slow motion. Craig saw the enemy's guns turn towards him and he shot at them, wounding one woman in her shoulder. He pushed desperately on the hidden door and it opened suddenly. The momentum carried him through and he fell on his knees into yet another featureless passageway. He kicked the door and it slammed shut. His heart was racing and he wondered how Andocia's soldiers had found out about the rescue mission.

Craig looked down at his device and groaned. The screen was blank, except for a message that flashed, mocking him. "Signal lost!" it proclaimed.

The man spoke urgently into his comm unit. "This is Craig

Carter. I have lost my satnav signal. Can you send some rein-forcements urgently?"

The communication unit remained stubbornly silent and Craig realized that he was now both deaf and blind. Obviously, the walls were now reinforced with some kind of material that jammed any communication.

Out in space, the technicians in Tanus's mother ship contacted the general. "Be advised, we have lost contact with Craig and his party. Can someone investigate?"

The general came online and they heard the sounds of gun-fire. "Mother bird, we are under heavy fire! I don't know what happened, but it looks like someone triggered a warning device. Andocia's people are all over us like fleas on a dog!"

The technicians stared wide-eyed at one another as they watched the fighting that was taking place. Tarmin was hyster-ical. "Our people are dying out there. We have to do something!"

Someone put their arms around the bird who now stood waist high to the people. "There is nothing we can do. All the trained personnel are down there. All we can do now is get ready to treat the casualties."

Tarmin stared at the drama unfolding on the screen and her voice shook. "What about my mistress? Will they be able to save her and my friend Constance?"

"Our soldiers are well trained Tarmin. We just have to wait and see."

Back on the red planet, Craig was unsure which way to go. Every passageway he entered looked like the one he had just vacated. He knew he had to go left, but so many doors barred his way that he feared he would run out of incendiary devices long before he reached Tanus. He was so engrossed in finding the right doors that he failed to see the small camera lens which at that precise moment was sending images back to Andocia's security control room.

On the top floor of the castle, Andocia stood with her employ-ees and watched angrily. "I should never have trusted Carter! He's a liar! Well he's going to pay for this!"

She placed a headset on her head and the controller jumped

hurriedly off the chair where she sat down. "Attention all troops. Take Miss Gregg to the cell block immediately and then I want you to double the guards on both Tanus and Miss Gregg's cells – no, triple them! If they are rescued you will forfeit your lives! Craig Carter has been seen in the tunnels heading towards the cells, but he must not be allowed to rescue his friends. Some of you are to go after him. Herd him into the labyrinth! Use whatever means you deem necessary, but no one is to harm him. If he makes it through the obstacles alive, then I will take care of him personally. The rest of you must deal with Tanus's army."

Craig walked nervously in the tunnels, but he knew he would have to go through whichever door he could open and try to rescue his friends when he had given Andocia's troops the slip. Suddenly the door behind him swung open and several guards came in. He fired over their heads, but they kept coming. They returned his fire and laser beams danced around him. He saw a door ahead and it opened. Craig ran through with the soldiers in hot pursuit. Once again, they aimed their guns and ordered him to stop, knowing he wouldn't obey. He slammed the door shut and locked it before continuing.

There was an explosion and Craig watched in dismay as the soldiers continued pursuing him. He saw two doors and tried to open the first one, but it was securely locked, so he ran for the second door. This one was open and he dashed through. Before he could lock the door, it shut by itself and he heard the lock click. His stomach clenched nervously when he realized that no one was coming after him. He felt as though he was a mouse caught in a trap. Craig glanced down at his device's screen, but it remained blank. He replaced it in his pocket and held his laser gun firmly in his hand.

The explorer walked cautiously, looking everywhere for sudden surprises, when he became aware of a soft slithering sound. He dodged to the left and turned around, where he came face to face with a large and deadly serpent. He fired, and slit the creature open from top to bottom and with a sharp hiss it died. The man moved forward slowly, checking the walls and floors for any other surprises.

He heard a grating sound further along the passage and watched in horror as the ground opened before him and he saw a pit of deadly spiders crawling quickly over the top heading for him. He assessed the gap, but decided it was too big to jump over. The explorer pointed the ring and a bridge formed, so he crossed harmlessly over the deadly surprise. He continued walking and found another door. The spiders were moving very quickly towards him so he blasted open the first door he saw and sped through it.

He found himself facing a large hallway where lights shone out of various containers, but as he got closer, he saw that the "containers" were the skulls of various beings. Further down the passage, he was flanked on both sides by the remains of many beings, some of whom he recognized, but there were many he had never seen before. He knew instinctively that these beings were friends of Tanus who had tried to rescue her and failed. Carter saw a tiny red light high on the wall facing him and knew he had been discovered. Andocia was obviously expecting him and he had walked right into a trap. He wondered what had happened to Tanus's army. It was quiet down in the tunnels and he could hear nothing at all. Craig hoped all was well above ground.

He decided not to waste any more time trying to blast through any more doors, certain that whatever Andocia had in mind for him would play out just as she wanted. The element of surprise was gone and he knew that his enemy was furious he had deceived her. As he walked cautiously up the passage, he saw two doors. The one on the left opened and he went through. It locked behind him automatically, as he suspected it would.

Carter heard the rustle of many wings and ducked as a colony of giant bats swooped down on him. He conjured up a number of rats and the bats forgot about him instead grabbing at the furry rodents, tearing them apart in a feeding frenzy. From her hidden chamber, Andocia watched Craig's progress on a screen and began to get angry. "If I could discover the source of his power, I could defeat him, but I still don't know how he makes those objects appear."

Now he was confronted by a winding passageway that had three doors leading off it and for a moment, Craig stood undecided, not sure which door would be his best option. No door opened for him this time and finally he settled for the one on the right. Andocia smiled gleefully and watched in anticipation as he tried the door. It was locked and he shot the lock out with his laser gun and went inside.

"Ah what a surprise he's going to get! Let's see him escape from my pets down there."

As Craig walked, he kept a watchful eye all around him, expecting things to come out of the walls and attack him, but he failed to look down at his feet. Suddenly he found himself slipping and sliding on a slippery floor, which sloped downwards and there was nothing to hang on to. As he got closer to the bottom, the heat became intense and he saw a pit of lava boiling and swirling below. He lost his grip on the gun and it slid down the incline and fell into the fiery pit. Thinking quickly, he thought about a rope and one materialized and coiled around the ceiling beams high above him and he held on for dear life and swung himself over the deadly pit. However, when he got half way, a fiery creature leapt from the depths and grabbed his ankles. Craig screamed in pain, as he smelt burning flesh. It tried desperately to pull him down into the boiling lava and for a while the struggle raged, but finally the young explorer managed to shake free and, with a furious yell, it fell back down into the fiery furnace. Craig swung, gaining momentum with every swing and finally fell, panting on the other side. Forcing himself not to think of his injured ankles, he went doggedly on.

Another door loomed before him and he went through it, but he came into an empty chamber. He blinked and suddenly there were many creatures all vile and ugly, reaching out to him and he stepped back to avoid their clutching arms. He didn't know which one to attack first, but then Tarmin's advice came back to him. *Things aren't always what they seem, so watch out! Andocia is a master of illusion.*

He took a deep breath and moved into the midst of the fearsome creatures who grabbed for him, but they were only illusions designed to make him panic and he walked through them all, completely unharmed.

When he had crossed the room, he couldn't find another door anywhere and began tapping the wall, hoping for a secret panel to open. As he looked back, the creatures all vanished and he found that the room was circular. A grating sound attracted his attention and he sprinted forward as the door opened, but stopped suddenly when an enormous creature shuffled inside and made straight for him. It towered over him and he backed away, keeping his eyes on it and trying to think of a way to get past it. The door behind him closed again, shutting off his escape.

While he and the creature were circling one another, three more doorways suddenly appeared and more of the creatures came inside and began to circle Craig. One lunged for him and he sidestepped, causing two of the creatures to take a swing at one another. Both screamed in rage as they fell and tried to disentangle themselves. He turned and stared and saw that he was standing right in the path of an oncoming monster. A quick glance at the two fallen ones convinced him that they were out of action for a while anyway. Taking a deep breath, he jumped over them and fled, with the other two in hot pursuit. He dodged from left to right, confusing the beings, that stretched their long talons out towards him in an effort to cause him injury, but he jumped nimbly out of the way. He looked quickly around but no more of the beings had come into the room. The first two were rubbing their heads and snarling. They began to get up and head in his direction. Desperately Craig summoned a huge log and swung it at the two behind him. He allowed himself a small smile of satisfaction when he saw the two beings fall senseless to the floor. But the distraction had cost him precious time ...

Before he could turn, he was grabbed from behind and his arms were pinned to his sides. Long fingernails dug into his arms and unconsciously, one of the being's fingers covered the ring on Carter's hand, trapping the power and the ring became useless.

Instead of wasting energy fighting the lumbering beings, he waited until one approached from the front, and then, lifting his legs high, he kicked out at it and it reeled backwards, but the one holding him didn't flinch. The being recovered quickly and began approaching again. This time it held his legs in a vice–like grip. He winced in pain as it grabbed his sore and blackened ankles and could only watch helplessly as the others came closer. They looked deep into his eyes and he saw the evil reflecting back at him. The one holding him dug its nails deep into his flesh and he bit his lip to stop the cry of pain from escaping. The second being held his legs still firmer, while the remaining two beings strutted around Carter and grinned maliciously. All of them licked their lips in anticipation.

One being tore his shirt open and placed its long, razor sharp nails against his chest. It extended a finger and traced a line down Craig's chest and Carter stared at the line of crimson that had begun to flow. It continued up and down his chest and he grimaced in pain. It felt as though they had lit a furnace inside his body.

With panic born of desperation, Craig managed to free his legs and he kicked viciously out at his tormentors, felling one. The adrenalin pumped in his body and he just wanted to get away, so he kicked and punched in all directions and managed to clear a space for himself. He saw an open door and ran for it, stumbling in his eagerness to get away. The door closed again and he stared miserably down at his body, which was a sorry sight. His arms were cut and bleeding and his chest had bloody traces all down it, while his ankles were badly disfigured. Craig leaned against a wall to get his breath back.

In another room, Craig saw lights in the shape of serpents, but the moment he entered, they stretched their long necks and spat deadly venom at him. Using the power of the ring, he conjured up a boomerang, which he flung at the first of them and the weapon scythed through them, cutting off their heads. The handsome explorer wrinkled his nose against the ghastly smell and jumped over the pools of green slime.

Another door then opened and he went through and tensed for

another confrontation, but instead he saw Andocia's followers frolicking in a glorious pool. They were wearing tiny bikinis and beckoned to him.

"Well done, Craig Carter, you've survived all Andocia's tests! She instructed us to clean you up a bit and then you'll be taken to her. Climb in and let us wash you; you look quite ghastly. You can't go to our mistress with all that blood on your body."

As Craig looked at them, he wasn't sure what to do. A part of him desperately cried out for a drink of water and he longed to be clean, but a small part warned that it might just be another trap, so he shook his head.

"No, I don't trust you! You're all as cold and calculating as Andocia. How do I get out of this place?"

"There's a door somewhere," grinned one of the girls, "you just have to find it."

He turned his back on them and was met by complete silence, which unnerved him, so he looked back, only to find the room was now empty and where the swimming pool had been, stood a deep pit. Curiously he moved to inspect it and saw that it wasn't very deep, but the bottom was lined with deadly spikes that would have impaled him, had he stepped into it. Carter walked away from the pit, but he could not find any doors leading out of the room. He heard the rustling of wings and spun around. A large, fiery bird squawked and flew straight for him. He thought about a bucket of water which he intended to throw at the creature, but nothing happened. The man ducked to avoid being incinerated by the bird. It flew over his head and then turned back to attack him once more. He dodged it and started running back to where he had started, hoping to get out through the door he had just entered, but he couldn't find it. An orange flash burst in front of him and he screamed when his left hand began to blister and bleed. He aimed the ring at the bird again, but nothing happened and the fire creature flew at him, its talons outstretched to attack the defenceless man. He dropped to the ground and dived away, causing the nasty claws to rake him across his back, and again he screamed in pain as the talons ripped into his flesh. Ignoring the terrible pain, Craig rolled onto his back and waited for the bird to approach. It screeched loudly, triumphantly, convinced its prey was doomed. The man waited until the bird's claws were almost on top of him and he could see that it intended to rip his insides out, but the bird was too eager to finish the job, and at the last moment, Craig lifted his body by using his hands and kicked the bird viciously in the throat. The bird made a gasping, rattling sound and then dropped to the floor, its neck broken. It flailed around on the floor and a few fiery feathers floated about. Some caught Craig on various parts of his body, causing small burn marks to appear everywhere. Some of his clothing caught fire, but he swatted it out with his bare hands.

Again he saw a door open and he ran out of the room. The door slammed shut and Craig stopped suddenly when he was confronted by several of Andocia's warriors brandishing weapons. He saw Andocia sitting on a throne, holding a sceptre that had a trident emblem on it. On her head was a crown of flames. Her red hair fell over her right shoulder and all around her, stood many of her followers.

"It would seem that congratulations are in order," she replied dryly. "Your prowess never ceases to amaze me, but this time you didn't get through unscathed. You'll carry those marks for as long as you live, assuming I let you live that is. Do you know what was drawn on your chest?"

Craig stared at her and shook his head.

Andocia smiled evilly and sent one of her helpers to get a mirror, which they held out in front of the injured explorer. His face contorted in misery when he saw the shape of a trident emblazoned on his chest.

"See, the mark of evil is upon you. If you live, everyone will know that I branded you, and you will never be able to remove that emblem. Your ankles are badly burnt too, and you'll be left with ugly scars."

She looked at his body, taking in all the injuries that he had sustained, and smiled cruelly.

Craig glared in hate at the devilish woman. "Why, you cold, calculating bitch!" he exclaimed angrily, taking a step forward.

In response, some women raised their weapons and aimed

them at him and he subsided into silence.

"Don't waste your time, Carter, for I doubt if the outside world will see you again anyway. I warned you not to come and interfere in my business. Maybe now you have learnt your lesson!"

Craig remained silent and Andocia continued talking. "I must say that your efforts caused us all quite some entertainment, but I have the knowledge to destroy you. Yes, I've found out the source of your power!"

Craig was horrified. *"You're lying!"* he challenged.

"Am I?" said she, grinning triumphantly. "When you fought with my friends, you always pointed your right hand in their general direction and on your fourth finger is a ring. That ring was your helper. When my pets seized you a short while ago, one of them accidentally covered the ring, and therefore you couldn't unleash its power, resulting in my brand upon your chest. Deny it if you can!"

"All right, so I had some help," he admitted.

"Take it off, Carter!" she demanded.

The explorer shook his head emphatically. "No, I won't remove it and you can't make me."

She gestured to some of her subjects. "Get the ring off his finger."

He struggled, but they overpowered him easily. One girl grabbed his finger and tugged with all her might, but she couldn't dislodge the ring. The others took it in turns, but the ring stayed put.

"Andocia, even with our combined strength, we can't get it off," complained one.

"Bah, I'll get it off!" said Andocia as she stood up and walked closer to Craig. He could feel her delving into his brain, and he tried to banish her voice from his mind, but he couldn't fight her and his arm refused to obey him. The right arm pointed straight at Andocia, the fingers outstretched and he watched helplessly as a red beam enveloped his ring finger. The ring began to move and try as he might, he couldn't get his fingers to bend. The gold ring moved off his finger and floated to

Andocia, who concentrated for a few seconds and then the ring disintegrated, leaving a tiny trail of gold on the floor. A cheer went up; Craig's power was smashed, and he no longer had the assurance that the ring brought him. Carter found that he could move his hand and he stared unhappily at the bare spot on his finger.

He recovered his composure quickly and smiled despite the circumstances. "It doesn't matter anyway! You can enjoy your moment of glory, but Tanus and Constance have been freed, so my task has been completed."

Andocia's followers stared at one another and they began to laugh. The evil woman laughed as well. "So, you think they have been released do you; well I'm sorry to disappoint you, but they are still my guests."

"You're lying! Tanus's army freed them."

"They tried to and it was a magnificent effort on their part, but the army also failed."

Craig shook his head. "No that's impossible! So many men and women came to fight. They must have succeeded."

Andocia slapped him through the face. "You are forgetting whom you are talking to! Because of you and your stupid scheme, many people died!"

His enemy pointed to a screen on one of the walls. "If you still don't believe me, then here is your proof."

Craig stared at the images on the screen. Half the screen showed a picture of Tanus still shackled, in her prison cell. She was sitting dejectedly on the bed. Her head hung down and she looked as though she had aged ten years since he had last seen her. The other screen showed Constance in a similar position. She was crying.

Craig gasped and suddenly his legs felt as though they didn't belong to him and he fell to his knees, and covered his face with his hands. "Ohh no! I thought the army had rescued them, but I was mistaken!" He looked miserably at Andocia and all her followers who were watching him, and he sighed. "All the planning and all the people who died – it was all for nothing! Now the situation is worse than it was before. I should have known this was an impossible mission, but I hoped that somehow it would all work out. It's all my fault! I made a terrible mistake and now many brave people have lost their lives!"

Craig stared at Andocia and her army and there were tears in his eyes. They ran down his cheeks, making streaks in the dirt and the blood on his face, but he was unaware of them. His entire body ached from the encounters with Andocia's pets. The explorer was compelled to look at Andocia and he found no sympathy in her red eyes. All her warriors stared stony eyed at him. Finally, he wiped his eyes on a part of his tattered shirt, and bowed his head while staring unseeingly at the floor.

Andocia spoke to him and he heard her voice, but it sounded far away. "That was a very passionate speech, Carter, but you were warned! This is the end of your mission. You are a tenacious but very foolish man, and you failed!! However, your problems are only beginning! Now I would hate to have you die of septicaemia from your many wounds, so you have a stay of execution for a few days, while your body is repaired and cleaned up."

Andocia gestured to some of the men in her army and they stepped forward. "Take Mr Carter away and clean him up. Afterwards you are to take him to the medical bay and have them do what they can to dress the wounds."

The men bowed to their mistress. "It shall be done, Andocia."

They reached down to Craig and helped him to his feet. Two of the soldiers stood on either side of the explorer and put his arms around their necks to support him. He went with them quietly and without a fuss. They took him to a public bath, where he was helped to get undressed and they cleaned him up as best they could. Despite their care in bathing him, several wounds on his body had opened up and begun to bleed again. He was given a robe to put on and then they took him in a wheelchair to the medical facility.

The doctors administered a painkilling injection and began repairing the damage. Carter drifted in and out of consciousness while they did what they could to ease his pain, but he could hear them muttering about the many scars he would have once the wounds had healed. When they were finished, he was taken to a private ward, where he finally fell into a deep sleep.

He woke up twenty-four hours later feeling much better. The pain was still with him, but the injections that were being administered helped a great deal. Lunch was brought to him and he found that he was very hungry. After the dishes had been cleared away, he asked one of the doctors if he could visit Tanus and Constance. The doctor replied that he had to ask Andocia's permission first, as she had left strict instructions that he was not to leave his room unless escorted by some of her elite soldiers. This didn't surprise the explorer, because he had seen two soldiers guarding his room. Also, every time anyone came to see him, the door was unlocked by the security guards, and locked when they left. Andocia it seemed, was taking no chances with him.

While he was waiting, his doctor came and examined him. "You slept for a full day, but that is understandable. How are you feeling now?"

"Much better I guess."

"Andocia wanted to see you after I had treated you, but apparently the medication made you sleepy, so I thought I would come and speak to you after I had done my rounds. I want to keep you here for a few days because your dressings need to be changed every day for a week. I'll change them now, while we wait to hear what Andocia says. This medical facility is quite a distance from the cells where your friends are being held, so it will take some time."

Carter's wounds were cleaned and dressed and soon afterwards a soldier arrived. "Andocia says that you may visit Tanus and your girlfriend, but only if your doctor feels you are well enough to leave your bed."

At that moment, the doctor returned, holding a syringe. "I will give you another painkilling injection and then you may go. If you feel tired or lightheaded, return here immediately. Many of your wounds are very deep and I don't want them to become infected. Also, you are to be taken to your friends in a wheelchair. Your body has received a shock and only rest will ease any discomfort that you have at the moment."

"I understand doctor."

The soldier issued instructions to the others waiting at the door and one of them obediently fetched a wheelchair. Carter got out of bed and stumbled. Pain shot up his legs when he put pressure on them. Immediately the doctor and the soldier had their arms around him and they put him into the wheelchair. A thick blanket was then draped over his shoulders, and his legs. The three soldiers present accompanied the explorer to the cell, with the most junior one pushing the wheelchair. No one spoke to him, or explained anything, not even when he was put into a medical hovercraft and flown part of the distance. They pulled up at the kitchen door on the ground floor of Andocia's home, where a doorway under the stairs led to the cells. The senior officer touched him on the shoulder. "Whom do you wish to see first, Mr Carter?"

"Could I see Tanus first?"

The man nodded and squeezed his shoulder gently. "I will leave you now. My two colleagues will proceed further and take you to her cell."

He saluted and the junior officers did the same. They continued down the winding passageways and Craig shuddered when he thought about his journey down some of these corridors. It was a labyrinth of passages that all looked alike, and he realized why the attempt to free Tanus had failed. The men stopped briefly at a room where a few soldiers were drinking coffee and eating their food. They were obviously off duty. His escort waved to them and then one of the men took a key off a holder and the threesome continued.

CHAPTER 10

The procession passed many identical doors, until finally they stopped at one of them. One of the guards went to open the door and the other gave Craig's wheelchair a little shove.

"We have arrived. You may go inside."

Craig held onto the wheels of the wheelchair and rolled inside. The door clanged loudly behind him and the key grated in the lock. He stopped for a moment to orientate himself, as it was very dark.

His eyes fell on a figure whose wrists were still encased in shackles that glowed red and he gasped in dismay. "Tanus?" he enquired nervously.

At the mention of her name, the woman looked up and their eyes met. He stared at her and could feel the incredible goodness flowing from her body, a sharp contrast to the evil in Andocia. He took in her features as he had done before. Her hair was black and she was dressed in a white garment that touched the floor. She had the bluest eyes that he had ever seen on anyone before, but what caught and held his gaze was the transparent veil about the lower part of her face, showing the outline of her mouth and chin, but the features were still unclear and this puzzled him. He looked closely at the woman and saw that she looked worse than he had imagined. Her face was lined and her eyes looked almost sunken into their sockets. She also looked as though she had lost some weight.

Her voice was a whisper. "Oh, Craig, I apologize for getting you into this mess. You look terrible – are you in pain?"

He nodded slowly, awed by the sight of this woman that he had spoken to often, and met very briefly not that long ago, and then he found his voice. "Oh Tanus, I'm so sorry – I failed you!" he replied dejectedly.

She smiled wanly. "I suppose I should've expected it, for others much stronger than you failed, but I had no one else to turn to. Please forgive me for involving you. I must admit, I was surprised to see you here. Andocia told me she had been in contact with you and you mentioned you weren't going through with your decision to rescue me."

"I lied to her Tanus. I wanted to help you, because of what you had done for me and Constance, but I had to have the element of surprise. Did she tell you anything at all about what took place here earlier?"

"She mentioned something about an army that tried to free me, but we saw no one. Constance and I heard gunfire but we didn't know where it was coming from. This place did seem to be rather busy though. There were more guards than usual down here."

Craig climbed awkwardly down from the wheelchair and kneeled in front of Tanus. "It was all my fault Tanus. I contacted your army and they wanted to help. The general made the tactical plans and landed here. I'm so sorry! I got separated from them and ended up in Andocia's throne room. She told me they had all been killed! I didn't know this would be the outcome when we planned this rescue mission. I knew I couldn't do it alone so I contacted them. Actually, I met your friend Tarmin and it was her idea that we put our heads together and come up with a plan to rescue you and Constance."

Tanus smiled for the first time. "Tarmin is alive? Oh, thank the stars! She tried to interfere when Andocia first captured me. I saw Andocia hit her with one of her red beams and my friend dropped out of sight. I thought she was dead!"

"She's fine," Craig assured his friend.

He became serious once more and stood up. "What happens now Tanus? The situation is worse than it was before. Your warriors are dead and you are still a prisoner! Tarmin is alive but I doubt she can rescue you on her own. Constance is also still here and I am Andocia's prisoner too. We have run out of options!"

"It would seem so Craig, but no matter what happens, I want you to know that you have my grateful thanks for trying to rescue me."

"I didn't have to do it Tanus, but I wanted to repay you for your kindness on previous occasions."

"I know, but you must be realistic Craig; Andocia won't treat you well."

He nodded sadly. "I realize that. Tanus, she discovered that my power stemmed from the ring and she destroyed it!"

"I saw what happened. That screen over there was switched on. All your movements were monitored and I watched every grotesque detail."

Craig looked morosely around him. "What happens now?"

"Andocia has won and we have been defeated. As I mentioned before, you were my last hope and there's no one else I can call on to help us. Craig, this may not be the time to bring this up, but Andocia admires you, despite her sending signals to the contrary. If you teamed up with her, she would treat you well and you could be the co-ruler over both universes. My time is nearly up! The longer I stay bound in this way, the weaker I will become. I cannot die, as I am immortal, but it will take me a long time to recover from my incarceration even if I am miraculously freed. These cuffs literally suck the life out of anyone unfortunate enough to be in this position."

"Tanus, I haven't known you long, but I know you are feeling depressed because of those armbands binding you. Once they are removed, you will be your old self again. If I had given up whenever I came face to face with one of my enemies, I wouldn't be alive today. I must admit though, I've never met anyone as powerful as Andocia before, but I try not to give up until I'm absolutely sure that the situation is hopeless. For a while I lost hope in myself and this mission. Andocia managed to put me into the deepest hole possible and she broke my spirit! I guess I thought I was invincible and that the legendary Craig Carter would fly to the rescue and free everyone! I learnt a hard lesson when I failed you, but I will never underestimate her again."

Tanus sighed heavily. "Your outlook is encouraging, but this is totally different. You saw what remained of my friends, and they were more powerful than you. Craig the tests she set for you were designed only to maim and not kill you. Hasn't it occurred to you that you would have been dead, had she done to you what she did to my friends?."

"But the ring ..." began Craig.

"Yes, even with the ring, you couldn't defeat her. It worked on anyone else, but not Andocia – in fact my people told you so."

Craig stared miserably at the woman in white. "Yes, I remember. Tanus, have you seen Constance perhaps?"

The woman sighed sadly. "Yes, I have – in fact Andocia let her come in and talk to me, just as she has done for you, but you won't recognize her any longer."

"I … I don't understand. Has … has Andocia tortured her?"

"She's just … different. I think it would be wise for you to avoid her at present."

Craig was confused. "I can't do that! Tanus I love her and I want to see her. I have already been given permission to visit her as well. How do I call the guards to come and fetch me?"

"If you look over there near the monitor, you'll see a red button. Press it and someone will answer."

The space explorer did so and he conveyed his request. He was told to expect an armed escort in five minutes. He looked questioningly at Tanus, but she didn't reply.

Shortly afterwards, his guards appeared, and he was ordered out. One of them pushed the wheelchair and he was accompanied to another cell and invited to enter. The door closed behind him and he heard it being locked. In a far corner, her back to him, Constance was weeping softly.

"Constance?" he asked gently.

"Go away!"

"Darling, it's me, Craig."

"Please go away Craig – I don't want to see you!"

He ignored her and put his arm around her shoulders and she sat stiffly, but didn't make any attempt to remove it, however she wouldn't look at him. He came to sit in front of her and she turned her head away, so he put his hand under her chin and lifted her tear stained face. Her eyes were red and swollen and tears leaked out of her eyes. He took some tissues out of a box sitting on a small table and brought them to her.

"Oh Constance, please don't cry! What has that evil woman done to you? Did she hurt you?"

His girlfriend shook her head. "How can you even bear to look at me!" she wailed. "This is my punishment. I tried to escape and she changed me into an old woman!" Carter stared at her, but the same beautiful face he knew and loved looked back at him.

"I don't know what you mean my angel! You are the same

woman I met and fell in love with."

Constance stared at him. "Thank you for being so tactful, but I look like a hag. You mean well, but I'm ugly. I have aged fifty years at least!"

"Constance, listen to me! You haven't changed at all! I don't know what Andocia did to you, but there is nothing wrong with you."

He led her to a mirror and forced her to look into it. She pounded on the mirror and tried to break it.

"I'm ugly! I wish that I could die! *How could she do this to me! I hate her so much!*"

Craig took her hands and held them tightly. "Constance, look at me!" he demanded.

She turned her head away and he repeated the request more forcefully. She stared at him miserably. He put his hands on both sides of her head and spoke more gently. "Just listen to me please! I don't know what Andocia did to convince you that you're an old woman, but you're not! She is a master of illusion and can make you believe anything she wants you to. I know, because she tried to do that with me when I was trapped in those awful tunnels. She's messing with your mind, so fight back! The one thing I have always admired about you is the fact that you have the uncanny ability to recognize friend from foe. Dig deep inside yourself and break this hold she has on you. I know you can do it."

He took her back to the mirror on the wall and made her look at it. She flinched from her reflection, but stayed where she was.

"Just imagine the image you are seeing is your true self, and concentrate on every feature of your body as though you were an artist about to paint a picture. Use your imagination!"

Craig watched fascinated as his girlfriend seemed to go into a trance. She stared at the mirror on the wall and remained completely still. Her eyes were open but she saw nothing in front of her. He kept his hand on her shoulder, willing her to break through the barrier that Andocia had built up. Several minutes passed and she remained still. Finally, she opened her eyes and stumbled backwards. Carter put his arms around her waist to stop her from falling. She looked at him as though seeing him for the first time and wiped away some tears.

"What happened?" she asked curiously. "Why was I staring at a mirror? When did you get here?"

"Some guards brought me to see you a little while ago. Do you remember anything at all?"

Constance looked at her boyfriend and a gasp escaped her lips. "You look awful! Why are you in a wheelchair?"

"It's all superficial my love. Everything will heal with time. How are you though?"

Constance looked at her boyfriend. "Oh Craig, she made me watch you fight all those horrible creatures and I suffered along with you, albeit mentally. Have you seen Tanus at all?"

"Yes, I have. I saw her earlier. I feel so bad for Tanus. She told me I was her last hope of rescue, now we are all Andocia's prisoners."

Constance sighed. "What's going to become of us now?"

She went back to the mirror and stared at her reflection. "I would kill for a hairbrush right now. My hair is so full of knots!"

Craig smiled. "Don't worry about it. I love the dishevelled look. It looks so sexy on you!"

She laughed at him and he put her on his lap, then took her in his arms and kissed her tenderly.

He continued to hold her and she rested her head on his shoulder. At that moment, he knew what he had to do. They had no hope of being rescued now, so there was only one thing he could do to save the situation. Craig took Constance's face between his fingers and looked tenderly at her. "There is one slim chance though. If this works out, you'll probably be freed, but Tanus will no doubt have to remain a prisoner. Constance, you know that I love you, don't you?"

She nodded.

"My darling, it looks as though it's going to be up to me to save the situation and I have the means, but promise me one thing."

"Anything, Craig, you know that!"

"Tanus told me that Andocia likes me. She suggested I offer myself to her as a companion. I would have to stay with her forever – or until I die I suppose. If I go through with this, it'll mean that I have to let you go. I'm sure Andocia will free you then, but it has to be a genuine commitment, for she would see right through me if I pretend. I beg you to forgive me in advance, but it's the only way."

Constance stared at her boyfriend and gently pushed him away. She pulled herself together with an effort and stood a short distance away from him. "Oh Craig, I love you so much! I don't want to lose you. Isn't there some other way?"

"I know of no other way. How I wish that I did," he replied fervently. "Oh Constance, I don't know how I'm going to manage without you, but I have to try."

They talked for a while longer, and then Craig pressed the button near the monitor and his guards came to fetch him. When the door closed behind him, he told the guards that he wanted to see Andocia. They contacted her and she met up with them in the lounge of the castle. He asked for a private audience.

She led the way to a comfortably furnished room and waved the guards away. Reluctantly they obeyed and she looked quizzically at him. "Well, you have my full attention, Carter. What did you want to speak to me about?"

He cleared his throat and decided to blurt out his suspicions.

"Andocia, Tanus told me that you didn't make the tests too difficult for me, because you admire me, even though I thwarted you once before. Is this true?"

"I suppose it is. You would never have survived the obstacle course the others went through no matter how good you are, even with the power of that ring. Tanus sent it to you, didn't she?"

"One of her followers sent it, on her orders," he admitted.

"Why did she choose you, a mere Earthling, to undertake this impossible mission?"

He shook his head. "I don't know and she wouldn't tell me, but it hardly matters now, for as you pointed out, I failed anyway."

"Yes, you did," she assented. "Where is this conversation heading?"

"Andocia, this is very difficult for me, but I'll try to explain it.

I've decided to stop fighting you and work beside you. You made me an offer once before about becoming your companion and helping you rule both universes. Does this offer still apply?"

"It might, but I need to hear what you plan to do," she replied cautiously.

"I've given it a lot of thought and I've decided that I'll do anything you ask of me. If you want me to commit to you, then I will. I won't pretend to love you, because that's impossible at this time, but maybe later – when I know you better."

She cocked her head on one side and regarded him quizzically. "What about your precious Constance? Do you expect me to believe that you'll just walk away from her?"

"I've spoken to her already and told her what I planned to do. Like me, she doesn't want our relationship to end, but she'll keep her word. All I ask in return is that you allow her to return to Earth. I also want to have permission to visit my friends whenever I desire it, in other words I don't want to be kept as your faithful lapdog, constantly under your scrutiny."

She smiled sardonically. "Tell me Craig, do you have any conditions regarding Tanus?"

He looked into her cold red eyes and shook his head. "All I want is for her to be free, but I know you'll never let that happen, so what's the point?"

"What do you think of Tanus?"

The question took him by surprise.

"I have the utmost respect for her and I'm really sorry she's your captive. I have only spoken face to face with her when she helped Constance to escape from your clutches once before. I never knew what she looked like before that time, but I feel as though I've known her forever. I don't know how you managed to trick her, but it's immaterial right now. Andocia, I'd really like your answer soon, because one way or another, I'd like to know what my fate is to be."

Andocia folded her arms over her chest. "Give me one good reason why I should believe you. You lied to me before. Maybe you have another escape plan and you are trying to make me lower my guard."

Craig sighed. "Andocia, if I had a plan, I wouldn't bother even discussing this with you. Believe me when I say this was the last thing I wanted to do. I take sole responsibility for the events that took place. I am even more sorry about the loss of lives on both sides. I have nothing personal against your people, but for the record it was Tanus's army that volunteered to fight for her freedom. I thought it was a good idea and I believed they would succeed, but I underestimated the might of your warriors."

Andocia stared at the man in front of her. "I have one more question. Answer me truthfully and then I will decide what your fate will be."

Carter nodded and she continued. "If you were given a choice, what would you do?"

"If you were merciful and allowed it, I would go back to Earth with Constance. I would then hope fervently never to lay eyes on you ever again, and just do my job as a space explorer."

The woman stared at her captive. "Well said! It took courage to say that to my face, but that's not going to happen."

"I understand. Please will you free Constance then?"

"Very well, I'll accept your terms, but I have my own conditions. Constance shall remain my prisoner for a little while longer. There'll be a celebration to honour our union and once you are truly mine, I'll set her free. You will be able to visit your friends, but I'll have to insist that you are accompanied by a few bodyguards – for your own protection of course. There will be no negotiation regarding Tanus."

"I suppose I will have to settle for that Andocia," Craig sighed.

"Good, then we are in agreement! I shall begin making arrangements soon."

Andocia's eyes roamed over his body as though she were seeing it for the first time. His hair was singed from his encounter with the firebird and he had many cuts on his face and body. His chest and back were covered with bandages. His left arm was also bandaged where the fire creature had burnt him. Both his wrists were covered with bandages and the burns around his ankles were also dressed, but blood seemed to be leaking through.

His adversary looked at all the damage and pursed her lips. "I think we are going to have to wait at least two weeks for you to look presentable for our union celebration. In the time left to you before that day, you can visit Tanus and Constance anytime you wish, but you have to ask for permission first. You will never be allowed to see either of them alone, but must be accompanied by some of my warriors at all times."

Andocia stood up and called the guards, and they took him back to his ward in the hospital.

CHAPTER 11

Craig lay in his hospital bed, but was far from happy about Andocia's decisions. Nothing was really going to change for at least another two weeks. He knew that despite his offer to combine ranks with Andocia, she still didn't trust him. Most of all, he feared for Tanus, knowing that every day she remained a prisoner, she would become weaker. It also wasn't fair to Constance, who was forced to remain incarcerated in a cell, just because Andocia wanted her to. He decided to be the perfect captive and vowed that no matter what he had to do to please Andocia, he would not question her methods. In that way she would hopefully give him some leeway, and perhaps he could still find a way to free Tanus. Whatever happened though, he vowed he would keep his promise to Andocia, as long as she kept her end of the bargain.

Two days later, Craig was discharged from hospital. He was told to return every day to have the dressings replaced. He was taken to one of the small guest suites in the castle where Andocia went to meet him.

"I still have my suspicions about you Craig, but time will tell I suppose. I wanted to put you in one of the cells but the doctor refused to allow it. He said you must stay in a warm and well-lit room so your wounds can heal properly. I am still going to have guards placed at your door overnight, and it will be locked.

However he has also advised that I let you sit in the garden because the sun will be good for your wounds. I'm not sure if I'm going to allow that, because you are a slippery character."

The explorer looked irritably up at her. "Andocia, what more do you want? I have promised to spend the rest of my life with you! I am giving up everything for you, yet you still do not trust me. Tanus and Constance are still your prisoners. They are my friends and I would sacrifice anything just to see them set free. You have no quarrel with Constance, but I agreed to let you keep her here as insurance until our union. So, if you don't trust me, then just let her go and I will trade my life for hers."

"What about Tanus? Would you like to plead for her?"

"Why? Would it help? If you are serious, what would you want in exchange for her life?"

Andocia smiled maliciously. "You have nothing to give me. She is far too valuable in my clutches."

"Not if you destroy her. Every time I see her, she is wasting away. What good is she to you in her weakened condition?"

"I have plans for her, but that needn't concern you."

"All right, but we have digressed from the subject. May I make a suggestion?"

"Why not! Let's hear it."

"At night you could continue to keep me under lock and key, but during the day let me walk in the garden for a few hours. You can have guards watching me, I don't care! I swear on Constance's life that I won't disobey you. If I try to escape, I know you will kill my girlfriend. Isn't that why you won't free her before we are joined together?"

Andocia laughed wickedly. "You are quite correct! Okay, you can have limited freedom in the garden and you will be locked in your room at night. If you disobey, I'll make you watch as I kill Constance slowly and painfully. However I cannot spare any of my soldiers to baby sit you, so behave yourself and I won't have to do something you will regret later. Just press the buzzer next to your viewing screen and ask whoever is on duty to come and unlock your door. Do the same when you have returned to your room and someone will come and lock you in. All your meals will be given to you in your quarters. If you are not there at the appropriate time, you get nothing to eat until the next meal."

Craig nodded in agreement, but as he walked out of the room, he was feeling depressed. Sighing quietly, he went to sit in the garden. "Oh, how I hate the idea of becoming her consort, but what else could I do? I won't even attempt to escape while she holds Tanus and Constance captive, so even if I can walk around freely, I'm just as much a prisoner as they are. My dearest wish right now would be to free Tanus and Constance, but it's impossible."

He went to a secluded corner of the garden where he was screened by trees and tried to imagine life with Andocia, but the idea filled him with dread. He knew that if there was any other choice, he would refuse to stay with the evil woman, but he could see no way out of the situation.

A soft rustling of wings disturbed him and Tarmin alighted on the ground near to him. Then she shrunk to the size of a large parrot and perched on a tree branch, next to him.

"Tarmin, what are you doing here?" he asked in amazement. "You're taking quite a risk."

The bird stared at him and pecked him affectionately. "Thank the universes you are alive! When we lost contact with you, I asked the general to send someone to find you, but Andocia's followers were everywhere. They took our troops completely by surprise! Everyone was too busy fighting for their lives to think about you. I guess the general thought you were already dead."

"I understand Tarmin. I would have done the same thing if I had been in his shoes. Someone must have tripped a silent alarm I suppose. This place is like a fortress! I missed the whole battle because I got lost in the tunnels. Andocia told me there were heavy casualties on both sides. I'm so sorry! Was anyone left alive? I saw no one when I got out of the tunnels."

"There were many casualties on both sides, but most of Tanus's soldiers were wounded. I don't know how Andocia's army fared."

Tarmin stopped talking and looked suspiciously at Craig. "How come you are walking around freely? What's going on? Why aren't you Andocia's prisoner?'

Craig sighed. "I *am* her prisoner. Tanus and Constance are locked up in the dungeons and I am powerless to save them. If I cause trouble, Andocia has threatened to kill Constance, and I believe her. You still haven't told me what you're doing here."

"I had to take a chance. I need to know how Tanus is getting on."

"She's alive, but Andocia still has her bound with those special restraints. I'm so worried about her! She seems to have aged in the last few days and she is getting weaker every day."

Tarmin made a hissing sound. "Damn that evil woman! Those chains aren't ordinary ones. They suck the life force out of any being who has the misfortune to be shackled with them. Tanus cannot die, but the longer she stays here the weaker she will become. Eventually she'll be too weak to fight back and Andocia will rule both universes. I would still like to know why there are no guards watching you. You seem to have come through your tests unscathed! I'm assuming she did test you?" the bird asked suspiciously. "So many of Tanus's friends tried to help and they died trying! Why are you still alive?"

Craig looked at the suspicion in his friend's eyes and he stood up carefully, unbuttoning his shirt as he did so. Tarmin gaped at the emblem on his chest. Then he lifted his trouser legs, revealing his bandaged ankles. "I have plenty of cuts and other wounds over my body as well, but you're right; I should have died, however Andocia had other plans for me. It's a really long and tedious story Tarmin, but Tanus persuaded me to take up Andocia's offer of companionship. It seems the woman likes me a lot, so I decided to do it, but I'm going to hate every minute of it. The only good part about this whole situation is that she'll release Constance and return her to Earth. I tried to bargain for some kind of leniency for Tanus, but she refused outright. If you have some better suggestions, I'd love to hear them."

"I can't think of anything right now," replied the bird. "I

wanted to know how Tanus was doing and you told me, so I had better go."

The man stared at his new friend and sensed her disapproval of his scheme. "Tarmin I know you are angry with me and I understand, but I'm sacrificing my freedom for Constance's sake, not because I want to upset her. You know that Tanus is being held underground in the cells. How would you get down there without being spotted?"

"I don't know! I planned to shrink to the size of a small bird. I can change into any bird I want to, big or small. I wasn't planning on being invisible! No one will see me as a threat! The guards won't shoot a bird. They might just think I got trapped in the tunnels."

Craig shook his head. "You have no idea where they are keeping your mistress and those tunnels are filled with hidden dangers. You might end up losing your life as well. It's far too dangerous. Do you have a message for Tanus? I'm sure I'll be able to pass it on for you."

Tarmin glared at him. "Can I trust you? I'm having doubts at the moment, especially since you are planning to join Andocia's ranks soon."

"Tarmin, I swear on my life that I am doing this under duress. If there were any other solution, I would grab the chance to get away from this place. Let me help you!"

The white bird looked around but no one else seemed to be present, except the two of them. "All right, I'll trust you for now. The general wants to try and rescue Tanus again. This time he will come in secret and bring only a few good soldiers with. He knows the location of the cells and he has a plan. I was going to tell Tanus about it."

"When will he come?"

"I don't know, but I'm sure it will be soon."

"Do you think he could include Constance in the rescue?" he asked hopefully. "She is only a few cells away from Tanus. Andocia has promised to free her after our joining ceremony, but I don't trust that woman at all!"

The bird was unsure. "I can't promise anything Craig! The

general's main objective is to free Tanus. Remember, he thinks that you are dead, and he has never met Constance, so neither of you are a priority. I'll tell him about the situation and see what he says, but I cannot come back here and tell you of his plans, because I don't know when he will execute them."

"Okay Tarmin, I'll try and find a way to free Constance myself. If I don't succeed then, perhaps the general would consider helping her."

"All right, Craig, I'll see what can be arranged. I had better get back before someone sees me."

He waved goodbye to the large white bird and then went back inside to look for Andocia. He found her poring over some charts in her communications room. "Andocia, could I ask you a favour?"

"What is it?"

"I was wondering if I may visit with Tanus for a while."

She looked up from her charts and stared quizzically at him.

"I suppose it can't do any harm, but I don't know why you would bother with her," she said as she handed over the keys.

He took them from her, unable to believe his luck, because he had expected Andocia to have someone escort him to her cell.

The explorer hurried to Tanus's cell and opened the door. She looked up, expecting it to be Andocia, but to her surprise, it wasn't. "Craig, what are you doing here? Did you put your proposal to Andocia?"

"Yes, I did and she trusted me with the keys. Tanus, I don't know if I can go through with this charade. I was sincere when I spoke to Andocia, but I don't want to be doomed to a life of seclusion in her shadow, but never mind about me though; I have encouraging news for you."

"Well anything to lighten my darkness would be appreciated. What news?"

"I forgot to tell you that I met your friend Tarmin a while ago. I had intended to tell you earlier, but when Andocia captured me and destroyed the ring, it slipped my mind. She was wounded when Andocia attacked you both, but she's fine now. She gave me a message when I saw her about an hour ago. A few of your followers are planning to come back again and rescue you."

For the first time since he met Tanus she brightened considerably. "Oh Craig, that's wonderful news!"

"I truly hope that they will succeed in freeing you this time, but Tarmin says they have a plan. Tanus, I have an idea, but I wanted to speak to you about it first. Andocia obviously trusts me, probably because she knows that I can't free you from those bands, no matter what I do. I'm pretty sure that the key to Constance's cell is on this bunch as well and I've thought of a way to free her without arousing suspicion. Andocia didn't put any restraints on her, so she can just walk out if I unlock her cell. Tanus, Constance won't be safe anywhere in either universe if Andocia looks for her, and I just wondered if you would mind sending her to your planet where I'm sure she will be well guarded."

"I don't mind at all. I want you to know that I really appreciate everything you did for me. I promise that I'll do everything I can to protect your loved one from Andocia. If you manage to free her, tell her to set her flight indicator to 100 and then just continue along that path until she reaches my planet. There she must identify herself and tell my people I gave permission for her to land, and they will take care of her. Now you had better return to Andocia, otherwise she may get suspicious. When do you think you'll be able to carry out your plan?"

"Tomorrow sometime I suppose. I intend to get Constance's ship ready for departure tonight."

That evening, just before supper, Craig sneaked quietly into the hangar and filled his girlfriend's ship with supplies and fuel to last until she reached Tanus's planet.

The following morning, he begged for the keys again and told Andocia he wanted to visit Constance. She stared suspiciously at him. "Why do you want to visit her? Before long she'll be history."

"I know that, but I owe her an explanation. I haven't had time to tell her about our proposed union," he explained.

She surrendered the keys and he went to visit Constance. Once inside, he spoke urgently to her. "Darling, please listen for we don't have much time. I'm going to free you and when you are safely away from here, I'll raise the alarm and pretend you attacked me in a jealous rage. I've spoken to Tanus and she offered her planet as a sanctuary. When you lift off, put your indicators on 100 and you'll go direct to her planet, but you must introduce yourself and tell them that Tanus sent you, otherwise they'll kill you for sure."

"But Craig, who's going to rescue you?"

He gently took both her hands in his and kissed them. "Don't worry about me! Andocia won't harm me – I'm to be her 'husband', remember," he replied bitterly.

"I don't like this at all," Constance complained. "We should both escape and to hell with that horrible woman!"

Craig held his girlfriend's hand tenderly. "There is nothing I would like more, but we are at a disadvantage here. Their ships are so much faster than ours. Even if we manage to make it out into space, they'll find us and then both of us will suffer. At least this way one of us has a chance. You have to get away because I don't really trust Andocia. She may decide to harm you even after I have done what she wanted. That woman knows I can't just stop loving you instantly. I'll always have feelings for you, no matter where I am. You are, and most probably will always be a rival for her affections. I don't want your fate to be in my hands, please understand this!"

"But Craig, will I ever see you again?" she sniffed unhappily.

He held her tightly. "I hope so my darling! Perhaps fate will be kind to us and we'll meet again."

He pulled gently away from her. "Go now, quickly before Andocia becomes suspicious and checks up on us."

Constance nodded in agreement and turned away from her boyfriend. Suddenly without warning she turned on him and punched him on the side of his head. He was dazed and fell to the ground, touching his aching temple. The skin had split open and was bleeding slightly.

"What did you do that for?" he grumbled.

"I'm sorry Craig, but it has to look real. If you just pretend I hit you, she'll read your mind and know you were lying. This is much better."

Carter rubbed his aching head and looked at the blood on his hand. "If I didn't know you better, I would think you did that on purpose!"

Miss Gregg's face showed no emotion. "Goodbye Craig," she said, and she was gone.

Craig waited until he judged it safe to raise the alarm, and then stumbled into Andocia's room, shaking his head and rubbing the wound.

Andocia jumped up in alarm. *"Craig, what happened?"*

"I'm so sorry Andocia, Constance has escaped! I explained about you and me, and I'm afraid she took it very badly. She complained that I was fickle and then she hit me. When I recovered my senses, she was gone."

Andocia's face contorted in anger. "Why the little … I'll kill her for that!"

"No Andocia, what's the point? You were going to let her go anyway, so why bother pursuing her. You wanted her out of the picture and she is, so forget it."

The devilish woman quietened down, but her eyes still flashed angrily. She placed her arm around his shoulders and his flesh crawled at her touch, but he pretended not to mind.

"All right, I'll leave her for now. I have some time in hand, so maybe we should spend it discussing our future together."

He went along with her, but he was so preoccupied he didn't really pay much attention.

CHAPTER 12

The next day, after Constance had escaped, the general executed his plan. He entered through a side entrance, masquerading as a delivery man. The real driver and his assistant had been knocked unconscious and lay bound and gagged behind a bush on a deserted road. They had been injected with some sleeping medicine which would ensure they stayed unconscious for the duration of the escape plan.

The general walked into the kitchen and his "assistant" followed behind, carrying a box of supplies. It was quiet in the castle and only one woman stood in the kitchen, cleaning the cupboards. She didn't look at them but indicated they should put the goods on the table. The "delivery man" came up behind her and swiftly put his hand over her mouth. He pressed a knife into her side. "Take it easy miss and don't scream or I will kill you," he whispered.

His colleague went to the kitchen door and looked out, but no one was around.

"All clear Sir," he acknowledged as he closed the door.

The girl dropped her sponge and raised her hands in the air and the general spoke again. "I don't want to hurt you miss. We are here to rescue Tanus and I won't hesitate to kill you if you scream, do you understand?"

The woman nodded slowly.

"I'm going to take my hand away. One wrong move and my friend will shoot you."

The general released her and she turned around slowly.

"Do you know the way to the dungeons?" he asked the maid.

"Yes. I have taken meals to the prisoners before. I'll be happy to help you Sir. I know a shortcut to the cells. Your timing was excellent. This is the quietest time of the day and no one will disturb you. There will be one or two guards down there, and the keys to the cells hang in the guard's lounge. Follow me please."

The two men put their heads out of the window and waved. A woman joined them and the foursome walked down the stairs that Craig had passed a few days earlier. The maid talked to the group as they walked. "I'm sorry the previous attack failed and I have to admit that I'm happy your soldiers came back for Tanus. Andocia is a she-devil and I don't like her! I didn't know what I was letting myself in for when I took this job. I'm going on leave today and everything is packed. I was just tidying up in the kitchen before I left, but I won't be coming back here ever again."

The general questioned her further. "Is Constance Gregg's

cell near to Tanus'? She isn't a priority, but a friend has asked me to include her in the rescue if we can."

The woman smiled. "She was here until two days ago. Her boyfriend came to see her and she managed to escape."

"Oh, really! Do you know how she got away?"

"No, I wasn't on duty then. There is a lot of speculation going around. Some of my friends say that Craig Carter freed her, while others think she just got the better of him. She is also quite amazing and very brave!"

The soldier's eyebrows rose enquiringly. "Do you have an opinion on what happened, miss?"

She shrugged her shoulders. "I don't really know, but I would say he freed her. Those two are so much in love, they deserve to be together."

The group continued down the passageways and the general whispered into his commlink. "Dave, I want to try and free Craig as well if I can, but I don't want to endanger the mission. Tanus is our first priority. Ask Tarmin to take a look around the grounds and see if she can locate him. If she does, tell her to take him to the agreed departure point immediately. Miss Gregg has flown the coop so we don't need to worry about her anymore."

The woman led them down another tunnel and then she stopped at a large wooden door.

"I have no key for this door," she explained. "What do you want to do now?"

"Knock on the door and tell the guard you were asked to check up on Tanus, then leave the rest to us."

The soldiers flattened themselves against a wall and indicated she should knock. She did this and a grate in the door opened.

"Yes, what do you want?" growled a guard.

"Andocia asked me to check how Tanus is doing and report back to her."

There was the sound of a bolt being drawn back and the door opened. The general fired his laser gun and the guard fell soundlessly to the ground. They looked at the maid and she pointed to a door not far away. "The guard's lounge is there," she whispered. The soldiers hurried forward, their shoes making no sound on the carpeted floor. She heard more gunfire and the general gave a thumbs-up sign. One of his companions held the ring containing all the keys to the cells.

The maid took the ring from him and searched quickly through the keys, then she separated one of them.

"Are there any other prisoners down here?" the man asked her.

"No, not at the moment. Just Tanus. Hurry before the guards are discovered."

The small group came to Tanus's cell and opened it. She was lying on her bed and didn't look up. The general touched her on the shoulder and whispered something to her. She stood up shakily and the woman soldier took out a strange weapon and placed the barrel against one of the cuffs. It split apart as though it was made of plastic and she quickly did the same with the other.

The general took Tanus by the hand, but she could barely walk, so he scooped her gently into his arms. She smiled wanly, put her arms around his neck and her head on his shoulder. The small group then hurried out of the tunnels and headed back to the kitchen.

While this was happening, Tarmin was looking for Craig and hoped fervently that she would find him outside somewhere because she couldn't risk going into the castle to find him. She knew he had no idea that Tanus was being rescued today so he would not be expecting anyone. If he was with Andocia, then she would have no choice but to leave without him. The bird flew around the castle and finally found him sitting under a tree. There seemed to be no one around and she landed close by, startling him. *"Craig, Craig, Tanus is being rescued as we speak! The general said I must find you and take you to the ship. Hurry, they will be leaving soon!"*

The space explorer jumped to his feet and hurried after her. She flew just above him and he followed her. He saw a ship hovering near the kitchen located on the ground floor, but there was a lot of ground to cover. No one seemed to notice anything and he hoped they would make it on time.

Craig was still quite a distance from the ship when he saw the general emerge with Tanus in his arms. Two more of Tanus's warriors were hot on his heels. At the same time, several of Andocia's soldiers saw what was happening and they drew their weapons, pointing them at the general, who was unable to fight back. The other two who had accompanied the general, drew their weapons, but the small group were hopelessly outnumbered. Carter turned away from the ship and Andocia's followers called to him. *"Don't let them escape Carter! Do something!"*

He ran up to them and held out his hand. "Give me a weapon quickly!"

The soldier in front handed over her laser gun, but instead of shooting at the escapees, he fired point blank at the woman in front of him. She dropped to the ground and before the others had recovered from their shock, he began to shoot at all of them. He laid down covering fire to distract Andocia's troops from the escaping party, who were running madly for the hovering craft. More soldiers came out of the building and suddenly the gun stopped working. He grabbed one of the fallen soldier's weapons and fired ceaselessly over the heads of the warriors that were streaming out of the castle. Miraculously none of the laser guns hit him.

Tarmin circled above him and he saw the general and his party climb onto a platform which began to lift up into the ship. She shouted at Craig to hurry, but the ship was lifting up and he knew it would be very close. The bird swooped down on him. *"Craig, grab my legs,"* she screamed desperately.

The explorer threw the laser gun at the remaining troops and ran swiftly towards Tarmin. He jumped as high as he could and managed to grab onto the bird's legs. She streaked upwards towards the ship and freedom. Carter gasped as he saw Andocia come rushing out of the castle, her face twisted in rage, and time seemed to stand still as he watched her raise her hand above her head and point it in their general direction. He looked upwards and saw the platform was very close to the hatch of the spaceship, the general's head already disappearing inside.

Craig screamed in agony as something slammed into his shoulder, causing him to lose his grip on Tarmin's feet. For a moment their eyes met and Tarmin's were wide with shock and misery. He heard her scream his name and then he was falling. Carter saw her shrink suddenly and dive into the ship. The hatch slammed shut and the ship took off into the sky and in a flash it had disappeared.

Craig's instincts took over and he instantly curled into a ball and relaxed every muscle in his body as the ground came swiftly up to meet him. He slammed to the ground with incredible force that made all the birds in the trees fly away in fright. He rolled on impact and finally came to rest near a tree.

The explorer cursed his bad luck and turned towards the angry soldiers who looked ready to kill him on the spot. Andocia was livid and also pointed a finger at him, taking careful aim. Carter got to his knees and put his hands on his head. The explorer remained still, knowing he had now sealed his fate. He closed his eyes in dread and expected a red bolt to slam into him and end his life. His nemesis stormed up to him. She had a murderous look on her face and his insides turned to jelly. He couldn't meet her malevolent gaze and turned his face away. Carter's head was forcefully turned until he was looking at her once more.

"I should just kill you but I have a much better idea. I'm going to make an example of you and all the worlds in both universes will know and fear me. It will cause grief amongst your friends and awe amongst your enemies. I was a fool to believe your lies, but it won't happen again."

Craig had never felt so nervous before and he knew he had made a terrible mistake! Before he had much time to consider his options, Andocia angrily hauled him to his feet and forced his hands behind his back. The explorer felt glowing red handcuffs snap shut on his wrists. He was shoved forward and several soldiers surrounded him, forcing him to walk ahead of them.

The group walked to the hangar where Andocia's ship was waiting and he was shoved ruthlessly inside. The soldiers formed a circle around him and led him along various passageways, until the group reached some cells. One was opened and he was pushed inside. The door clanged behind him and the guards made no attempt to take off the handcuffs, but walked away without a backward glance. Craig looked at his shoulder and saw blood was still trickling down his arm.

Some time passed and he slept fitfully for a while. Much later, Andocia came to sit on a chair near his bed. Her face twisted into an evil sneer. "You fool, Carter! All you had to do was co-operate with me and I would have laid the worlds at your feet, but you lied to me and I detest that. The manacles around your wrists are the same as those I used to bind Tanus. She couldn't escape from them and neither can you. Now there is no room in my heart for you."

"I don't care anymore," Carter replied. "Tanus and Constance are safe and that's all that matters."

"Before this day is over, you'll have cause to regret that statement, because I'm going to make an example of you. Both universes will fear me!"

"Where are we going?" he asked curiously.

"I am taking you to one of my many hideaways," she replied.

She stood up abruptly and walked away from him. No mention was made of the wound in his shoulder, and no one came to clean it. His eyelids grew heavy and he fell into a dreamless sleep.

When he woke again, he saw Andocia regarding him intently from outside his cell.

"Is something wrong?" he asked groggily.

"I just had an overwhelming urge to kill you!"

Her prisoner said nothing and she continued. "I am so tempted to end you once and for all, but I have a much better idea. However, I want to ask you some questions that have been bothering me."

Once again, Craig remained mute.

"Were you sincere when you pledged allegiance to me, or was it just a lie?"

Craig struggled into a sitting position. "Andocia, we are worlds apart and I really couldn't see us together, but I was prepared to do it for Constance's sake. She means more to me than life itself. If you had killed her, I would never have agreed to any kind of alliance. However, I meant what I said when I promised to be your partner. I was honest with you and told you I would have to learn to love you. We hardly know one another, but I was prepared to keep my promise. When Tarmin gave me an opportunity to escape, I discovered my freedom was more important than an alliance with you and I decided to risk it. I never lied to you – I just ... changed my mind."

"You knew Tanus's followers were going to rescue her, didn't you?"

"Tarmin told me, but even she didn't know when they were planning to do it."

"I'm curious, Carter; what made you decide to undertake this impossible mission? Surely you must have realized you would come off second best?"

"I did it because I was asked to. I owe Tanus my life, because she warned me about you on various occasions, thus I managed to escape your clutches."

Andocia smiled coldly. "Until now that is! Tanus won't be able to help you, because we are far away from my planet now and she doesn't know where all my hideouts are. If you are hoping to be rescued, it won't happen. Anyway, Tanus is weak from her confinement and even if she did locate my ship, there's nothing she can do about it until she regains her strength. You see, not only are these handcuffs functional, but they also begin affecting one's nervous system. They cause acute depression, so the longer a person is confined, the more depressed they become. I don't know if it'll have the same effect on you, but that's immaterial to me, for soon it won't matter to you either way."

A servant bringing some food on a tray to Andocia interrupted them. Another plate was placed in front of Craig and he stared at it reluctantly. He looked expectantly at the devilish woman and held out his hands, but Andocia shook her head.

"I'm sorry, but I'm not taking any chances with you. You stay bound until I decide otherwise."

Craig sighed. "Andocia, where do you think I can run to? I am imprisoned in a maximum-security cell, on a ship going to heaven knows where."

Andocia glared at him, but she removed the manacles from around his wrists.

The man pulled a wooden chair up to the small table in his cell, picked up the knife and fork and began to eat the food. Despite his misgivings, he found he was ravenously hungry and realized with a start, that he hadn't eaten for most of the day. When the plates had been taken away, he got back onto the narrow bed. Andocia held the cuffs out again and Craig shook his head unhappily. For a moment she glared at him, but relented and stood up to leave.

By this time his shoulder had begun to throb, and he struggled to get comfortable, but no relief was offered. One of Andocia's followers went over and whispered in her ear, pointing at Craig, then the girl disappeared and returned with some soap and water and began to clean the wounds that were leaking. His shoulder was also attended to. The girl sponged him down as best she could and put clean dressings on them. She took the bowl away and returned with a syringe. "Mr Carter, don't be alarmed, this is just a sedative to calm you down and ease the pain."

He smiled gratefully at her and allowed her to plunge the needle into his arm. When she turned to leave, he reached for her hand. "Wait, please," he pleaded. "Do you know what Andocia has planned for me? The suspense is killing me."

She shook her head and averted her eyes, and then she gently extricated herself from his grasp. "Sleep now! The sedative is fast acting and you should have a quiet night."

Obediently he lay down on the bed and was soon fast asleep.

During the night, he had a dream in which Tanus came to him. "Craig, I'm too weak to help you at the moment and I don't know where you are, only that Andocia has you in her ship. She's planning something diabolical and I fear for you. I have the power to send a special bird to you, which can kill with a single peck. If you wish to end it this way, tell me now and it will latch onto your brainwaves. Or would you prefer to go with Andocia and take your chances?"

Craig's lips moved, but no sound came out. "No Tanus, I'm not ready to die just yet! I gave up once before when Andocia blinded me and thanks to good friends, I survived that ordeal. There may still be a chance for me. Besides, I want to see Constance again. Is she all right?"

"She is doing fine Craig. I have her here with me and I swear to you that no one will harm her as long as I'm around. You just take care of yourself."

"I plan to do exactly that. Give Constance my love, and tell Tarmin that what happened wasn't her fault. She did her best and it just didn't work out. I'm grateful to her anyway for trying to help me."

"I'll pass your message on. You are a brave man Craig and I respect you for that. I'm so sorry I got you into this mess, but when I'm feeling stronger, I'll find out where you are and free you. I consider you one of my friends, always remember that."

When he woke again, it was morning and he felt much better. Andocia told him they were arriving on another of her planets. Before landing, she manacled his wrists again and he walked with her. The sky was a murky colour and he wasn't sure what galaxy he was in. As he walked, Andocia's people stared at him. There were both men and women followers on this planet. Carter was taken to a cell and locked inside, then Andocia removed the bonds and he stretched his cramped muscles.

CHAPTER 13

Back on Earth, Commander Simms paced the floor time and time again.

"Why haven't I heard from Craig? Three months and no word from him since he requested I get Constance away from Earth. Where the devil *is* he? Is he alive or dead? Has he rescued that woman? All this waiting is driving me crazy!"

His secretary came in and handed him some computer disks. "Sir, you've been pacing back and forth for the last half an hour and you'll wear a hole in the carpet. Shouldn't you sit down and rest?"

"You expect me to rest? How can I relax, knowing that my best space explorer is missing?! Constance contacted me from some place not so long ago, but the message wasn't clear. At least she's alive though, but what of Craig?"

"I'm sure we'll get news of him soon," she remarked soothingly.

How right she was, but they were totally unprepared for the way in which it would influence the people of both universes and the impact it would make on them all.

⁂

Craig Carter sat mournfully in his cell, contemplating his fate. He looked out of the window and sighed. He saw grass and sky and the sun burned brightly. The explorer wished fervently that he could walk outside but he knew it would not happen anytime soon. He crossed his arms over his chest and rubbed the goose bumps.

"What does that evil woman have planned for me?" he wondered. *"I interfered with her plans and lied to her and she hasn't taken it well at all. I have a stubborn streak that just won't quit even when the time is right. Maybe I should have asked Tanus to send that bird of death to me and it would be over now."*

Even as Craig thought the words, he admonished himself for being so foolish. "I've been in worse situations than this and made it through. I'll do it again! I *will* see Constance again! My life is far from over."

He went to the window and put his hand outside as though to catch the breeze that blew on his skin. It felt warm and inviting.

The door to his cell opened and his food was brought in. The woman warrior avoided his eyes and placed the food down on the bed. At the doorway, many soldiers stood ready for action in case he tried to escape, but he stayed at the window until the door had closed and locked behind him. He noticed the cutlery and crockery were all plastic and useless as weapons. The explorer ate his food although he didn't have much of an appetite.

Much later, Andocia came into the cell and sat down on the bed. Carter remained standing near the window. The woman stared quizzically at him. "You know I hate you so much for what you have done to thwart me in the past, but at the same time I must be honest and tell you that you fascinate me as well. You have no hope of escape, yet I sense your reluctance to give in to despair. I can see why your boss holds you in such high esteem. So, tell me Craig Carter, are you always so stubborn or is it that you are too foolish to know the difference?"

Craig glared at his captor. "I know the difference all right! I suppose that I am stubborn, but friendship means everything to me, so I do what I can to help those in need. It's one of my better characteristics."

"Then I suppose you get into a lot of trouble because of it," she remarked dryly.

Craig smiled mischievously. "I guess I do, yet despite the perils I enjoy my job. I get to meet new people almost every day and swap ideas with them. Some however aren't all that willing to share ideas."

Andocia smiled wickedly. "Like me, I suppose."

Carter shrugged. "I suppose so, but there are others as well. My job does have a down side, I have to admit."

The explorer paced in the confines of his cell and looked at his captor. "One of my faults is that I'm very impatient and therefore I hate waiting for things to happen, so tell me Andocia, what's going to happen to me? I know you're angry with me and I suppose I would feel exactly the same if our positions were reversed but I'm not sorry that Tanus and Constance got away!"

"Do you have any regrets Carter?" she asked curiously.

Craig thought about it and shook his head. "No, I have none. If I had to live my life over again, I would most probably do exactly what I'm doing now. Despite everything, I would really like to stay alive, however, I won't plead for mercy because you have no heart. All I want to know is when will you kill me?"

Andocia laughed evilly. "Who says you are going to die? You said it yourself; everything you hold dear means more to you than your own life, so I'll grant your wish."

Craig went cold from fear. "What do you mean?"

"It's very simple Carter. You won't die, but the rest of your friends most certainly will. There is a fairy tale that has lasted through thousands of human generations and no doubt you know about it as well. It concerns a princess who was put to sleep for one hundred years and in that time, everyone she knew died of old age. She was revived by a handsome prince and began her life anew. It was called *Sleeping Beauty* I believe.

That's my plan for you, except there'll be no handsome prince, or in your case, princess who brings you back to life with a kiss and there will be no happy ending for you. When I choose to wake you up again, you are going to awaken in a very different world – the world I will have created!"

Carter was speechless and he stared in horror at his captor.

Andocia smiled at his discomfort. "Enjoy the last few days of your life as you know it. Something this elaborate needs time to prepare. We'll talk again."

Carter could only stare helplessly as the door slammed and locked behind him and he was left to contemplate his fate.

↲ ↲ ↲

The next day Andocia visited him again but he was still shocked by what she had told him the previous day and had very little to say.

"It seems you are reticent and have no wish to speak with me. I came to tell you that you have three days left before I put my plan into operation. Have you any final requests? I'll try to implement them so that your last few days are comfortable. By the way, being released isn't an option."

Craig looked longingly outside and visualized flying away in his spacecraft, but he soon put that idea out of his mind.

"I do have a request," he replied. "If I'm to be taken away from those I love, at least let me sit outside. I don't want to spend the last few days of my existence in a jail cell."

Andocia laughed spitefully. "Do you think I am an idiot? You are a very sneaky person and now that you know what I have planned for you, you'll do anything to escape. Sorry, think of something else."

Carter was silent and Andocia broke the silence. "Look let's compromise! I'll let you go outside, but you remain bound outdoors. You'll never be left alone, not even for a moment. Whatever you need, within reason of course will be provided by those who guard you. Does that satisfy you?"

"It will have to do," he replied.

Later that day he was escorted outside as promised. His hands were handcuffed in front of him and many of Andocia's followers escorted him. He sat down on a bench and they released his handcuffs, but they fastened one of them through a wrought iron armrest, while the other remained attached to his wrist. He sat down on the bench and looked heavenwards. "I wonder how you are my darling Constance. Are you missing me as much as I'm longing for you?" he thought miserably.

He closed his eyes and thought about his girlfriend. He imagined he was kissing her soft lips and he sighed.

"Mr Carter?"

"What! Oh, sorry I must have been daydreaming," he replied hastily.

One of Andocia's followers was standing close by holding a mug in her hand.

"It must have been a good dream," the woman replied. "You were smiling."

"It was," he confirmed. "I was thinking about someone very special."

The woman offered the cup to him. "Andocia thought you would be thirsty so she had me make you something to drink."

"Thank you," he replied gratefully. He sniffed it but couldn't make out what it was.

"This is herbal tea and is very popular here. It also helps you to relax a bit. Anyone can see you're very tense. I suppose given your circumstances, it's understandable," replied the woman. "If you don't mind my asking, what did you do to make Andocia so mad at you?"

"I thought everyone knew! I helped Tanus's followers to rescue her, amongst other things," he replied vaguely.

"*You did that?*" she replied incredulously. "I heard about the space explorer who has been a thorn in Andocia's side for quite some time now. By the way people have talked about you, I thought you must have been about ten feet tall and equipped with super powers."

Craig laughed. "You must be joking! How did that rumour spread?"

The woman shrugged. "Oh, you know how it goes! Someone tells a story and then another person embellishes on it a little and the tale becomes more extraordinary every time it gets relayed down the line."

"Sorry to disappoint you! No super heroes here, just me."

She reached for the cup and took it away from him. "I'll just take that back to the kitchen now."

Carter smiled at her. "Thank you, I enjoyed that tea."

She went away and the explorer stretched out on the bench and looked around. He took in every detail he could and imprinted it on his memory, stored away for further use. Even as he sat docilely on the bench, he was planning how he could escape from the planet.

The next day he asked to go outside again and his captors complied. The same girl served him his meals and he chatted to her. "What's your name?" he asked between mouthfuls of food.

"It's Misha," she replied.

"That's an unusual name. I like it!"

"Thank you," she remarked.

"How did you end up working for Andocia?" he asked curiously. "You look like a really nice person, not like the rest of these people. No one else even wants to speak to me."

"Don't be offended, but I think they are in awe of you. As I said before, you have quite a reputation. I shouldn't say this," she whispered, "but I think you are just wonderful. Personally, I think Andocia is being too harsh on you. I wish you hadn't been caught, because she isn't known for her patience."

"Thanks for the advice Misha, but it's too late now. Tomorrow will spell the end for me and I'll never see my girlfriend again. You know, you remind me a lot of her. She's kind and loving and I sense the same characteristics in you. If Constance wasn't in my life, I would have been proud to know you. Someday you'll make someone very happy."

"Thank you," she purred.

"You still haven't told me how you ended up working for Andocia."

Misha shrugged indifferently. "I needed a job and Andocia was advertising for helpers. I too believed in a cause and knew how to defend myself. At the time I was out of work and so I applied for the job. I met Andocia's criteria and here I am. I don't intend staying here forever either. Once I have learnt all I can, I'll move on to something better."

Craig looked around and found the rest of his guards were standing out of earshot. He stared earnestly at the woman.

"Misha, why don't you look for another job somewhere else? I know of a number of countries on Earth that would welcome your services as a bodyguard. Help me to get away from here and I'll see you get a good job in a less stressful environment. You have my word and I always keep it."

Misha looked nervously around. "I don't know about that! You know how Andocia feels about traitors and I don't want to end up sharing your fate. I like living!"

"I do too! Do you think I want to be put into a coma until all the people who mean anything to me, are dead?! I have a life too. Help me to live it. You said it yourself, you don't approve of Andocia's decision. Misha, I have no desire to live in a semi-comatose state for an indefinite period of time and then have to return to a universe that is completely different to the one we live in now."

Misha bit her lip. "I don't know …" she began hesitantly.

"At least think about it!" he begged. "I only have tomorrow and then it'll be too late. Will you give me your answer by tonight?"

"I need to think this through," she replied vaguely.

Misha took the tray away from Craig and walked off with it.

That evening she brought his supper to him in his cell. She was nervous and accidentally banged the tray down a little too hard. She was shaking. "I'm so frightened! I realized this afternoon that you made perfect sense, so I'll help you to get away if you promise me I'll be protected. Did you really mean what you said about finding me a job on Earth or was that just talk because of your tenuous situation?"

Craig put his hand on his heart. "I swear I meant every word. I haven't lied to you once and I'm not about to do so now."

"All right, I'll think of a plan tonight. Tomorrow morning ask to come outside again. I'll see what I can do to find you a weapon."

The explorer squeezed her hand gratefully. "Thank you. I owe you my life!"

"I'll collect payment when we're away from this accursed place," she replied seriously.

That night as Craig lay on his bed, he felt more at peace than he had over the last few days.

CHAPTER 14

The next morning several guards came to his cell and hand-cuffed him. When he questioned them, they replied that he was to have breakfast with Andocia. He was taken to another building where Andocia met them. She stood up silently and didn't greet him. Immediately, Craig knew something was wrong.

"What's going on Andocia?" he queried.

"I have something to show you," she replied.

Her people took hold of Craig and marched him outside. They led him to a tree, around which stood many of Andocia's people. The man gasped in horror when he realized that someone was tied to it. The figure's head was bent and the hair hung in tangled strands. As the party approached, she lifted her head and Craig groaned aloud. "Misha, what have they done to you?" he gasped in dismay.

"See what you've done Craig!" Andocia remarked angrily. "You have caused another person to suffer because of you. You corrupted one of my employees and now she's going to pay the ultimate penalty for your sin. I knew I couldn't trust you and I was right. I know all about your scheme to escape from my planet! Misha was only too willing to confess when we tortured her."

The grip on Craig's arms tightened as the guards restrained him. Desperately he pleaded with Andocia. "Please don't kill her! It's my fault, not hers! I just wanted to get away from you and all you stand for. You can send her away somewhere else if you don't trust her anymore. I'm the one you're angry with so kill me instead!"

Andocia was furious. "You'd like that of course, but I have other plans for you. Death will be too lenient for you. I want you to suffer!"

Craig looked miserably at Misha. "I'm so sorry! I never wanted you to get hurt! I meant every word I said to you, I swear it on my life!"

Misha looked at him through tortured eyes and a tear escaped and ran down her soiled cheek, making a stripe through the dirt on her face.

Andocia raised her hand and pointed her index finger at her hapless victim. Coldly she addressed the rest of her soldiers gathered around. "See how I deal with traitors! Let this be a lesson to anyone who is entertaining thoughts of deceiving me."

Carter tried to turn his face away from the sight, but someone put an arm around his neck and forced him to look.

The beam seemed to come from Andocia's hand in slow motion. Craig gasped when the beam hit Misha in the centre of her chest. Her body arched in a spasm and her eyes opened wide. Her mouth opened in a soundless scream and her life blood spurted out as her heart ceased to function. Misha slumped down and it was all over. Craig stared miserably at the dead woman.

Andocia walked up to him and dealt him a vicious backhand across his face. "When you're lying in your casket, I hope you dream of this moment, because this was your fault. I lost a good soldier and good help is hard to come by. From now on, all your privileges have been revoked. In fact, I am not going to take any more chances with you! The casket is ready and now your time is up."

Craig struggled furiously. "No! You promised me another day!" he complained, as he tried to wrench his arms free.

"Today, tomorrow, what does it matter?" she snapped. *"Take him away!"*

Carter managed to free his arms. He kicked out viciously at the guards who had been restraining him and ran for his life as they tripped and fell. He had taken note of the layout of the planet and knew in which direction Andocia's ships were stored. He ran for the hangar, intending to steal a ship and get away from the evil woman who now pursued him.

"Don't let him get away you fools! If he escapes, Misha won't be the only one who dies today. I want him alive, so shoot only to wound."

Beams danced around his legs and kicked up dirt on the ground, but Craig ran faster. A few red beams were aimed at him and he managed to avoid them.

Several of Andocia's soldiers headed him off in the hangars, but he refused to accept defeat and cleaved a path through them. Andocia was furious and she screamed obscenities at her staff. The sea of bodies grabbed at his clothing and tried to drag him down, but he used his arms and legs as very effective weapons. Finally, he reached a spacecraft and yanked the door open, praying fervently that the craft was fully fuelled.

He had just begun to close the door, when a red beam slammed into his leg, bringing him down. Blood began to fill the wound and he tried desperately to close the door. Andocia however was ready for him and she hit him in the arm with another beam that flew from her hand. Before Craig could stop himself, he was tumbling down the ramp and landing at the devilish woman's feet. He tried to struggle to his feet but his injured leg gave way and he fell again. He was unceremoniously dragged to his feet and forced to look at Andocia.

Her red eyes flashed dangerously and she glared at the would–be escapee. "I should just kill you, but I have to make an example out of you and that is the only reason why you are still breathing." To her followers she said, "Bring him to the labora-tory and let's get this over with."

He was marched into her laboratory and gazed at a glass

container standing nearby. It didn't take much imagination to see it was designed to hold a human occupant and his eyes opened wide in horror. Andocia's followers pushed him down into a chair.

"What ... what are you going to do to me?"

"It won't hurt! I'm going to put you in a coma and place your body in that container. In that state, you shall circle the universes and orbit the planets until I decide to revive you."

Craig shrank back from the device in horror. "No please don't! There has to be another way," he pleaded.

Andocia laughed spitefully. "I tried that but you refused my offer of companionship. All you had to do was say yes to the best job in both universes. There is no more to say on this subject for my word is final and I have made my decision. Don't worry! When you wake up, you'll be as young and as handsome as you are now, while your friends grow old. Maybe in fifty years, I'll revive you."

"Dear heaven, you're mad!" he replied. He glared at her in hatred and she stared compellingly at him.

"Look into my eyes, Carter. You have no will of your own, for I own your mind. I'm strong, much stronger than you."

He turned his head away from her, determined to fight her influence, but someone stood behind him and forced him to look at Andocia. He felt a sharp pain in his neck and the room began to swim in and out of focus.

Her voice took on a deeper tone and the man felt as though he was speeding down a dark tunnel. The world started to dip crazily as Craig fought desperately to remain conscious, but Andocia was stronger and his eyes closed. The devilish woman felt his pulse and examined him until she was certain his breathing was normal and regular. She spoke telepathically to him. *"Say goodbye to your life as you know it, Carter! I'll see you in perhaps fifty years or so."*

He heard her and answered, although he could feel himself drifting into unconsciousness. *"It doesn't matter what you do to me! When you finally decide to revive me, I'll still hate you! You should just kill me and save us both the trouble!"*

Everything seemed to be happening in slow motion and Craig renewed his efforts to fight the unconsciousness creeping up on him, but the drug, together with Andocia's powers were too strong and everything went dark. Andocia tried to make contact with him once again, but there was no response.

"So, it's done! Place him in the casket!"

The explorer was lifted into the container and Andocia bent down to unbutton his shirt, revealing the trident emblem, which now shone a deep red. She spent the next hour attaching various tubes to his body. One contained oxygen, while another would feed him intravenously. Another would take care of his bodily waste. When she was sure that everything was working satisfactorily, she compiled a note and placed it on the lid of the container. It read:

CRAIG CARTER
SPACE EXPLORER

The toughened glass container was then blasted into space.

"Now let the planets know the wrath of Andocia! Let them tremble at the sight of the earthman!" She laughed loudly as the casket began its journey.

CHAPTER 15

It floated away as if controlled by some invisible mechanism. On Bartha, the scanners picked up the shape of something oblong. When they focused their screens on it, they saw Craig's body and the emblem engraved on his chest. They wrung their hands in grief, for they had come to respect the young explorer.

"Andocia is making an example of the Earthling. He saved us but we can't help him. Oh Craig, I pity you! You don't deserve this! We dared to go up against Andocia and look what she did to us when we disobeyed her. She turned us into monsters. Only Craig Carter saw the beauty within us. We'll always remember him, because we owe him so much."

ù ù ù

On the Meltonian planet, the people gazed in fear at the box. They watched miserably as he floated around in space and they discussed his plight in their own language. For a while they watched the glass container circle the planet and finally, they turned their eyes away from the sight.

Then it moved onward and approached the white planet, where Tanus and Constance watched the screen in trepidation. It came close to the planet and they recognized Craig. The effect on Constance was disastrous and she collapsed in a dead faint, her face a deathly white. Tanus stared sadly at the spectacle and sighed. "Oh Craig, if only I had full use of my power, then I could bring that capsule down here and treat you, but alas it's not possible right now. You tried to help me even though you never really knew me all that well. It took great courage for you to stand against a foe like Andocia. I suppose you never really knew the extent of her power, but you've learnt the hard way. Even now I'm struggling to get better. I'm so weak and tired because of my prolonged incarceration. My heart grieves for you and your beloved Constance because I have never before seen a love so pure and true."

Tanus got slowly to her feet and went to see how Constance was doing. She was conscious, but very distressed. Tanus heard her sobbing even before she had turned down the long corridor that led to Constance's bedroom. When she came into the room, Miss Gregg wiped her swollen, red eyes and Tanus gently put her arm around the young woman's shoulders and tried to comfort her. "My dear, I grieve for your loss as well. I blame myself because if it wasn't for me, neither of you would be in the mess you are right now. I don't know what came over me when I asked for your boyfriend's help! I shouldn't have bothered him at all. Now he is in an induced coma and being paraded around like a trophy and you are a fugitive! You cannot return to Earth, because she will seek you out and destroy you."

"Why has she done this?" Constance blew her nose. "What did we do that was so bad? Craig doesn't deserve to be in this position. He should be here in my arms. I miss him so much!" she wailed.

Tanus sat down near the distraught woman. "I have known Andocia for a very long time so I can safely say I know her better than anyone else. You and your boyfriend were targeted because she didn't like the way you both stood up to her. This was a new experience for her and she was caught off guard by your aggression I suppose."

Constance sat up straighter and there was fire in her eyes. "She had no right to try and take over Earth. No one wanted her to rule over them like a dictator. We were just doing our jobs!"

"All of you were doing a very good job too!" Tanus remarked. "Everyone combined their efforts and that was why she didn't succeed. I promise you something my dear; when I have recovered my strength, I'll personally search for your boyfriend and when I find him, I'll return him safely to you once again."

"I'm truly grateful to you Tanus, but if you don't mind, I would like to return home soon. I have a job to do and I can't expect Commander Simms to let me stay here indefinitely. When you have rescued Craig, I'll be happy to come and fetch him and I'm sure my boss won't mind. Until then, I have to get on with my life."

"Ultimately that's your decision to make my dear, but I would advise you to be careful. It's true, Andocia has succeeded in capturing one of the beings she detested, but never forget the role you played in her life. Craig may have caused her more irritation, but you certainly made her angry too. Maybe she'll forget about you and just move on, but then again, maybe not. Are you willing to take that chance? I would advise caution at this time. Once you leave my planet, I cannot protect you. Stay another month perhaps and if you still feel the same way, then you must go. Does that sound fair?"

Constance sighed. "I love Craig so much, but I don't want the same fate to befall me. Does that make it wrong somehow?"

"No, of course it doesn't, Constance. Just wait a little longer, okay. Besides I like talking to you and catching up on the news about Earth. Will you stay a while longer?" she pleaded.

"Okay," Constance agreed. "I must admit your planet is very peaceful and the rest is doing me good."

Tanus took her hand. "I know you were devastated by the sight of Craig in that container, but he is still in orbit around my planet. Do you want to take another look before he leaves this orbit? You don't have to if you don't want to," she remarked hastily.

"I would like to," she replied decisively. "It may be a long time before I see him again."

They went back to the control room where the image was magnified and Constance looked at the face of the man she loved.

Tarmin flew to the capsule and perched upon it. She raised her head and sang a soft, clear tune of mourning. While the container orbited the planet, the bird stayed with it, as if guarding it. When it moved off to enter the black universe, she reluctantly took her leave. Head drooping and tail pointing downward, Tarmin returned to the white planet and came to rest beside Constance, giving vent to wails now and again, for the bird had come to love the handsome explorer in the little while she had known him.

Both women and Tarmin cried, each taking comfort from one another. Tanus handed out the tissues and everyone blew their noses. Tarmin put her wings around the two women she loved so much and pecked them both gently on their cheeks.

"Mistress, I placed the device on Craig's box as you requested. You should be able to trace him when you are feeling stronger."

Tanus hugged her friend. "Thank you Tarmin. It will help when the time comes to rescue him."

Constance smiled and hugged the white bird. "Thank you so much!" she replied gratefully.

Miss Gregg looked at the vidscreen and managed to catch another glimpse of her boyfriend's casket just before it went out of range. She turned to the woman in white. "Tanus, did you see the expression on his face?"

"I did, yes," she replied gently as she put her arm around the woman's shoulders.

"Do you think that he is in pain, or suffering somehow?" she wanted to know.

"I don't think so Constance. He's just sleeping. If he was in pain you would see that reflected on his face."

Constance was comforted by that and then they left the control room.

The container entered the universe Craig knew and loved and began to orbit Sonambra. Sonambro and his followers were struck dumb by the emblem and they were filled with fear. Usually a happy and outgoing people, they were reduced to sadness and regret. They mourned the loss of a good friend. Sonambro was upset that things had gone haywire when he had tried to give Constance sanctuary on his planet and was racked with guilt. "I had no idea that such an odious being existed," he thought miserably. "We are energy beings, yet Andocia was unaffected by us or our planet and she tried to capture Constance despite this. I am truly glad that Miss Gregg got away, even if they caught her later. I hear that she is under the white being's protection – Tanus I believe her name is. I hope all is well with her. I hope Cragus will be all right. Maybe someone can save him. We can only hope for a miracle."

The casket continued on its journey and orbited Mercury before making for Tyrome.

On Tyrome, the silver creature saw Craig lying in the container and was both pleased and angered. "I'm glad that he's in a coma because he was nothing but a nuisance, but I would've enjoyed being the one to destroy him. However, that woman terrifies me and therefore I won't question her actions. I found Mr Carter to be quite tenacious and he thwarted me as well when I tried to make the Saturnians work for me. He did it again when I tried to do the same with Sonambro. That man never knew when to quit, but he met his match when he tangled with Andocia."

Then the container headed for Mars. After orbiting around, it passed through the asteroid belt to Jupiter. The inhabitants weren't really sure what was happening, but they recognized Craig and shook their heads sadly. Then it made its way to Saturn.

On Saturn, an alarm sounded and Jorrel was hurriedly called to the communication centre. "Jorrel, there's an unknown object floating about near Saturn," Karnd warned him.

"Zoom in for a close up and let's see what it is," Jorrel remarked.

This was done and Craig's body came sharply into focus and filling the screen. Lara gasped in horror and fled tearfully from the sight. The Saturnians held an emergency meeting to discuss the situation.

"Lara, you are the most learned of us all. What do you suggest we do? Craig is our friend and I can't bear to see him like that," Jorrel complained.

"I want to do everything I can to help him, because he was always ready to help us in our time of need, but I don't know what I can do. We can certainly bring the container to Saturn, but it might be booby trapped," Lara sighed.

"Do you really believe Andocia would do that?" asked Karnd incredulously.

"Yes, I do. She is evil and won't like anyone meddling in her affairs. Look what happened to Craig because of it. Even if we managed to open the container, how can we revive him? Any interference on our part could result in his death. I'm not prepared to chance it."

"Must we leave him to float in space like a piece of junk then?" Karnd complained.

"Leave it for the moment. I'll get to work on the problem though and if I think of a solution, I'll discuss it with you, okay."

No one liked her answer but they decided to defer it for the time being.

⚷ ⚷ ⚷

The capsule made for Uranus and orbited once before continuing to Neptune.

The Neptunians could only stare at their comatose friend and Lolita wiped away the tears that spilled from her eyes. "It's so unfair! How long will he remain a human exhibit? Will Andocia ever revive him? I can't stand to see him like this!" She began to cry brokenheartedly and her mother led her out of the room.

The King of Neptune spoke with his advisors and also his family. "Unfortunately our expertise does not encompass human beings. We have no idea how to fix any problems that humans encounter. We are so different to humankind."

"But Father, Craig has always been good to us. In fact, everyone on Earth is wonderful and so helpful. Surely we can do something? We must." Lolita cried.

"I would do anything I could to help him, you know that, but all we can do is offer our help to Earth."

Lolita swam back to their control room, hoping to catch one last look at the glass container, but when they looked again, it had already disappeared.

↙ ↙ ↙

Then onto Pluto. The Plutonians, enemies to all because of their deadly powers which enabled them to grow to gigantic proportions, laughed as they recognized the explorer.

"It serves him right. I always hated that man. It's a fitting punishment!"

Another turned to his companion. "We hate everyone, except our own species."

The creature laughed. "You are right of course – we most certainly do."

↙ ↙ ↙

The orbiting space stations watched in awe as Craig floated by. They too mourned the loss of someone they had come to respect a great deal. On the Russian space station, Ivan Petrovsky stared out the window and shook his head sorrowfully. "I have no love for Craig Carter but I have to admit he's a welcome distraction when I'm pursuing him. He always managed to get away from me though, but it looks as though he has met his match this time. That Andocia woman is certainly a force to be reckoned with and I'm glad I haven't crossed her path."

↙ ↙ ↙

It went to Venus next and again his condition caused great sadness. It was now several months since Andocia first placed Craig in his coma and he was given up as dead. Constance continued to remain with Tanus and her followers.

One fateful day, Commander Simms was at the observation post in the control centre, when a tiny blip began to flash on the screen and he locked the scanner onto the object, which became larger as it approached the atmosphere. It came closer and he pressed the "'magnify" button, which brought the object sharply into focus. The computer hummed and spoke calmly. *<Object scanned. Confirm, one human occupant – vital signs stable.>*

A collective gasp of surprise and dismay rang out as the technicians recognized their colleague. Craig lay on his back, arms by his side and the expression on his face was one of absolute calm. All eyes were riveted to the mark on his chest.

"Andocia! She was responsible for the state in which he's in. It says here that he'll remain in this condition until she decides to reverse it!"

Commander Simms gasped as a sudden pain knifed through him and he clutched at his chest. The paramedics were called and he was rushed off to hospital, suffering from a heart attack. As a final tribute to Craig, all his friends on Earth and the Moon fired objects into the sky and there was a cascade of glorious colours that lit up his casket. Then heads were hung in sorrow and tears were shed for the well-known and loved explorer.

CHAPTER 16

The container continued its tour of the universes, but what of the occupant? Craig slept soundly, but while his body remained unmoving, his mind wandered constantly and he dreamed, and dreamed, and dreamed.

He relived his life over and over again, from the beginning of his career with Mission Control, right until the present time. Images came to him of his parents and their home and the love he knew they had for him. He had always been an only child, but he had never been bored. His inquisitive mind had got him into trouble on more than one occasion and he remembered fondly how his parents had often found him lying on his back in their garden, gazing up at the stars.

"One day I'm going to be flying in space, Dad," he used to say. "Sometime when I'm older, I'll see those stars close up. There are so many exciting things up there in space and I want to see them all."

His father had tousled his ash blond hair and laughed kindly.

"You must do what you must do," he had responded. "Let your dreams take flight and make them your own!"

"I will," he had promised both himself and his parents.

Even though he knew his parents were just indulging him, he knew what his future held. Craig Carter achieved his dreams, but some nightmares followed as well.

When Craig had turned seventeen, he tried to become a space explorer. Commander Simms had sent him away and told him he was far too young and inexperienced to go out into space. He was told that while it seemed a noble thing to do, exploring space was dangerous and the commander felt he wasn't ready.

Craig was despondent and had wandered over to where the spacecrafts were housed. He had watched in fascination as the mechanics fixed broken ships and while the staff knew he was intruding, they left him to wander around and gawk at the different crafts. Some of the staff kindly explained the different types of spacecrafts and took him on a tour of the premises.

From that moment on, Craig was determined to explore space. He returned to Commander Simms' office and the man glared at him. "Why have you come back here Mr Carter? I already gave you my answer and no amount of pleading on your part will get me to change my mind."

Craig smiled at the man. "I know that Sir, but space has fascinated me all my life. If I can't go up in space, could I at least learn to fix the ships?"

Simms' face had split in a wide grin. "I don't see why not young man. You are very determined and I like that about you."

They had shaken hands vigorously and the commander had made the necessary arrangements.

Two years later Craig finally achieved his dream and became a space explorer. The training was brutal and very hard work, but he had persevered, despite this. He found out later that very few people who trained as space explorers ever completed the course, but he was one of the lucky ones and finally he had achieved his dream! From that moment on his life had changed. He made many friends out in space, but also several enemies.

One of the first foes he had met was Tyrus. The silver humanoid-like beings were electrical beings he had outwitted when they had tried to take over Saturn and later they tried the same thing with Sonambra, but the young man had stopped them both times. Tyrus would do anything to kill him, he recollected with a shudder. Even though his body remained immobile, Craig felt the revulsion run through his system.

There was Colonel Ivan Petrovsky too of course, but Craig had never divulged any secret information about the spacecrafts that America was building, even though he had been tortured. Idly he wondered where the man was. He was unaware that as he dreamed, his Russian counterpart was watching him from Moscow's Mission Control.

He had to admit though that Andocia was by far the most wicked adversary he ever had the misfortune to meet. Her powers were awesome and he wondered how it came about that she had such incredible abilities. The woman scared him, but he had to admit he had a sort of morbid fascination of her as well. Craig knew what she had done to him and hated her for it, but try as he might, he couldn't get his body to respond and he remained in the chemically induced coma. If only he might wake up, he thought desperately, maybe he could help himself.

His memories of Constance were vivid and he felt as though

she was standing beside him. "Don't give up!" he heard her urging him. "You *will* get through this, like always. I love you!"

His mind drifted to their first meeting. He had seen this gorgeous woman and had tried to speak to her, but she had given him the cold shoulder. She had been one of the newest recruits the year before he had become a space explorer. Constance had also helped Commander Simms on the odd occasion when his secretary was sick or away on leave.

Craig had to admit that he was probably very cocky in the beginning when he had first tried to speak to her which was why she had refused to go out with him. It was only when Craig had undergone the same training as her that they began their relationship. She, unlike him, had started her training at seventeen, for she had been really gifted and did well on her missions. Sometimes they even got to go into space together, but those occasions were few and far between. Now Carter wondered how he had ever lived without her. He yearned to hold her; to feel her lips on his and her arms around him, but he knew he was far away from her and he cursed Andocia with every cuss word he could think of, but still he orbited the planets, controlled by Andocia's diabolical invention. He hoped that if he was found and revived and everyone he had known and loved was indeed dead, he would somehow take revenge on the woman who had made this all possible.

CHAPTER 17

By now, Tanus had recovered fully and prepared to recover the capsule. It re-entered the Golden Way once again and she went out in a ship with some of her followers and intercepted it. Summoning all her powers, she concentrated on reclaiming it. A white ray shot forward and enveloped the capsule in which Craig slept deeply, and guided it into her ship. It was placed in the cargo bay where Tanus went to see it.

She stared down at the inert figure inside the glass container and stroked the glass near his head. "I blame myself for this. I should never have involved you in my problems, especially knowing what Andocia was capable of. I'll do everything I can to revive you though, I swear it."

One of her followers interrupted her thoughts. "Tanus, should we take him to the medical bay?"

She turned to her follower. "No, leave him for now. I have a well-equipped laboratory on the white planet and we can work on him there. I don't know what would happen if we suddenly opened this casket. He might suffer some kind of trauma. Monitor him and report any change in his condition to me immediately."

"Yes mistress," replied her follower obediently.

Tanus left the woman in the cargo bay and returned to the front of the spacecraft. A few hours later, the ship landed softly on the ground outside Tanus's palace. The cargo bay door was opened and Tanus levitated the container out and into the laboratory.

The casket was placed on a nearby table and she stared at the sleeping figure for a few moments and then concentrated on the casket. First the woman in white examined the casket and checked if Andocia had somehow booby trapped it, but she found no such devices. Tanus placed her hand on the glass casket and concentrated deeply, sending out her consciousness to touch the sleeping man. She was afraid that the incarceration might have damaged his brain, resulting in madness, but she had not shared this detail with any of her doctors or other inhabitants of her planet.

All was quiet in the laboratory for Tanus had dismissed everyone. She wanted to give her full attention to Craig before anyone else could come in contact with him. The woman in white closed her eyes and concentrated deeply. No sound came out of her mouth because she spoke telepathically. *"Craig Carter, this is Tanus. Can you hear me?"*

She waited a while but received no answer, so she repeated the question. *"Craig Carter, this is Tanus. Can you hear me?"*

She caught a few faint stirrings from inside his head. However, she could feel the strain and tension building inside him.

"*Tanus?*" he asked tremulously. "*Tanus, is that you or am I dreaming?*"

"*It's really me,*" she replied. "*You are safe now. I have brought you to my planet.*"

"*Constance! ... How is Constance? Is she still alive?*"

"*Hush now and don't upset yourself! She's fine,*" Tanus replied gently.

"*How ... how long have I been sleeping?*"

"*You have been asleep for several months, but you are still asleep. This is only a dream, but you will be awake soon I promise you. I have brought the casket to my planet and I'll take care of you.*"

"*Another dream!*" he replied sadly. "*I have been dreaming about many things!*"

Tanus stiffened but kept the conversation light. "*What have you been dreaming about, Craig?*"

There was no answer and she began to worry that she had lost him, but he answered slowly, as though he was remembering the dreams. "*I have dreamed of so many things! My parents ... my past ... my life in general. I have dreamt of Constance ... and of you, Tanus. Good things mostly, I suppose.*"

"*Have you had dreams of Andocia?*" Tanus asked kindly.

"*Yes, but not many. I have to wake up – to come back to my life – to the woman I love.*"

Tanus smiled for the first time since she had begun the conversation with the comatose man. She projected calming images into his mind and slowly he began to relax.

"*Listen carefully Craig. I assure you that all is well, but you still need to sleep for a while longer. I'll see you soon. Now I want you to sleep so that you can heal completely. When you wake up you will forget this conversation ever happened. You will not have any more disturbing dreams I promise.*"

The kindly woman felt his consciousness slip away and she knew he would no longer feel stressed about the situation. She went outside and called the doctors.

The lid was opened slowly and Craig was put on a bed in the hospital. Constance was asleep and Tanus didn't want to disturb her, deciding that she would tell her the good news in the morning. Then she called a conference with her advisors.

"My loyal friends and subjects, I have managed to bring the Earthling, Craig Carter here, but he is still in a coma. Andocia wasn't very tolerant of him and she branded him with her mark. His ankles too are badly scarred. I have also found wounds on his left arm and leg, and various others all over his body. Although they have healed, there are ugly scars. The wounds on his wrists have also healed, but there is plenty of scar tissue that will need to be cut out. Carter went through all that horror in order to help me; someone he hardly knew. Don't you think we should try to rid him of these ugly reminders?"

A hum of agreement went up amongst her supporters.

"I propose we contact all the scientists of the friendly planets in both universes and see who can help us. I think it would be advisable to first work on his body before we try to wake him up, or we'll cause him needless pain."

The technicians went back to their stations and contacted all the scientists and doctors of Earth, Venus, the Moon, Saturn, Neptune, Sonambra and even Jupiter. The volunteers were ferried in Tanus's own ships.

When everyone had arrived, they discussed the best tactics to use and the Saturnians were chosen to begin operating. They had invented an artificial skin that combined with the human DNA and restored defects in the human body. It had already been used successfully on other humans and had helped them make a full recovery. Firstly, the emblem on his chest was removed and the artificial skin was placed carefully over the mark, which began at his breastbone and ended just above his pelvis. He was bandaged up and then they began working on his ankles and wrists. These too were bandaged up and left to heal. Afterwards the doctors began working on his scarred arm and leg. He lay in the coma for another month, while his body healed, and then they decided to bring him out of it.

An X-ray was taken of his head and the colour photograph clearly showed what the problem was. Andocia had put a red shield around his brain so that no one could bring him round without dissolving it first. They all scratched their heads in bewilderment for a while, but then the Jupitarians came up with the solution. They cut a special plant in half and extracted the juices from the fleshy object. The contents were placed in a pot, which was then put on to boil. The juice changed colour after which the Saturnians made a tiny incision in his head and injected the solution via a syringe, directly into his brain and waited nervously for the results. The next day, another X-ray was taken and the red mist had dissolved. A quick but thorough examination revealed that Craig was no longer in a coma, but simply unconscious. Tanus sighed gratefully and he was left to recover by himself. From the time Tanus had told her about Craig, Constance kept constant vigil by her boyfriend's bed, never leaving his bedside for a moment, except to sleep.

Tanus meanwhile went to sit outside on a bench under a shady tree. Tarmin joined her a little while later. "I'm so glad everything is all right with Craig now. Is he going to be okay?" she asked nervously.

Tanus smiled at her friend. "Yes Tarmin, he is going to be fine once he wakes up. Why do you look so worried?"

The bird looked at her mistress. "I know you so well! We have been together for a number of years now and you have also been very stressed lately. I know that you were very worried about Craig when you brought him here – we all were, but there's something else that was bothering you."

Tanus stroked her friend's wing. "You don't miss much do you Tarmin? I admit, something was bothering me a great deal."

"And …?" prompted the bird when her mistress fell silent.

"You know what Andocia is like and frankly I was very worried about Craig. I knew that when she put him in that coma, his brain would not shut down. He was helpless to move a muscle, but his mind was active. I was concerned because he could have gone insane and even if we had managed to rescue him, he would be crippled emotionally."

Tarmin looked at her mistress and understood why she had been acting so strange and aloof. "So that was why you had him taken to the laboratory before anyone was allowed to see him."

Tanus smiled and stroked her friend. "I had to do it! I *had* to know!"

She looked down at the ground and Tarmin gently lifted her mistress's face up.

"What did you find?" she asked nervously. "Is ... is he ...?" The white bird couldn't finish the sentence and waited anxiously for the answer.

"He is fine Tarmin, just fine! We got to him in time though because I could sense he was starting to become alarmed. When I questioned him, he said he had been dreaming, but that most of his dreams were good ones. He only had a few nightmares, but he was working through them."

Tarmin wasn't aware that she had been holding her breath and let it out with an audible whoosh. "Oh, but that is good news then! I'm so happy!" she chirped excitedly.

The woman in white fell silent once again and Tarmin gently wrapped a wing around her arm. "If he is mentally stable, then why are you still worried?" she wanted to know.

"*I HATE ANDOCIA!*" she stated with such vengeance that Tarmin was dumbfounded.

"I despise her too! But this is nothing new; both of you have been enemies for many centuries."

"I know that Tarmin, but the fight between her and me is understandable! We left Earth many years ago and now she is causing them harm. They have done nothing to her and yet she has terrorized them. I know Craig was the link, but he just happened to be in the wrong place at the wrong time. He didn't ask for this to happen, nor can anyone blame him. She knew where the jump vortexes between both universes were long ago, as I did, but she made it seem as though it was his fault she found this out."

"I know that mistress, but no one blames him for this. Everyone knows that it wasn't his fault."

"Every planet in Craig's galaxy believe in him – now; but think how he must have felt when everyone thought he was a criminal."

"That is past history Tanus. His reputation is intact now and no one will ever doubt him again."

Tanus picked up a rock and flung it at a nearby tree, where it slammed into the bark before coming to rest on the ground. "The thing is Tarmin, as much as I have always despised Andocia, nothing can compare how I feel at this moment. She hurt him – she hurt someone in my *family!*"

Tarmin drew back in surprise and then answered cheerfully. "I understand completely! Craig risked his life to save you and landed in this predicament. Tanus you may not be my real mother, but you are my family too, and because of who Craig is – well then he is my family from now on as well."

Tanus smiled but she was still thoughtful. Tarmin sensed there was more that her mistress wanted to say so she perched close by and massaged her friend's neck. It was knotted and full of tension. She spoke telepathically to her mistress. *"Please Tanus, tell me everything. I have never seen you so sad and yet so angry at the same time. You are starting to worry me."*

The woman nodded and her eyes became wet with tears. "I'm sorry I lost my temper like that, but as I said, I have been stressed. I couldn't bear the thought that Craig might have become emotionally unstable because of what Andocia had done to him. I blame myself for his predicament, because I was so desperate to be freed that I risked his life. I had no right to place him in such danger. I know now that Andocia influenced me when she captured me and I became depressed and lost all reasoning. I'm a match for Andocia at the best of times, but she still managed to upset me and I lost control. Craig is just a mortal, so you can understand how guilty I feel. That young man is very stubborn and tenacious! If it had been anyone else, they would have gone insane, but he's going to be fine."

Tarmin nodded and cleared her throat noisily. "Uh ... Tanus ... can I ask something?"

The woman nodded and the bird continued nervously. "I'm glad that he'll make a full recovery, but what if things had been different and you found out that he had in fact gone insane. What would you have done then?"

"I would have ended it! I would have put him out of his misery!"

"You would have ... *killed him?*" she gulped.

Tanus nodded and the tears poured down her face. "I would have had no choice! I was going to do it if it became necessary and then I was going to blame Andocia. Everyone would believe me if I had said that the strain of being cooped up for so many months had caused him to have a stroke! I feel terrible just having thought of that and I wonder if Andocia and me are really all that different."

Tarmin was visibly shaken, but she put a wing around her friend's shoulders. "I must agree with you. I know you would've done it out of love, not deceit. If Craig had been emotionally scarred, he'd have expected nothing less. I know that if something like that happened to me, I would want you to do the same thing."

"You don't think I'm a monster then?" she wanted to know.

"Never! I love you and I would do anything for you. You are nothing like Andocia."

Tanus dried her eyes and smiled wanly. "Well let's go and see how the patient is, shall we?"

They went to the hospital and found Constance sitting by Craig's bed as usual. Her head had fallen forward onto the duvet and she dozed. She was awoken by a movement and saw both Tanus and Tarmin enter the room. They were just about to ask her how he was when they looked at the bed and saw Craig's head moving from side to side. He groaned and his eyes flickered open. He looked around in confusion and slowly his vision began to clear, and he found himself staring at the two women who were standing on either side of his bed, each holding one of his hands. Everyone cheered loudly. Craig was helped to a sitting position and stared around at the people he loved most.

"How ... how did I get here? The last thing I remember was being with Andocia."

Constance hugged him gently and the tears ran down her cheek. "Oh Craig, it's a long story and when you're feeling better, we'll tell you everything that happened."

Tarmin hopped up and down excitedly, emitting shrieks of joy, before she ran over to Craig and pecked him affectionately on the cheek. He smiled and stroked her soft head. He stared lovingly at his girlfriend and pulled her gently towards him. Their lips met in a warm embrace and Tarmin gave vent to a mischievous "ooooh", jumping nimbly out of the way as Craig's hand moved to smack her. Tanus laughed. "All right Tarmin, that's quite enough. Go and tell my people that Craig Carter has recovered."

Tarmin flew outside and perched on the roof of the palace, where she sang a clear, sweet melody and the people gathered to hear her announcement. "Now hear this! The Earthling, Craig Carter, has woken up! Andocia's spell has been broken!"

The cheering crowd drowned her voice out.

On the advice of Tanus's doctors, Carter was instructed to stay in bed and take things easy for a few more days and then the bandage around his head was removed. He examined his body thoroughly and was grateful to find that all the scars were gone. The doctors of the various planets had done their work well.

However, Craig's confinement in the casket had taken its toll. Because he had been asleep for so long, his muscles were weak and he found it difficult to do anything even remotely strenuous. He had to receive extensive physiotherapy just to walk properly. He was impatient to return home, but knew it wouldn't happen in the very near future.

Commander Simms was notified of his recovery and he insisted that Craig only return home once Tanus's doctors pronounced him fit enough to travel. No one said anything, but Craig knew they feared Andocia's wrath when she found out about his escape from the fate she had intended. Carter knew he could not fight even one of his weakest enemies as he was. He foresaw many hours of hard work in the gymnasium once he returned home to Earth.

When he felt strong enough to walk around unaided, he went to see Tanus. Constance held his hand and they sat down on the couch. The woman in white poured them something to drink. While her back was turned, Constance again wondered about the lower half of Tanus's face, for while the features were there, they seemed blurred. Tanus read her mind but said nothing. Some things would have to remain a secret she decided.

She turned to the two people she had grown to love and smiled at them. "Craig you have been through a terrible ordeal and I just wanted to thank you for what you did for me. I know I'm repeating myself, but you are amazing! At the same time though, I want you to know that I feel very bad for making you do what you did. I was so desperate to regain my freedom and so many of my friends had died trying to help me that I wasn't thinking straight. I got you into this mess and I want to apologize. Andocia is my problem, not yours and I had no right to endanger you or Constance the way I did. Will you forgive me?"

Craig smiled at the woman in white. "There is nothing to forgive! I was glad to help and I'm sorry I messed it up. Your people freed you in the end, not me. Anyway, it was a good thing, because we got to know you. Besides, you helped us to get away from Andocia when she kidnapped Constance and me."

"Yes, and you warned us when she was coming to get revenge on us for interfering with her efforts to take over Earth," Constance reminded her.

"I did what I had to," Tanus replied modestly.

"Well so did I," Craig replied. "Now let's just call it even, agreed?"

"Agreed," Tanus smiled.

"What happens now?" Constance asked curiously.

"Well Craig has to regain his strength before he can go home. I have told your superior of his progress. Constance if you want to return home however, you may. Craig's ship was picked up months ago by another astronaut. Yours is still here in my hangar. I'll see that your boyfriend gets home safely when he has been pronounced fit enough to travel. You have been here a lot longer than him and you must be very homesick."

"I am but I'm staying right here," Constance remarked stubbornly. "Craig and I will return together if that's okay with you."

"I have no problem with that, my dear! It has been wonderful talking to you and I look forward to spending more time with you in the future. I know that both of you have many questions and I feel I owe you some explanations. What would you like to know?"

Craig and Constance exchanged looks and turned back to their friend.

"I was wondering about your similarity to human beings and I wondered where you came from originally," Craig asked. "Have you always lived here on the white planet?"

"No Craig, I haven't. Many eons ago I lived on Earth, just as you do. I grew up on a farm long before space travel was even invented."

Constance spoke up. "Andocia told Craig that she was hundreds of centuries old as well. Is this true? Are both of you immortal as Andocia claimed to be?"

"Yes, we are," Tanus confirmed. "Andocia is also originally from Earth."

"She is?" But how come she has green skin then, or does she paint her body that colour, just to stand out in a crowd?" Constance wanted to know. "In all the time we were forced to spend with her, she never once told us that she was born on Earth."

"Oh, that's Andocia! She loves to have a little bit of mystery surrounding herself. She came from planet Earth just as I did, but she really has green skin. It's a long story, but in return for her immortality, that was the price she had to pay. You have been through so much, so perhaps I should leave that story for another time."

Craig stared at the woman but he didn't want to press her for any more information, so he left it. Constance however still had questions. "Tanus, Andocia managed to capture you and that was why we landed up in this predicament in the first place. She has incredible powers, but what of you? You obviously have powers too, but I wanted to know if Andocia is stronger than you."

"We both have incredible powers and I would say we are evenly matched. We have been enemies for a long time and I don't expect anything to change in the future. She's obviously evil, as you have found out, while I work for the good of the universes. The battle between good and evil is always present and I don't have to tell you both about that, because you see it in your work almost every day."

They nodded in agreement.

Constance however was still very curious. "Tanus, you say that you are human and I believe you, but why is the bottom half of your face hidden from us. Is there a reason for this perhaps? Were you injured sometime maybe and have a disfigurement that you don't want anyone else to see?"

Tanus laughed at this. "Not really my dear, but I do have my reasons. There is nothing wrong with my face – in fact I like it just the way it is. People see me the way I want them to and it is different with everyone. It's a sort of party trick I suppose."

Constance wanted to question her further, but she got the feeling that the subject should remain closed, so she left it at that.

They had a few more questions but were interrupted by one of Tanus's followers who reminded her that she had a meeting in a few moments. Tanus stood up and looked benevolently at the two people who were so special to her. "Please forgive me, but this meeting is important. We will talk later. Meanwhile enjoy yourselves!"

Craig grimaced. "I would like to but that tyrant of a physiotherapist wants to see me soon anyway."

"Well you need to strengthen those legs Craig! You still have a long way to go. See you later!"

She waved at the couple before disappearing out of the door.

⚓ ⚓ ⚓

Much of Craig and Constance's time was spent exploring the white planet. They found there was always someone willing to spend time with them in order to show them the sights and they appreciated it a great deal. Wherever he and Constance went, they were treated with kindness and respect, for word had got around that Craig had gone out of his way to save someone he hardly knew, at great risk to himself. They also spent plenty of time with Tanus. Yet even though they were always close to Tanus she didn't seem very forthcoming about her life. Apart from what she had previously told them, she simply changed the subject discreetly when their questions became too probing or personal. Craig and Constance wondered about this, but they never asked her any more awkward questions. She had done a lot for them and they were grateful for her help.

CHAPTER 18

Another month passed and Constance went to talk to Tarmin, leaving Craig alone for a while. The guards were still around, for they feared retaliation from Andocia. By now the news of his complete recovery had reached the planets in both galaxies and the good wishes had come pouring in. The space explorer was touched by the gestures.

Not everyone was pleased by the news. Tyrus stormed out of his control room and aimed a blast at one of the hapless trees on his planet. He generated electricity and the unfortunate tree was burnt right through the middle, fell to the ground and withered immediately. His people looked nervously at one another.

"What's his problem?" whispered one of Tyrus's subjects.

"Sssh!" cautioned another, moving out of earshot. "He has just heard that Craig Carter is alive and well and resting on Tanus's planet. He was so excited when the Earthling was lying in that glass container. Naturally he wanted to be the one to kill that meddlesome explorer, but Andocia got to him first. He assumed the human would remain in a comatose state forever and now that he is well again, Tyrus is furious. He wants revenge for what the human did to him."

His companion nodded sagely and they walked off together.

↙ ↙ ↙

Back on Earth, Colonel Ivan Petrovsky was smiling. "I see that the esteemed Mr Carter is recovering from his ordeal. I'm not sure if he's just very brave or very foolish! It took great courage to go against the most powerful creature in both universes. He certainly has interesting friends though. I have never met the one known as Tanus, but it would seem she is as good as Andocia is evil. I look forward to renewing my acquaintance with comrade Carter in the very near future. After all, my country would love to see him again. He has so much information we are dying to relieve him of."

He smiled ecstatically and looked at the stars in the sky. "I wish you well comrade, for when you have fully recovered, I'll be seeing you again."

Petrovsky whistled a tune as he buttoned his overcoat and went out into the falling snow.

♪ ♪ ♪

Back on the white planet, Craig sat alone and thought about his life. He knew he was very lucky to be alive, but his ordeal had not left him unscathed. He wondered if he would ever see Andocia again and hoped fervently that he wouldn't. He knew he had many deadly enemies but they all paled in comparison to Andocia. She may be human, as Tanus had told him, but she was evil incarnate, he had no doubts about that.

He sat in the brilliant sunshine and looked up at the clouds scudding by, when suddenly he heard a voice that dripped with menace. He spun around on the bench and found he was staring straight at Andocia. He rubbed his eyes, not sure if his vision had been affected in some way, for although she was there, he could see right through her.

"It seems you are alive after all! I heard about your miraculous recovery but I had to come and see for myself."

"What do you want?"

"I want you Carter and I'll get you sooner or later. I've never forgotten what you did to me and sooner or later you will have to pay for your meddling. At the moment you are hiding behind Tanus's skirt, but she cannot always protect you. I'm very patient and I will wait for the right opportunity."

"You took a chance coming here Andocia. Tanus has guards stationed not very far away. I just have to call out to them and they will be here in a moment."

Andocia laughed evilly. "Call them if you want, but it won't help in the slightest. You see I'm with you only in spirit form. You are looking at a hologram of me, but I am projecting my thoughts to you. Every word you say can be heard by me, just as you are hearing my voice, but if Tanus's guards arrive, I'll simply disappear!"

"Leave me and Constance alone Andocia! I want nothing to do with you and neither does she. Go and bother some other hapless beings!"

"I will," she promised, "but I'll be returning for you sooner or later. Never relax your guard Craig Carter, because when you least expect it, I'll be back for you."

She disappeared suddenly and Craig saw Constance coming towards him. "Are you all right Craig?" she asked kindly. "You look as though you have seen a ghost."

"I saw Andocia – well it was a hologram of her. She threatened me and told me never to relax my guard."

Constance was visibly upset. "Damn her! I hate her so much! Why won't she leave us alone! I have to tell Tanus!"

Her boyfriend took her hand and squeezed it. "Just forget about Andocia for now. She isn't nearby or she would have come in person. Tanus has enough to worry about and she is still not strong enough."

He pulled her onto his lap and kissed her gently. "It looks as though we are always going to have trouble with Andocia, so we have two choices. Either we give up exploring space forever, or we live with the situation. What do you want to do?"

Constance shook her head. "No, this is my life and yours too. We have both wanted to explore space and make a difference – and we do! Every time we bring a criminal to justice, we make the universes a better place to live in. I don't know about you, but I refuse to let her win!"

"I feel the same way, sweetheart. I won't let her shatter our dreams. Life must go on!"

Her boyfriend pulled her closer and she snuggled into his arms. They held one another, taking comfort from each other's presence.

⊥ ⊥ ⊥

A few days later, Constance went to prepare their ship for a triumphant return to Earth. Tanus went to Craig and took his hand, and then led him to her private chamber, away from prying eyes. She motioned him to a seat and sat down opposite him.

"Craig, I need to speak privately with you. I've already thanked you for the way, in which you put your life in jeopardy to help me, and I'll always be grateful to you for that, but I needed to speak with you about something else. Craig, you may think that I'm being very forward, but I have some advice for you; you and Constance are so right for one another and it's my feeling that you should marry her as soon as possible. You and she are meant to be together forever and I'll explain why in a few moments, but firstly, I would like to give you this ring as a gift. I had it specially made for Constance and it will fit her perfectly," said Tanus as she reached into her garment and brought out a gold ring that glittered and sparkled.

"This ring is made of the purest gold and has been treated with a substance which makes it indestructible. The diamond set in it is the purest and most precious stone ever created. Even in this day and age, a diamond is still a girl's best friend."

Craig stared at the ring in wonder. "Oh Tanus, thank you so much, but I didn't need you to tell me how precious Constance is, because I know that already. I was going to ask her to marry me, when I had completed my mission to save you, but Andocia kidnapped her before I could ask. Then I failed miserably when I came to your rescue and was also taken prisoner. That left such a void in me and I just wanted to die. My life means nothing without her!" said Craig as he took the ring and put it safely in his breast pocket and zipped it up.

Tanus smiled and held his hand. "Craig, I feel that I owe you an explanation. Didn't you ever wonder why I chose you to rescue me?"

Craig nodded his head. "Yes, it did puzzle me quite a bit but I was grateful for your confidence in me and I dearly wanted to prove myself to you."

"For which I owe you my life! But I had an ulterior motive and it actually concerned Constance more than you realize. I know you have often wondered why you can't see my face. I think it's about time I show you my true features!"

The explorer watched fascinated as the mist that seemed to blur her face around the mouth area, began to clear. Craig gasped, blinked twice and then stared open mouthed at the woman in white. "Oh good ... good grief, you're Constance's exact twin!"

"Yes, I am and that's why I've never shown my face to her. I don't know how she would react to this knowledge and I must respectfully ask you not to reveal what you have found out. However, just make sure that it's the only secret you keep from her. Will you give me your word?"

"I promise!" he replied solemnly, "but I just wondered, do the rest of your people know what you look like?"

"Yes, they have seen my true features. Even Tarmin knows this. Now can you understand why I asked for your help? I was very depressed when I chose you to come and rescue me, but there was an ulterior motive as well. When I was a young girl growing up on a farm, my family meant everything to me. We were all very close. I know how precious Constance is to you and I knew that one day you would want to be her partner for the rest of your life, so I consider you as a member of my family as well."

Craig smiled at her. "Thank you, Tanus! You are a very special person too. I'm honoured that you think of me as family. Everything I went through with Andocia pales in the knowledge that I can count on you, no matter what."

Tanus took both his hands in hers. "No, you don't understand!"

The explorer stared dumbly at her. "What do you mean exactly?"

"Well, I guess I had better explain this to you. Constance is my cousin, many times removed of course. That is why we look so much alike. Centuries have passed and she is the only one who resembles me so exactly that she could be my twin sister. When

I was living on Earth, my surname was also Gregg. You love my cousin and have already told me that you plan to marry her, so therefore we will be related by marriage. That's why I said you are family. You will be just as soon as the two of you get married, but I'm proud to say that you are already my friend!"

Craig was dumbfounded and he shook his head to clear it. "Am I dreaming?" he asked. "That was some coincidence!" He stood up suddenly and seemed to sway for a minute, then he grabbed onto the back of the couch to steady himself. Tanus watched him carefully as his face became serious and she knew what he was thinking.

Tanus smiled secretively and patted the couch next to her. "Come and sit down for a minute! You look as though you might pass out."

He sat next to her and for a moment was lost for words.

"Now do you understand why both you and Constance are so special to me? I left Earth behind so long ago. I had other things to do and I just never went back home. Then you came into the picture and suddenly I remembered my roots, so I researched your family. Imagine my surprise when I heard that you were involved with a Gregg. I knew it was not a coincidence. It was meant to be! When I found out that you were in trouble and Andocia was behind it, I had to get involved."

Carter smiled happily. "I knew it somehow! When I heard your voice for the first time and Andocia was pursuing us, I knew I could trust you implicitly. Constance felt the same way. There was – a connection."

Tanus nodded. "Now you know why."

Craig hugged her tenderly for a while and then his face became serious. "Did you have any siblings?"

"Only one," she replied. "I had a sister."

"What happened to her?" he enquired.

Tanus looked sadly at him. "She died!"

"I'm so sorry!" he replied contritely.

"It doesn't matter. It happened a long time ago! One day when I have more time, I'll tell you the story of my life, but now you must return to your planet and resume your duties. The Space

Control Centre needs you both, for you are exceptional space explorers."

"One last thing Tanus. Do you want me to tell Constance that you and her are related?"

The woman shook her head. "Constance has also been through a lot lately and I'm sure that you will agree with me, it's a lot to take in. She's just getting used to the idea that you have come back to her alive and well. I would like to tell her personally if you don't mind. I'll leave the story for another time."

Impulsively Craig hugged Tanus again and then left the woman in white. At the doorway, he turned to wave, then left to join Constance in the ship.

When they were well on their way, Craig went to his girlfriend and hugged her tenderly. "Darling I wanted to thank you for standing behind me all through this terrible ordeal. You had no way of knowing if I would ever come out of the coma that Andocia put me in, yet you stayed true to me. You are a very attractive woman and many men would be glad to know you. You also suffered because of me and I'm truly sorry for putting you through that."

Constance took his face in her hands and stared deeply in his blue eyes. "My darling, don't worry about it! Being chased by criminals is our life and you know it. I can take care of myself. The most important thing of course is the fact that everything turned out all right in the end."

"I suppose it did!" he confirmed.

Then he went down on one knee and took her left hand in his.

"Constance, you know that I love you with all my heart, don't you?" he asked tenderly.

She giggled and replied. "I love you too, but why are you kneeling?"

He took the ring from his pocket and opened the box. She looked at it and the ring sparkled and flashed with a brilliance that made rainbow puddles of light reflect on the interior of the ship.

"Constance, will you marry me?" he asked lovingly as he slipped it onto her ring finger.

She stared at him and her eyes were bright with happy tears. "Yes! Yes! I will! You are my life and I'll always love you." She looked at the beautiful ring and smiled happily. "Craig, it's gorgeous! Where did you get it?"

"Tanus gave it to me. It's her gift to us. She also mentioned that we are welcome to spend our honeymoon on her planet if we want. Well my darling, looks like we'd better get busy and start planning this event! We'll celebrate when we return to Earth. I know this spaceship isn't the best place to propose to you, but I just couldn't wait a moment longer!"

Constance smiled at the man she loved. "No, it is the perfect place! We spend so much of our lives exploring space so it seems fitting somehow. I love you sweetheart!"

Sometime later, the happy couple arrived on Earth and were met by Commander Simms. When he had heard that Craig had been rescued, he made a speedy recovery and returned to work.

Six months later, the happy couple sealed their union in the presence of all their friends and family, including the aliens on other friendly planets. Constance wore a white brocaded dress made of satin, with a very full skirt, and Craig looked stunning in his dress suit. There was an expectant hush as the ceremony began.

"Do you, Craig Carter, take Constance Gregg to be your lawful wedded wife?"

"I do!"

"And do you, Constance Gregg, take Craig Carter to be your lawful wedded husband?"

There was a slight blush on her cheeks as she answered, "I do!"

The wedding ring was placed on her finger and a kiss sealed their union. Afterwards, a huge reception was held and many of the planets were there to wish the young couple much happiness. Many speeches were made and their friends toasted the happy couple. All Mission Control's staff was invited as well and the party went on until the early hours of the morning.

When all the excitement had died down, Craig and Constance took their leave in a spacecraft that was covered with flowers. They planned to visit all their friends, including Tanus. As the craft soared into the sky and vanished from sight, the happy crowd turned and made their way back to their homes and planets.

CHAPTER 18

Out in space, the newlyweds stood by the observation window and stared at the planets floating about. Craig had his arms around his new bride. "Well Mrs Carter, how do you feel?"

"I feel just wonderful Mr Carter," she giggled. "I still can't believe that you and I are married!"

"Believe it my love. I feel as though I have waited a lifetime for you, yet we have only been dating for three years. I am so lucky to be your husband."

"And I love the idea of being your wife," she smiled happily.

"I'm glad, because we'll have the rest of our lives to be together. It doesn't get better than this!"

Constance looked at the black sky and all the stars seemed brighter somehow. "No, it doesn't get better than this," she echoed.

Craig held his wife's hand and kissed her gently. "My darling, you are so precious to me, but I still have my doubts about the 'happily ever after' part though – not with you," he replied quickly, "but with my enemies. Because you and I are man and wife now, they could use you as bait to make me do what they want."

Constance smiled at her new husband. "My darling they have already done that, so nothing is going to change. Besides I'm not exactly helpless you know! I can take care of myself. There will always be criminal types in our future, unless you plan to change jobs soon. Are you prepared to do that?"

"No," her husband replied. "I love my job. I like the challenges that space throws at me. I enjoy the thought of meeting new beings and establishing friendly relations with them. We learn so much from one another."

"Then we'll learn to deal with it. Now I want to concentrate only on you. Can we do that?" asked Constance coquettishly.

"We most certainly can Mrs Carter," he replied laughingly as he swept her into his arms and took her to their sleeping quarters. "Let's begin right now!"

"That is an excellent idea my dear husband."

They lay together, entwined in one another's arms and the world ceased to exist as they found pleasure in one another. They passed planets as the ship serenely made its way through space and headed for Neptune where they were to spend the first leg of their honeymoon with the King and Queen.

Out in space Andocia was brooding. She had heard of the union between Craig and Constance and was displeased. "That man must have very good luck. I put him through an ordeal that he won't easily forget, yet he still managed to find happiness despite this. If he thinks it is over between him and me, he is very much mistaken. We will meet again! Next time I won't be so lenient with him."

Andocia smiled wickedly and went to find her advisers. She wondered what mayhem she could cause in one or both universes.

Craig and his new wife Constance hovered above Neptune and contacted the planet. They were welcomed and told that someone would be up to escort them personally to the King and Queen. They climbed out of their spacecraft and waited patiently.

Soon afterwards some of the King's guards came to the surface and climbed out. They bowed to the new husband and wife. "Welcome to Neptune once again you two. It's always a pleasure seeing you."

They were each given a set of "gills" to help them breathe underwater and once the couple had placed them in their mouths and noses, they prepared to dive underwater. One of the guards jumped in first and waited for Craig and Constance to do the same. Once they had begun swimming, the second guard dived in and swam behind them, while his associate led the procession. The two honeymooners looked at one another and Craig shrugged his shoulders at Constance's questioning look. This was new to them because it was usually Lolita who came to meet them every time they arrived on Neptune.

When they arrived at the palace the guard who had swum ahead of them, lifted a horn and blew into it several times. Immediately the palace staff lined both sides of the impressive hallway. A door opened and the King and Queen of Neptune came down the aisle personally to meet them. At the sight of the royal party, everyone bowed reverently.

The King came up to Craig and shook his hand vigorously. "Welcome to Neptune Craig, Constance! It's always a pleasure to see you both."

The Queen smiled and hugged Constance. "Yes indeed! Welcome my dear. You both honour us with your presence."

The royal couple dismissed their staff with a wave of their hands and the newlyweds were asked to follow them to the guest lounge, where they were offered some refreshments. They were relieved of their luggage which was taken to their room.

When they were finally alone with the rulers of Neptune, the King's face became serious. "I must say you gave us such a fright some months ago with that terrible stunt Andocia pulled. I thought we would never see you again."

Craig smiled and waved away the King's concern. "Thank you, Your Majesty. It was a difficult time for us, but it's over now and I'm very grateful to be alive and sitting here with you. I don't really remember much about it. It seems that everyone else who witnessed what Andocia did to me was more traumatized by what they saw than I was."

The King clapped his hands and smiled. "Well that's over now and we aren't going to discuss unhappy things here while you are our guests. Simply enjoy your time with us and if you need anything, just ask any member of my staff and they will see you have everything you need. Lolita extends her deepest apology for not being here to meet you, but she has other commitments. She should be back in a few days."

"Thank you for telling us your majesty. We look forward to

catching up with her later then," Craig replied.

The King smiled. "There's just one more thing I wanted to discuss with both of you and then you can go and amuse yourselves."

The couple looked expectantly at the ruler of Neptune. "What is it?" Constance asked curiously, especially since the King's face had become solemn once again.

"Well my dear, I am sure both of you must have questions as to why I sent two guards to fetch you. Both of you probably expected one of the palace staff, or Lolita."

"We were curious," Craig affirmed and Constance nodded.

"I hope you don't mind, but we are concerned about both of you. While you stay here, it's my responsibility to keep you safe and I'm afraid that Andocia will come after you again and try to finish what she started. That's why I have assigned some guards to take care of you while you are our guests. They will not encroach on your privacy in any way!" he remarked, "Just bear with us for a while. Is that okay?"

The couple exchanged looks, touched by the King's gesture.

"We understand and thank you," replied Craig gratefully.

The King stood up and nodded. "Very well then that's settled. You have the rest of the day to amuse yourselves and I'll expect you at suppertime when you are to be our guests of honour."

The ruler of Neptune rang a bell and a servant appeared. "Noah, escort these young people to their quarters."

Noah bowed to his King and the young couple followed him out. He walked down a long passage and then climbed a stately flight of steps. They walked for a while longer before the servant opened a door and they went inside.

Constance and Craig stood in the doorway and gasped at the splendid room. A huge four-poster bed dominated the area. There were huge cupboards on both sides of the room. A dressing table in the same wood as that of the bed stood at another wall. The servant opened another door and they found themselves in a tasteful lounge cum dining room. The servant then opened another door and the newlyweds gasped at the sheer size of the bathroom. In the centre of the room stood a bath the size of a swimming pool. There were jets on every side that would turn the bath into a spa.

"This is so beautiful!" gasped Constance in amazement.

"The view is incredible as well!" exclaimed her husband.

The entire suite was surrounded by water and everywhere they looked, they could see the beautiful flora and fauna that shared the planet with the Neptunians. Rainbow coloured fish darted about and there were fish of every shape and size swimming outside their quarters. Several beautiful plants swayed gently as the water currents ebbed and flowed.

The servant bowed and smiled at the couple. "If you need anything then please do not hesitate to contact me," he said, indicating a rope near the bed. "Just tug on this and someone will come and attend to you."

Craig thanked him and he closed the door behind them.

Constance turned around and around and just stared at the incredible view that met their eyes. "I can't believe that all this is ours for a while! This suite is bigger than our whole apartment back in America."

"It most certainly is my love, but this planet is mostly water, so there is plenty of room for development. I'm going to enjoy our holiday here amongst our friends."

Constance smiled in agreement. "What about Andocia, Craig? Will she try and spoil things for us do you think?"

"I hope not, but I doubt it somehow. I think she'll keep a low profile while we are with any of our friends. She knows that they will protect us and I doubt if she'll cause any trouble for us in the near future."

"Yes, but what will happen when our extended honeymoon is over?" Constance asked nervously.

"Well we are fooling ourselves if we think she'll leave us alone forever. Once we are back at work she will most probably come after us again. We just have to use extreme caution then. While we are guests of the Neptunians, I want to forget about every enemy we have ever made and just concentrate on us. We can worry about her later. Don't let thoughts of her cloud your mind my love. Let's just enjoy the time we have together."

Constance smiled at her husband. "Well we have a few hours to amuse ourselves before we are expected to dine with the royal family. I wonder what we should do?"

Craig smiled wolfishly at his new bride. "Well I can think of a few things," he grinned as he scooped her up and put her on the large bed.

His new wife giggled. "What a good idea!" She sighed as she pulled him down as well.

Much later after they had bathed in the huge bath, Craig stared at his new wife as she dressed for the evening festivities. He took in the slim, athletic, hourglass figure and sighed inwardly. They had come a long way together and he still found it hard to believe that they were finally married. She was fussing with her makeup and Craig took in every feature as though he was afraid she could vanish in an instant. She was wearing a rose pink off-the-shoulder dress that clung to her figure like a second skin. It hugged her waist and then flared out, ending in a scalloped hemline that reached her ankles. She wore silver high heeled sandals that shone in the light. Her shoulder length hair was piled on her head in a sleek topknot, held in place by a diamante hair clip. She wore a simple diamond necklace around her neck and matching earrings sparkled in her ears. He remembered they were a wedding present from her parents. His reverie was interrupted by the intercom ringing next to the bed, and he picked it up. They were requested to join the royal family for dinner. Carter bent his arm at the elbow and Constance put her arm through his. Arm in arm they went to join the royal family.

When they reached the entrance to the banquet hall, a servant announced them. As they made their way to the royal table, the Neptunians stood up and clapped. Craig felt very humble and Constance surreptitiously wiped a tear from her eye. Only when they had been shown to their seats by the attendant, did the people sit down. The young couple were amazed and humbled to see the banquet hall was full. The newlyweds were seated on the right of the King. The Queen sat on the left of her husband and next to them sat Princess Lolita.

Craig stared at the princess and she smiled at him. She was a vision of loveliness in a form fitting emerald dress. Lolita wore satin shoes the same colour as her dress. Her long hair was braided and piled on top of her head. The princess's long neck was accentuated by a necklace that held the largest emerald he had ever seen. Emerald earrings flashed and sparkled in her ears.

The King clapped his hands and servants appeared, carrying trays laden with food. There were breaks between the platters of food when they were entertained by the best singers and dancers that Neptune had to offer. Several magicians also held them enthralled, as well as actors who had written a very special story. The festivities went on for many hours and finally the newlyweds made their way back to their room. Just before they closed their door, two palace guards saluted and took up their places at opposite ends of the doorway. The couple were so tired and full that they fell asleep as soon as their heads touched the pillows.

The next morning, they were served breakfast in their suite and then invited to join Princess Lolita in her solarium. While they were still tired from the previous evening's festivities, Lolita looked as fresh as the flowers that bloomed in her special garden. She held out her arms and embraced both her friends excitedly. "I'm sorry I wasn't here to greet you when you arrived!"

"Your father said you had meetings to attend, so we understand," Craig replied kindly.

Lolita smiled at the happy couple. "I know I was present at your wedding – which was fabulous by the way, but I have to say how happy I am for both of you. You two are perfect for one another."

Constance smiled at the princess. "Thank you! We are honoured to count you among our friends."

"Think nothing of it! You have both gone out of your way to help us when we were in trouble and we count Earth as one of our allies," Lolita replied.

They exchanged news for a bit and then one of the Queen's maidservants came and bowed to the group. "Forgive me your highness, but your mother wishes to speak to Constance."

The young woman smiled. "I'll see you both later then."

Craig smiled at his new bride and pecked her gently on the lips. "Okay; see you in a while."

When they were alone, Lolita's smile disappeared. "Craig, forgive me for bringing this up now when you are both on your honeymoon, but I am worried about you!"

"Why do you look so concerned? Is something wrong?" Craig wanted to know.

The princess shook her head. "No nothing is wrong, but I'm still worried about you. You went through a very harrowing experience when Andocia paraded you around in that glass container. I just wondered if you are having any side-effects at all?"

"Tanus asked me the same thing when she rescued me, but I remember nothing. I must have been in such a deep sleep because I never had any dreams. While I was asleep Tanus invited various scientists over and they fixed the scars on my body."

Lolita clasped her friend's hands. "I'm glad! I was so worried."

Craig squeezed her hands gently. "Lolita, we have known one another for quite a long time now. Is something else bothering you?"

The Neptunian princess looked down at her feet. "You know me so well and yes, something else is worrying me."

The space explorer put his hand gently under her chin and made her look at him. "What is it? You can tell me."

Lolita blushed. "I … I feel so silly! I meant it when I said that you and Constance were meant for one another, but you are my best friend in the whole universe. I just don't want things between us to change."

Craig laughed and hugged Lolita. "You are so adorable Lolita and you know that I love you. It is not the same sort of love that I have for Constance, but more like the love I have for my parents. As I have told you before, I love you like a sister and that is never going to change. I'll always be here for you if you need me."

Lolita smiled gratefully at her friend. "Thank you so much. It means a lot to me."

Carter smiled and took her hand. "Now that is enough doom and gloom. This is a happy occasion so let's not have any negativity. I was talking to your father earlier and he mentioned you have a secret garden that you are cultivating. I would love to see what you have achieved so far. I could use some exercise because at the rate your parents are feeding us, I can already feel I have put on some weight, so let's go outside and you can show me where it is."

Craig put on his swimming costume and placed the "gills" in his nose and mouth. He met Lolita at the servants' entrance to the palace and they swam away together. Behind them, two palace guards followed. The young man waved and they waved back.

Meanwhile back in the palace, Constance and the Queen were drinking tea in the guest lounge. "Forgive me my dear, for stealing you away from your new husband, but I needed some advice."

"I don't mind," the woman replied. "What can I do for you Your Majesty?"

"Well actually after we have had our refreshments, I need your opinion about a few things. I have an engagement I must attend with my husband and I wanted your advice on what I should wear. You have excellent taste in clothes so you are the perfect one to ask. Do you mind?"

Constance smiled at the Queen. "It will be an honour!"

The two women finished their refreshments and the Queen led the way to her chambers. Once inside, Constance was struck by the sheer luxury of the place. The furnishings were done in pink and gold. The double bed was round and filled with scatter cushions in a soft pink, while the bedding was also pink, but slightly darker. The dressing table was inlaid with gold and was made in a pale brown wood with pink undertones. The colour scheme was very similar in the private bathroom and large dressing room.

Constance looked around at the various cosmetics and skin

products in the room, but there was no evidence of anything belonging to the King. As if reading her thoughts, the Queen smiled. "We have separate bedrooms my dear. This is necessary as sometimes my husband is out until very late at night and he does not wish to disturb me, so he has his own suite."

She went to another door and opened it. It led to the King's chambers. Constance didn't want to impose, but a quick glance around the room showed her that the King had his own private bathroom as well. He also had a large office that led onto a small porch.

The Queen smiled. "That door is never locked my dear. I love my husband too, you know!"

Constance smiled. "I understand of course. It certainly does make sense."

The Queen smiled and her face grew soft as memories of her marriage surfaced. "I remember the day we got married. We were so much in love and we just couldn't keep our hands off one another. My husband was not the King of Neptune at the time, but his father became ill early on during our marriage, so we didn't have much time to spend on ourselves. Duty called, as it must when you are a member of the royal family. So far it has been a good union, thank the universes. Lolita was born four years after we got married. I tried to have more children, but unfortunately it didn't happen. Neptune has grown and prospered over the years and we have learnt much from the various planets we have befriended. Now enough reminiscing! Time is passing by and we have yet to find a dress for me to wear tonight!" the Queen exclaimed as she took Constance firmly by the wrist and led her to the huge dressing room where she opened the wardrobe doors, causing Constance to gape in surprise at the many outfits hanging in the closets. "Oh my!" gasped the young woman. "We should have started doing this yesterday already. There are hundreds of outfits in there."

The Queen chuckled. "Well come along then, let's begin!"

Fortunately for Constance, everything was in a specific order and the Queen had an idea of what she wanted to wear. They spent a few hours going through the Queen's wardrobe and finally settled on something smart and elegant for the Queen to wear. By this time, it had grown late and the Queen hurried to bathe and get ready. With a sigh of relief Constance left the Queen's chambers and went to find her husband.

She found Craig nursing a drink in their suite and put her arms around his neck. "Busy day huh?"

"Absolutely," he confirmed. "I spent most of the day with Lolita. You must see her garden Constance. It is amazing!"

"Perhaps tomorrow I'll go with her if she has nothing planned."

"How did it go with you and the Queen?" her husband asked.

"Very hectic. You won't believe just how much clothing that woman has in her closet! I'm sure she could clothe the whole of Neptune!"

Craig chuckled. "Can you imagine how much clothing Lolita must have in her closet as well."

His wife giggled. "She probably has twice as much as her mother! Just as well we have only a small apartment on Earth. We can only keep the bare essentials and that's fine with me."

"That's absolutely true!" Craig commented. "I like the minimalist effect of our place. Remember though, Neptune doesn't have the number of buildings on the planet that we have on Earth, so they have plenty of room to expand."

"They certainly do," Constance agreed. "What should we do tonight? The King and Queen are attending a royal function and Lolita is busy as well."

Craig smiled at his wife. "Well I think it would be nice to visit one of the incredible restaurants here. I don't want the palace staff to wait on us all the time either and we need some alone time."

"Okay, then that's settled. I'm just going to have a shower and change my clothes and then we can go out," replied Constance as she made her way to the bathroom.

That night they were taken to a restaurant that was highly recommended to them. They were accompanied by two guards as usual but they didn't mind as they knew the King had tightened the security on his planet, fearing that Andocia may come back and try to harm the young couple.

They spent a few more days on Neptune and they bid farewell to their hosts. Lolita and her parents hugged their friends tightly and told them to be careful out in space.

CHAPTER 20

Soon they were on their way to Saturn. They were in constant contact with Commander Simms who was also very worried about a retaliation from Andocia. Craig was looking pensively out of the observation window as the planets and stars whizzed by. Constance came up behind him and put her hands around his waist. "What are you thinking about my love?" she asked gently.

"The same thing that has been worrying me all along I suppose. I was wondering what Andocia will do now that we are married. Is she still going to bother us?"

Constance sighed. "The answer to your question is yes, she will still keep bothering us, but hopefully not in the near future. Usually once she has bothered us and caused havoc, she seems to ignore us for a while. I'm sure we aren't her first priority any more. She seems to have a lot to do in her own universe."

Her husband turned around and kissed her gently. "How did you get so philosophical my love? You seem to know how she thinks."

"I'm beginning to recognize a pattern in what she does. I can understand her moods – up to a point, but not always. I hope she'll leave us alone so that we can have a decent honeymoon at least."

"Well let's just do the best we can and enjoy our time together, shall we?"

Constance smiled at her husband, "Yes, let's do that!" She took him by the hand and led him to their sleeping quarters. "I want to spend as much time alone with you as I possibly can. Things are going to be very different when we return to Earth."

Craig turned around and smiled at his lovely wife. "I agree

with you my darling," he replied as he followed her.

A few days later they were close to Saturn and Craig contacted his friends. "Craig Carter calling Saturn. We request permission to land."

"Permission granted Craig. Please go to landing bay 3 and someone will meet you there."

"Understood control. Beginning landing procedures now."

Their ship touched down on Saturn and almost immediately Karnd came to greet them. He shook Craig's hand and fluttered up to kiss Constance on her cheek. "Congratulations on your union!" he exclaimed happily. "We are honoured to have you spend time with us for a short while at least."

"Thank you! We feel very privileged to be here," replied Craig.

He led them to a vehicle and they climbed in. As soon as they were settled, another vehicle pulled up behind them. Constance and Craig looked curiously as they followed behind.

Karnd smiled sheepishly. "Forgive me, but they have orders to guard you while you are here on Saturn. I hope you don't mind. They will be very discreet I assure you," he hastened to add.

The couple exchanged looks and shrugged. "It's okay Karnd. We understand perfectly. We had the same thing on Neptune so are getting quite used to it," Constance remarked.

"It's for your own protection of course. We all fear a reprisal from Andocia."

The couple smiled and thanked Karnd for his kindness.

They were taken to a hotel and given the honeymoon suite. Even though it was not as luxurious as the one on Neptune, it was still breathtaking. The door closed behind them and they were left to settle in. Later that day they were going to have lunch with Jorrel and Lara.

Once they had unpacked, they sat in the small living room and discussed their stay.

"It looks as though we are getting the royal treatment again," Constance smiled. "I wish they wouldn't fuss over us so much though."

Craig sighed. "I know! I want to spend time alone with you but I'm conscious of beings always looking out for us. I guess

Andocia really got everyone in a knot when she tried to make an example out of me. The Saturnians are scientists, not bodyguards."

"You made a lot of friends when you began exploring space, Craig. You are responsible for helping them when Tyrus tried to take over Saturn so they feel they owe you. I'm sure everything will be fine, but we have to humour them. They will be very offended if you refuse their bodyguards."

"I know," he sighed, "but they have jacked up their security since I was last here. Their weapons look quite dangerous."

Constance nodded. "They certainly do. Well I think it is time for lunch. I must say, aside from the fact that we are going to be shadowed everywhere, I'm really looking forward to seeing Jorrel and Lara, It's always so interesting talking to them."

"It certainly is," Craig agreed.

The couple joined their friends for lunch and both Saturnians hugged them happily.

It is wonderful to see you both again!" Lara enthused. "We were at your wedding of course, but it seems like ages ago already. You both look well."

"Thanks, Lara. We are fine and very happy," remarked Craig.

Constance smiled and hugged her husband. "We are truly happy Lara! I feel as though I was missing something very important in my life, but now I feel – complete somehow."

Jorrel grinned at the happy couple. "I have to admit, you two make a fine couple. You were truly meant for one another. It shows in your eyes."

The woman held Jorrel's hand and squeezed it gently. "Thank you, dear friend. It's so good to be here amongst friends."

The afternoon passed quickly and later when they had returned to their rooms, Constance moved over to the large picture window and stared outside. "You know something my darling – we are very lucky to have such wonderful friends. We have powerful enemies as well, but somehow having so many beings that care for us, makes up for all the anguish and stress we go through during our various missions."

Craig moved over to the bed and sat down. He held out his

arms to Constance who crept gladly into his embrace. She put her head on his shoulder and he stroked her hair softly.

"I was wondering what's going to happen in the future, Craig," his wife said pensively.

"We are going to have a very happy and fulfilling life," remarked her husband.

"I know that, but I was wondering … Do you think now that we are married, Commander Simms will send us out on missions together?"

Her husband shook his head. "I doubt it my angel. I suppose it will happen sometimes, but not always. That's why our honeymoon is so precious to me. Once we return to Earth, things will be pretty much as they were before we got married. Why, will that be a problem for you?" he asked worriedly.

Constance shook her head. "No. I was just thinking aloud."

"Constance, it isn't a good idea for us to travel together all the time anyway, because my enemies will now become our enemies, and vice versa. If we travelled together all the time, we would also be easy targets."

His wife nodded in agreement. "When did you become so clever!"

Craig looked offended. "Huh, I've always been clever – and also pretty dogmatic. Do you remember how aloof you were when we first met? You ignored me most of the time. You were one of the rising stars in the astronaut fraternity and I was just a lowly spaceship technician. I wanted you from the first day I met you and you didn't know I even existed!"

Constance giggled. "I remember! I must say I'm very glad you never gave up on me. I have a good intuition about these things, but somehow I never saw just how good you would've been for me."

Her husband smiled and pulled her closer. "I love you Mrs Carter!"

"I love you too Mr Carter!" she affirmed.

His grip on her became firmer and more insistent and she responded by kissing him hungrily. They lay down on the bed and for a while nothing mattered but their love for one another.

The next day they went on a tour of Saturn, accompanied by a guide who showed them parts of Saturn they had never explored before. When they got back to their hotel, Jorrel contacted them. Craig looked at the display on his mobile device and answered the call. "Hello Jorrel, what can I do for you?"

"The Saturnian was very apologetic. "If it isn't a good time, we can do this later."

"What is it?" he asked curiously.

"Lara wants to know if you can come to the Science Building, as she would like to discuss some important issues."

Craig and Constance exchanged looks.

"Does she want to see us now?" asked Constance.

"If it's convenient, otherwise we can schedule it for later on today," Jorrel replied.

"Now is fine," Craig replied. "We'll see you soon."

The couple went to the scientists' meeting place and waited for Lara. She kept them waiting for about fifteen minutes and then came to greet them. "I hope you don't mind, but my colleagues and I have been working on something and I wasn't sure if it would be ready yet, but I put in some extra time and I have a prototype to show you."

"A prototype of what?" Constance enquired curiously.

The scientist led them into a large room and indicated two chairs. The couple sat down and Lara pulled up a chair to face them. "I know you are on honeymoon and I didn't want to bore you with space business, but this is important."

Lara picked up a remote control device, which she aimed at the computer. Immediately an icon flashed on the screen. She took her place on the chair opposite her friends and smiled at them.

"What I am about to show you is top secret. This device is complete, but we have not tested it as yet. For quite some time we have studied NASA's space program and all the ships that have been built over the years. All the countries on Earth have their own versions of spacecrafts. There are many models and some have better features than others. Some are more luxurious than others, while some are faster. Some are just plain and simple with no outstanding features."

Both Carters nodded their heads in agreement. "I follow what you are saying, but what are you getting at?" remarked Craig curiously.

Lara pressed a button on the remote and a holographic view of the latest fighter crafts in America came to life in the empty chamber. It rotated around slowly, showing the craft from all sides.

"This is the best spacecraft that NASA has invented so far, yet even with its streamlined features, it's still not as fast as Andocia's crafts. It occurred to us that even though the technology has improved in leaps and bounds on Earth – even outstripping those you used to work on, Craig, back in the day when you were still repairing the older crafts, there is still one glaring fault that has never been fixed. The reason Earth's astronauts are always at a disadvantage is that you have very weak cloaking devices to shield yourselves from being pursued by your enemies. Your time lapse features are not bad, but the fuel leaves a signature trace which can be picked up by enemy crafts. Not many ships can follow this trail, but Andocia's can. Ours can also pursue anyone in time lapse.

"There is another problem as well. You have no devices on board your crafts to warn you when someone else uses a cloaking device and is sneaking up on you."

While Lara was explaining everything to her friends, various holographic images were displayed in the room.

Constance nodded as a memory surfaced. She recalled that one of Andocia's followers had managed to sneak on board the craft that Craig was piloting and kidnapped her without him even being aware that she was gone.

Lara continued. "We have designed a cloaking device especially for the spacecrafts of Earth. It should help you all tremendously in the future, if you have these installed in every craft on your planet. Naturally we will have to test it out first so that we can fix anything that might still go wrong. We were wondering if we could place one of these devices on your spacecraft as a trial. If it is successful then we will endeavour to send all the relevant information to Mission Control. The videos are very easy to follow and your mechanics will be able to fit these in no time at all. We have one condition however and this is non-negotiable. Although we will first give this technology to Commander Simms, if it is a success, you must share this information with other countries as well. Andocia is all powerful and it's not fair to keep this technology to yourselves. This could make other countries vulnerable to her reign of terror. Is this acceptable?"

Craig leaned forward and smiled at Lara. "It sounds wonderful, but we'll need official approval from Mission Control. It would be best if you discuss this with Commander Simms first. He also needs to discuss this with the security forces, as well as the Minister of Defence. It could take a while."

"Okay, but before you contact him, we wanted to discuss something else with you as well."

Both astronauts nodded in assent and Lara continued. "We have also devised a way to increase the speed of your ships marginally. It occurred to us that you cannot outrun some of the other planets' ships when you are being pursued by them. At this point in time though, we are doubtful if we can make them a great deal faster, but as your country designs better ships, this can be incorporated into them, thus making them extremely fast. If we tried to run this program at its fullest capacity right now, your ships would literally break apart."

Both astronauts exchanged glances with one another.

"Lara that's wonderful news!" Constance commented. "Every little bit of speed will be an advantage. I know Commander Simms will be delighted to obtain this technology from your planet, but as Craig has said, we'll have to inform our superiors. They are the ones who have to give the go-ahead for this."

The scientist nodded in agreement. "There's no time like the present, dear friends. Will you contact Commander Simms so we can begin the negotiations?"

"It'll be our pleasure, but first we would need to see an actual trial of this. I have the utmost faith in Saturn's abilities, but before I contact the commander, I must have something plausible to discuss with him. The chain of command is very important on Earth. Can you organize a demonstration for us?" Craig requested.

"Very well, I'll organize this for tomorrow morning."

Both explorers got to their feet and shook hands with the scientist.

"Thank you for wanting to help us Lara," Constance smiled. "There shouldn't be a problem because we know your species is the smartest in the universe. We are very excited to be a part of these trials."

The couple left the scientist and made their way back to their hotel. They were very excited about the demonstration and discussed it while they were travelling.

CHAPTER 21

The next morning the young couple met Lara at the testing grounds where they noticed two Saturnian fighter crafts waiting on the asphalt. Craig and Constance exchanged surprised looks and Lara smiled. "I know! I know! We have never had fighting crafts before, but we thought it was about time we built some. This is top secret and we must insist you don't tell anyone about these just yet."

Craig was impressed by the streamlined ships and commented on them. "These look amazing Lara! They are so simple, yet so functional. Are these crafts fitted with the cloaking device you want us to install on our ships?"

"Yes, they are a standard feature of these ships. We have also fitted them with the speeding device I told you about. Our ships are extremely fast – faster than yours will be once the device is fitted, but at least you'll have a good idea of what to expect in a tense situation. We haven't had a chance to use them out in space yet, but we have conducted exhaustive trials here on Saturn and all were very satisfactory. Naturally we aren't really fighters, so we would like both of you to give us some pointers in the art of combat. We have trained some of our people to be pilots and all seems to be running smoothly so far."

Lara beckoned to some beings in the background and they came forward. "Craig, Constance, allow me to introduce you to two of our best pilots so far. This is Aneeda," she remarked, putting her hand on the woman's shoulder, "and this is Jacob."

Both pilots bowed slightly and then shyly shook hands with the two space explorers.

"It is an honour to meet you," Jacob remarked and his companion nodded.

"It's good to meet you too," Craig replied.

The scientist turned to her guests. "What we are basically going to do is stage a mock battle using these ships. I would like one of you to partner with Aneeda and the other can do the same with Jacob. We won't be using live ammunition for the tests of course, so we have armed these crafts with laser lights. The idea is that when the weapons are discharged, the laser will guide the 'weapons' to the ship being targeted. The beams will ping harmlessly off the hull of the ships, but the computer will register this as a hit and give us a damage report. Both of you can instruct your pilots on the best means possible to ensure supremacy in the air, just as long as you don't put our pilots in danger by doing nearly impossible stunts. During this demonstration, our pilots will use every function they can, including the cloaking device. Is everything clear?"

"Yes, it is," Constance replied. "When should we begin?"

"You may begin now if you wish."

Craig smiled and beckoned to Jacob. "Let's team up against the ladies, shall we?"

The Saturnian smiled. "A very good idea. I'm looking forward to this."

Constance put her arm around Aneeda's waist. "Well come along then Aneeda. Let's show the men what we are made of."

As she passed her husband, Constance pulled him close to her and kissed him on the lips. "Don't go easy on us because we are females," she smirked.

Craig grinned challengingly at her. "Oh no ma'am. In this battle you are the enemy, so no mercy!"

Jacob's eyes were huge and Craig smiled good naturedly at him. "Take it from me, Constance is a very sneaky person. You'll have your job cut out for you up there."

Aneeda's shoulders slumped and she gulped at the exchange of words. "Easy would have been fine for me!" she mumbled under her breath.

Constance patted her reassuringly on her back. "It's going to be fine, I promise! You just pilot this craft and I'll guide you."

When they were seated in the spacecraft, Constance wriggled a bit to get comfortable. "This space is a little cramped! Luckily I'm thin enough to fit in here."

"Oh dear, we are much smaller than humans and therefore do not require much space," Aneeda replied.

"It's fine," Constance assured the pilot.

In the other fighter craft, Craig was having the same problem. He managed to squeeze into the co-pilot's seat and folded his long legs underneath the legs of the chair. They waited patiently for Lara to signal that the demonstration should begin. While they waited, Jacob pressed keys on the keyboard in front of him, bringing the entire system online. Craig watched fascinated as everything lit up.

Lara's voice came clearly to them. "All right I'm going to hand over to our control tower now. Good luck to both teams."

A momentary silence and then a new voice spoke. "This is control! Jacob, you are team one, and you Aneeda, are team two. Start ignition now. We go on a count of ten. Begin countdown: 10 ... 9 ... 8 ... 7 ... 6 ... 5 ... 4 ... 3 ... 2 ... 1 ... GO!"

Both ships lifted up horizontally. Jacob's ship went left and Aneeda's turned right. They rose up high into the sky and began turning back towards one another. Craig watched as they flew past each other and he looked at the screen facing him. He was already looking for weak spots on the other ship and he knew Constance would be doing the same. Jacob looked at him for guidance.

"Let's do another pass. I managed to have a look at the left side of the ship, but I want you to approach from the right this time. Start from the rear end of the ship and then move to the right, ending your sweep in front of the other craft. By that time, I'll be able to pinpoint any weak spots on the ship."

Jacob seemed confused, but he began his turn anyway. "If you're worried about them shooting at us, it won't happen this time. Constance is going to ask Aneeda to do the same as we are doing," Craig explained. "Afterwards though, we'll have to keep our wits about us. As I mentioned before, Constance is a very sneaky person."

Jacob nodded in understanding and did as he was told. Once they had completed their circuit of the other ship, they split up and flew off in opposite directions.

Craig put a cautionary hand gently on the pilot's shoulder. "Okay here they come! Now watch out! They are coming in for the kill. Begin evasive manoeuvres now!"

Jacob gulped and managed to swerve as a beam passed very close to the left wing of the craft.

<Team two – narrow miss.> The computer announced.

Jacob looked at his co-pilot and grinned wickedly. "Aha, I see what you mean! Well let's give them something to think about!"

The pilot swerved the craft and it turned sideways. He pressed a key on his console and the ship shot forward at an incredible speed. They were within firing range and Craig pressed the button on his console. Immediately a red beam shot out and they heard a pinging sound as the beam glanced off the tail section of the other craft.

<Team one has scored. The tip of the tail section has been hit. Minimal damage. Continue with demonstration.>

Jacob and Craig watched as their opponents turned around and headed straight for them. Jacob pulled on the throttle, sending the ship higher into the sky and a beam narrowly missed the underside of their ship.

Just as he was levelling off again the other ship mirrored his move and came alongside them. Craig and Jacob watched in astonishment as Constance waved at them and then a warning light blinked on the dashboard.

<Cargo door damaged. Effect immediate repair!"

"Oh no. Can you fix it Jacob?"

Jacob nodded. "I can try but we'll only have a two-minute interval."

He pressed some keys on the console and a picture of an oxy acetylene torch appeared on the screen and immediately an image of the damaged door was brought into focus. Both men groaned when they saw the computer-generated image. The door was hanging on one hinge and flapping wildly in the air. Both men looked miserably at one another. Jacob shook his head.

The control tower interrupted them. "Jacob, what is your decision?"

He sighed and pressed a button on his helmet. "We concede defeat, control."

"Very well then. The first round goes to team two. Take a short break and reset the system please. We will begin round two in ten minutes."

In the other ship, Aneeda was jubilant. "That was fantastic! I never thought it was possible to beat them."

Constance grinned. "You haven't seen anything yet! Next time we mustn't give them a chance to breathe. We have to attack very quickly. Craig won't get caught like that again."

Aneeda looked at her companion in disbelief. "Are you always so competitive in real life? I thought you would go easy on Craig seeing as he is your husband, and vice versa of course."

Constance smiled at her companion. "I'm very competitive when I'm out in space, just as Craig is. Remember, what we are doing here is duplicating real life situations that can happen out in space. Your enemies aren't going to go easy on you when they have you in their sights, so you must be very aggressive and smart at the same time in order to gain the upper hand. Therefore, these demonstrations have to be based on the fact that we have to adopt a kill or be killed attitude."

Aneeda nodded. "I understand! So, we have to treat this demonstration as though we really are fighting an enemy who means to harm us."

"Precisely! Now you know what has to be done. No mercy!"

"No mercy!" she echoed.

The women high fived one another. "All right then, let's get them!" she exclaimed.

"This is round number two," the control centre informed them. "We begin in 10 … 9 … 8 … 7 … 6 … 5 …"

Constance nudged her companion. "Go now!"

"But …" Aneeda gulped, "the countdown …"

Constance pointed at their opponents. "Look they are accelerating; *Go now!!!!*"

Obediently Aneeda shot forward. "Excellent! Don't give them a chance. Lock on so that I can fire on them." Constance ordered.

The pilot's face was set in a grimace. "Target locked! Fire now."

The space explorer fired her laser beam, but it missed the oncoming ship.

"Huh? What happened?" asked the pilot.

"That was a clever manoeuvre! They obviously anticipated that move and the moment we locked on them, they swerved out of the way. We won't find it easy to fool them again. Craig is determined not to lose this time."

Aneeda began to ask a question when Constance's hand tightened on her wrist. "Look out! They are coming in to attack!" she warned.

Immediately an alarm went off on the console and instinctively Aneeda swerved out of their path.

<Warning! Left side damaged!>

A picture of their ship showed up on the screen. Both women groaned when they saw a hole in the left side, close to the base of the wing.

"How bad is the damage? Can we continue?"

Aneeda pressed keys in front of her and a damage report was displayed. *<Left wing compromised! Imminent fuel leak detected.>*

Immediately Aneeda pressed another key and an identical dashboard display popped up on Constance's side.

"Constance, I need to seal this leak. I'm handing control over to you. Can you manage to fly this craft and shoot at the same time?"

"I'll do my best. You do what you must. Uh oh, here they come again!"

The Earthling pressed a key and the ship shot forward immediately. She swerved, and a green beam shot across in front of their windshield and disappeared into the distance. As soon as it disappeared from view, a number of green beams danced around their ship. She glanced over at Aneeda whose face was set in a grimace. Her fingers flew over the keyboard at incredible speed and Constance found it difficult to follow what the Saturnian was doing.

"Uh Aneeda, how's it going over there?"

"Nearly done," she snapped. "Don't bother me right now!"

Another beam danced across the front windshield and Constance made a sudden decision. *"Hold on tight! I'm going to buy us some more time!"*

She turned the nose into a downward spiral and sped downwards at breakneck speed. Aneeda looked at her in horror. *"What are you doing?"* she screamed. *"If we stall at this angle, we'll slam into the ground!"*

"Trust me! I know what I'm doing!" she replied calmly.

Aneeda looked in horror at her co-pilot and the blood drained from her face. She felt as though she was going to be sick.

Constance's eyes were closed and her face was calm and serene. She spoke quietly so as not to alarm Aneeda further. "Breathe deeply and close your eyes! You must become as one with the craft. Listen carefully to the sound of the engine. When we're about to stall, the turbines will whine a little louder. When that happens, I'll slow us down and we'll level out."

Aneeda's eyes grew huge and she tried to do as she was told, but her hands stayed frozen on the keyboard.

A few minutes later, Constance opened her eyes and pressed a sequence of keys. Immediately the ship levelled out.

"Aha, did you hear that?!" Mrs Carter remarked triumphantly. "Right on cue, just as I said!"

"You are completely insane; do you know that?!" the Saturnian gasped. Immediately afterwards a huge grin broke out on her face. *"My stars! That was totally AMAZING!"*

Aneeda took a deep breath and shook her head. "You know that was also completely illegal don't you?! We are probably going to be disqualified and lose this round."

"I know, and I'm sorry, but I just couldn't resist! The others never expected that, I guarantee it. Have you fixed the fuel leak though?"

"I managed a temporary repair, but we have to end this particular demonstration very quickly. It will remain a weak spot and I'm sure Jacob and Craig will take advantage of this. Another hit in that spot will mean we have lost the battle. Where are they by the way?"

Constance pointed upwards. "Here they come! Can we use the cloaking device now? I have another plan."

Aneeda took control of the ship and a blue light began flashing on the console.

"Okay, we are invisible,' she confirmed. "What should I do now?"

"Bring this ship alongside theirs and hold it steady. I want to shoot out one of the stabilizers."

"You know they can track us?" she remarked.

"Yes, I do, but they won't know which end is facing them and that will give us an advantage."

"You realize of course that the stabilizer is a very small target and well hidden. You will only have one chance to hit it," the pilot cautioned. "Unfortunately, I have to deactivate the cloaking device just before you fire your weapons though. You see, most of the power flows into that device so the weapons cannot be optimized when we are invisible. There is just enough power to run the essential services when the cloaking device is active."

Constance smiled reassuringly. "I know! I have to make this shot count."

Aneeda pulled up next to their opponents and her hand hovered over the keyboard. "Okay, tell me when you want me to deactivate the cloaking device."

"Do it now!!" the woman exclaimed.

Aneeda pressed the key and immediately Mrs Carter aimed the laser light at the ship. She adjusted the trajectory slightly and pressed the triggering device.

The console lit up and the computer showed a picture of the other ship. *<Direct hit! Stabilizer damaged!>*

Meanwhile on the other ship, Jacob and Craig were staring miserably at the screen in front of them. "Well Craig, looks as though we have lost this battle as well. I really thought we had finished them off when you damaged their craft's wing, but I was mistaken. I have misjudged your wife – again!"

"She is good, isn't she?" Craig remarked admiringly. "This fight can still end in victory for us if we manage to hit the wing again. Can this ship still fly?"

Jacob shook his head. "I'm sorry, but we cannot risk it. As you can see from the diagram on the screen, we will not be able to fly in a straight line. I know you are a good shot, but you can't hit anything while this ship lurches from side to side."

Carter nodded. "We might still have won this round though, because Constance performed an illegal move by going into such a steep dive. Lara isn't going to let her get away with that."

"I suppose it depends on what Lara decides is legal. Whatever the outcome of this battle, I think Constance is absolutely incredible! Not many pilots can do what she did and survive. So, do we concede defeat? Control is waiting for an answer."

"Yes, we have no choice."

Jacob passed the message on and turned to his companion. "Lara says we must reboot our systems and return to the landing bay. We can have a break and enjoy some refreshments. Afterwards she will discuss the battle at length with us."

Both crafts returned to the surface of Saturn and landed in the allotted spaces. The four pilots made their way into the hangar. The moment they appeared inside, the Saturnians stood up and cheered loudly. Lara glared at them, silencing them immediately. The staff sat down again but they were grinning excitedly.

The scientist put her hands on her hips. "Just what was that demonstration about, young lady?" she addressed Constance crossly.

The young woman looked down at her shoes to hide her grin. When she looked up again, her face was penitent.

"I apologize for that stunt, Lara. I knew what I was doing, but I shouldn't have taken such a risk with your spaceship. I know you said we were not to do any crazy things, but I'm very competitive by nature. Even though the battle was only a simulation, I didn't want the 'enemy' to win the round."

Lara shook her head. *"Humans!* Yes, I forgot how stubborn you all are. It is in your natures. Well I'm sorry to tell you, but that was completely illegal as far as we are concerned, so you have been disqualified. I'm awarding the second battle to Craig and Jacob by default."

There was an audible groan from mission control staff.

"I understand," Constance replied quietly. "Does that mean you'll delete this fight simulation from the records? I assumed you were going to use these fight sequences to train your own pilots."

Lara stared at her friend and there was a hushed silence. She shook her head as though unsure what to say. Suddenly she flew to Constance and hugged her tightly. "Oh, dear universe, I cannot stand this," she squeaked happily. *"That was the most amazing, incredible stunt that I have ever had the pleasure to witness!"*

Everyone stood up and clapped. Lara wiped happy tears from her eyes and became serious once more. "No of course I won't delete this fight sequence! I will however make a note on the footage that this is not what pilots should attempt to do. Oh, and you are still disqualified."

"Yes Lara," Constance replied. "You're the boss and I accept your decision."

"Good, now you must all be famished. Let's go and eat. After lunch I'll give you one more chance to get even with Jacob and Craig."

The party sat down to enjoy their lunch. While they were waiting for the food, Lara turned to Craig. "Were you aware that Constance could execute that move?"

"Yes, I was. On Earth that's one of the tasks our pilots are asked to perform during simulation. They don't actually have to do this in real life, but it's used as a test to see how competent the fighter pilots are. It's an advanced course and doesn't have to be done by all the astronauts at NASA. Obviously, one cannot execute that move when piloting a passenger craft for example, so the commercial pilots don't have to do it. It's a very difficult course and is not undertaken lightly."

"Has anyone else managed to perform that stunt?" Lara enquired.

"Yes, over the years several pilots have passed that advanced course," Craig answered. "However, Constance was the only one in her class who managed to perform that manoeuvre, *with a perfect score of 100%.*"

Constance raised her eyebrows in surprise. "How did you know I was the only one?" she asked curiously.

Craig grinned at her. "I may have been a space technician when you qualified but I was always interested in you. I had access to all the information, so I snooped."

Lara turned to Craig. "I'm curious. Did you also do the advanced course when you applied to become a space explorer."

"Yes, but I didn't have a perfect score like my wife. I can perform that manoeuvre, but I did crash during simulation. Constance got it right every time! That is something no other pilot has ever accomplished," he replied as he raised his glass and toasted his wife. "It is almost as though she has a sixth sense!"

Constance laughed. "I was just lucky!" she exclaimed.

After lunch, the pilots returned to their ships to perform the last test.

"All right this is what I want you to do," Lara explained. "I want to focus solely on speed and manoeuvrability. In this exercise both crafts are to engage one another in battle and try to cause as much damage as possible to each craft. We will record the number of hits on each ship and the craft that causes the most damage will be declared the winners. You'll have ten minutes only to perform this task. This time I want only simple evasive manoeuvres, not death-defying stunts!"

The two teams climbed on board and the countdown began. Both ships waited patiently for the countdown to finish before they took off at incredible speed. The laser lights danced around both ships as they ducked and dived and it was hard for the control tower to make out who was winning. On board both crafts, the pilots groaned as their opponents scored hit after hit, but all four pilots lost count as to how many hits they had sustained or scored. Neither group said much as they concentrated on the task before them. Lara interrupted them. "Time is up! Return to base please."

Both teams went to sit in the lounge while the data was analyzed. Fifteen minutes later, Lara came in with an electronic tablet device. "We have reached the end of this exercise and I want to thank you both for allowing us to use you as guinea pigs in this experiment. I know you are on honeymoon, but I hope you forgive me for taking up some of your precious time."

"I'm glad we could help," Craig replied. "This was important to us as well."

"Excellent! Now for the final score! Team one managed to score ten hits and team two scored nine. The winners are team one. Congratulations Jacob and Craig!"

Constance hugged Craig and shook Jacob's hand. "Well done both of you."

Aneeda shook Craig's hand and patted Jacob on his shoulder. "Yes, that was incredible. It was close but you deserved to win." She smiled at Craig and Constance. "It was an honour working with you both. I can see why you have such incredible reputations!"

"We have learnt a great deal from you," Jacob agreed.

Jacob and Aneeda shook hands with them once again and they left the control centre.

Lara sat down next to her friends. "You must be tired from all that activity so I won't keep you much longer. I just wanted to know if you have any questions or you want to know more about our technology."

Husband and wife exchanged satisfied looks. "I think you have covered everything," Craig remarked.

"Well in that case I have one last request," Lara replied. "Can you contact Commander Simms and see if he can arrange a meeting for us?"

"I'll do that at once," Craig promised.

Constance yawned. "You go ahead Craig and I'll see you later. I want to have a shower and relax for a while."

Thirty minutes later, Craig returned to their suite and found his wife drying her hair. "What did Commander Simms say, honey?" she asked.

"He's happy to hear about this breakthrough and he has promised to contact the Minister of Defence, and the head of the space police security detail. Our boss is going to let Lara know when they can arrange a three-way conference call to discuss everything with Saturn."

Mrs Carter sat down next to her husband. "How long do you think it will take for Commander Simms to organize this? We are only staying here another week and then we have to go and spend some time with Tanus."

"Commander Simms said he should have this organized by tomorrow evening at the latest."

Constance sighed and snuggled up to her husband. "I don't know about you, but I intend to spend some time just watching television, or else I might download a book to read. Today was a very busy day."

"It certainly was," her husband agreed. "I have to say it was very kind of Lara and the other scientists to think of us. This new technology will give us a bit more of an advantage when we are being pursued by our enemies."

"Do you think the officials on Earth will agree to have these devices placed on our ships?"

"I'm sure that they will," Craig replied. "After all, any advantage that we can have out here in space is a good idea. Things can get very hectic in both universes."

His wife agreed, "It certainly can."

Both Earthlings were quiet for a while. Each were occupied with their own thoughts. Constance yawned and stretched. She put her head on her husband's shoulder and was soon fast asleep.

The next afternoon, Jorrel came to call them. "Commander Simms is online and wishes to talk to both of you. He has asked for your input into the discussion of the new technology we are offering Earth. Follow me please."

Both space explorers went into the control centre and greeted Lara, Jorrel and Karnd. Everyone stared at the giant screen on the wall in front of them. There was a bit of static before their boss's image became clear. He nodded at his employees. "Good afternoon Craig, Constance. Lara has kindly shown me the footage taken yesterday. Your mock battle sequences with Saturn's pilots was – ah – very interesting to say the least. I would like to comment on some of them, but time is short and my colleagues are in a hurry. Therefore, it would be prudent if we just got on with the matter as discussed with Lara."

The vidscreen then split into three sections and the Minister of Defence and the head of the space police came into focus. Commander Simms introduced the Minister of Defence to the explorers and they nodded. "Pleased to meet you Sir," both replied politely.

"Likewise," he replied.

"You know the head of the space police of course," Simms beamed.

"Yes indeed!" Craig replied, smiling. "It's been a while Keith. Congratulations on your promotion by the way."

"Thank you, Craig. I believe congratulations are also in order for you. You finally took my advice and married that amazing woman. If you hadn't done so, I might have asked her myself."

Constance blushed and Craig laughed. He remembered how Keith and several others had risked their lives to fight against Andocia when she tried to take over Earth. Many good people had lost their lives, but they had not died in vain. Andocia had been stopped and had left Earth alone since then.

His thoughts were interrupted by Commander Simms. "Okay then, let's get on with our discussion ..."

CHAPTER 22

While the delegates were discussing the technology Saturn was offering to them, another discussion was also taking place in the blue universe.

Andocia was sitting alone in her office when her smart phone rang. She looked at the display and her eyes opened wide in surprise. "Well hello there! You are the last person I expected to contact me. To what do I owe the pleasure?" she asked as she went to close the door, flipping over a "do not disturb" sign as she did so.

"This isn't a social call!" Tanus snapped. "I've been meaning to contact you, but I haven't had a spare moment until now."

"I know, I've heard rumours of you flitting from planet to planet and having meetings with the inhabitants."

"Yes, well mostly I've gone to smooth lots of ruffled feathers. You are usually the cause of most of their problems."

Andocia smiled lazily. "What can I tell you? I get bored very easily and I need some distractions."

Tanus shook her head but didn't comment.

"Why are you contacting me Tanus? Obviously, something is bothering you, but then there's always problems, aren't there! What's on your mind?"

"I'm getting tired of having to explain to different beings why you are just so wicked. Tell me Andocia, have you broken up with your latest boyfriend again? Is that the reason for your boredom?"

Andocia glared at her. "Mind your own business. Anyway, I don't have boyfriends – I have conquests. As with everything else, I get bored with the men who come into my life so I move on."

"I thought so!" Tanus commented. "Maybe you should go on holiday somewhere and leave these poor beings alone for a while."

The wicked woman smiled evilly. "You know, that is good advice. Perhaps I should pay another visit to Earth. The last time I was there it was very entertaining."

Tanus glared at her. "Leave Earth out of this! You have done enough damage there as well."

Andocia sighed. "Tanus, I know you very well. You and I have been enemies for as long as I can remember. Just tell me what's on your mind and then I can get back to work."

"I think you know why I am phoning. I want you to leave Craig and Constance alone! They are married and the last thing they need is to be hassled by you for no apparent reason."

"What makes you think I'm even interested in them anyway? Like I said, I get bored very quickly and therefore I lose interest."

"You aren't bored with them and you know it. Craig fascinates you, because he refuses to obey your ridiculous commands, and Constance is not a threat."

"Well, you are just as involved in their lives as I am!" Andocia countered.

"I'm interested in them *because* of your behaviour and interest. If you left them alone, then I would do the same."

Andocia smiled wickedly. "No, you wouldn't! You will do everything in your power to help them. I know you have looked into their backgrounds – well so have I. Their dossiers make for fascinating reading, don't you agree?"

Tanus was silent and Andocia continued. "We were friends once – long ago! Have you forgotten that we shared each other's secrets? There isn't much about you that I don't know. The same goes for you of course. You know more about me than anyone else *alive!*"

"I suppose I do, but even so, you changed long ago and chose your current path. Afterwards things were never the same between us," Tanus replied.

"You also changed Tanus. It's not my fault you chose to go off in another direction."

"I never had a choice – unlike you Andocia. You still had the opportunity to refuse what was offered to you."

"Yes, I did, but I liked what was being offered to me so I agreed."

Tanus sighed. "Well enough about that. I hope your decision has brought you much happiness and satisfaction, but I doubt it. You are lonely and constantly looking for distractions. That is what Craig and Constance are – a distraction."

"Well perhaps they are," conceded Andocia, "but both of them are worthy opponents."

"They are very good at their jobs, that's for sure, but neither one of them is different to any other astronaut who explores the galaxies. Earth's training programme is excellent and many space pilots can do what those two are accomplishing, so why single them out especially?" Tanus enquired.

The evil woman laughed uproariously. "You've got to be kidding! Both are extra special and you know it, just as I do. As I mentioned before, I studied their dossiers as well and found some very interesting things out and you know exactly what I mean! I know *everything about them.*"

Tanus glared at her enemy. "If that's true, then you know they aren't a threat to you. I understand why you captured Constance and it had nothing to do with Craig's mission. He just assumed you kidnapped her because I asked for his help, and you just let him believe it. You wanted to make sure – didn't you?"

Andocia crossed her arms over her chest and smiled. "I had to be certain that Constance wasn't going to be ... troublesome, yes."

"What did you find out?" Tanus asked patiently.

"Well she's not a threat ... not at the moment anyway. I was happy with my findings."

"If that is truly so, then why are you still so fixated on her?" enquired Tanus curiously.

"I'm interested in her because she has an above average intelligence. She's capable of things I have never observed in a normal human being."

Tanus sighed heavily. "What experience do you actually have with human beings Andocia? You left Earth a long time ago and have never really interacted with anyone human. It's true you were once a human being, just as I was, until the *changes* we underwent. Constance is very intelligent, I know that too. Why else did you think she became a space explorer at the tender age of seventeen?"

For the first time, Andocia looked uncomfortable. "I thought it was because of her father's influence."

The woman in white laughed. "Yes, even Craig thought that at first, but he was also proven wrong. That young woman never used her father as a stepping stone into her career. She did that all by herself. You don't need to worry about her, Andocia."

"Well, when you put it like that, I suppose you're right."

Tanus nodded vigorously. "There's something else I want to

discuss with you. When you had Constance in your clutches, what did you do to her?"

Andocia looked guilty. "Nothing much! I just probed her mind."

"Are you sure that was all you did?" Tanus replied suspiciously.

"Yes. Why are you asking?"

"When I rescued her, I also did some probing of my own. I sensed some trauma lingering behind. There was a memory that was obviously bothering her. Her grandmother had just died and no one was explaining to her exactly what had happened. I sensed something like disbelief that the woman had killed herself. Someone – a doctor perhaps mentioned it could have been a stroke. The woman's name was Elizabeth, but Constance called her Beth."

"I know who she was," Andocia replied. "She was a formidable lady who possessed incredible power. She was a very astute person who happened to be telepathic – amongst other things."

Tanus's eyes widened in surprise. "How do you know that Andocia? I knew she was Constance's grandmother long before I probed that young woman's mind. There was never any mention of anything unusual. According to the records, she was a normal human being."

There was an uncomfortable silence and Tanus glared at her enemy. "I asked you a question and I'm waiting for an answer. How could you have known that Elizabeth was telepathic?"

"I ... I ... uh ..." Andocia stammered, lost for words.

Tanus was horrified by a thought that came to mind. "*No! I never realized it before – until now. You were very thorough, but not thorough enough.*"

The evil woman had regained her composure and stared blankly at her enemy. "I have no idea what you are talking about."

Tanus shook her head. "I know you are evil, yet at one time you were just – undisciplined. *You killed her didn't you! She didn't die from a stroke and she didn't kill herself either. How could you be so ... so ... unbelievably WICKED?!*"

Andocia examined her nails placidly. "Yes, I killed her! She was incredibly powerful! It amazes me how she kept her ... talents ... from her husband and daughter."

Tanus spread her hands out in a gesture of misery. "But why did you do it? She was never a threat to you!"

"Yes, she was! I went to visit her in the old age home. At first, she didn't know who I was, but then she recognized me. She said she knew about me and she threatened to tell Constance. That crazy woman was going to tell her granddaughter about her powers – and everything else. I couldn't let that happen, so I ended her miserable life."

Tanus shook her head in disbelief. "It wasn't necessary Andocia, it just wasn't! You should never have gone to see her in the first place and then she wouldn't have realized who you were. If she was as powerful as you claim, then she obviously read your mind and that's how she knew everything about you. There is no way she would have known who you were if she had never laid eyes on you."

Andocia looked chastened. "Oh! I guess it makes sense, but no one can read my mind, except you and maybe a few others. I guess I let my guard down and she found out about me that way."

"Dammit Andocia, how could you have been so stupid and irresponsible?!"

"But Tanus, you don't understand! When she found out who I was, she attacked me! She wasn't just a telepath – there was much more to her than you could imagine. She had powers – like us. She fought like someone possessed and left me with no choice. I managed to knock her out and then I slit her wrists. You should have seen what her room looked like when we had finished fighting!"

Tanus was still angry with her rival. "What you did was unforgivable Andocia. You should never have gone to see Beth. The horrible chain of events was entirely your fault. If you had not meddled in their affairs, her family could just have gone on thinking Beth was a bit eccentric and not crazy. Beth could have lived out the rest of her life in peace. Alexis would still have her mother and Constance would still have her grandmother."

"I did her a favour Tanus! She said that her powers were a curse and she hated having them."

"She didn't understand them!" Tanus exclaimed angrily. "You

and I also have those gifts, but others taught us how to use them productively. Many people on Earth probably have those talents and some of them know how to use them properly. It isn't common knowledge of course because no one wants to stand out in a crowd. Even in this day and age, telepaths are looked upon with suspicion."

"I guess that was stupid of me," Andocia agreed. "I never expected such a reaction from an elderly lady. I was just curious in the beginning. I never realized she was so strong."

The woman in white shook her head. "This is getting worse and worse! Now I understand what Craig told me a while back. He said that after Beth had died, the Greggs donated a large sum of money to the old age home. They built a wing in Beth's name, but the incident was reported as a suicide to avoid further scandal. That money was a bribe! That means they knew what Elizabeth was capable of and kept it quiet. I suppose we cannot blame them. They didn't understand her at all."

"Do you think Constance or Craig know about this?" Andocia asked.

"I doubt it. Well they won't hear about this from me. Some things are best left unsaid. As much as I love Craig and Constance, they must never find out about this," Tanus remarked.

"Well my lips are sealed as well. I won't say anything either," Andocia promised. "Well I have things to do so I had better get on with them ..."

"Not so fast Andocia. There's something else I need to discuss with you first."

"What is it now?" she asked impatiently.

"I meant it when I said you must leave Craig and Constance alone. What were you thinking when you put Craig into that induced coma? That was also unnecessary and downright foolish!"

"I wanted to make an example out of him. I find that Earth and my other enemies don't seem to take me seriously."

"Earthlings were never your enemies Andocia. You made them despise you when you tried to take over Earth. They are not pushovers as you undoubtedly found out. You cannot blame

Craig for doing his job. I wonder, did you ever stop to consider what would have happened if his life-support had failed? How long did you intend to leave him up there, floating aimlessly in space?"

"I was going to revive him, but you got to him first!" she replied defensively.

"It was just as well I rescued him! You should have checked before you sent him out into space! His comatose state wasn't deep enough! You incapacitated him, but you couldn't stop his mind from wandering. He had nothing but memories to keep him alive and it was fortunate he had the good sense to banish negative thoughts from his mind. The man knew what was happening to him, but his tenacity kept him sane. Craig does have an incredibly strong mind, just like Constance has. I guess that's what makes them so good at what they do. He could easily have gone insane up there. I had to wipe everything from his mind, now he only remembers that you put him into a coma, but nothing else. I want this insanity to stop, do you hear me? No more stupid stunts!"

"Okay, fine! Are we done now?" Andocia asked impatiently.

"Almost! I have just one more thing to say. I want you to leave them alone while they are on honeymoon. I've had ships guarding them from the time they began their journey and if you make any attempt to harm them, I will retaliate. They'll be coming to spend some time with me after visiting with the Saturnians. Make sure you stay away from them. Promise me that you will!" Tanus demanded.

"I promise!" Andoicia replied.

The woman in white nodded and then cancelled the call.

CHAPTER 23

Meanwhile back on Saturn, Craig and Constance were enjoying some refreshments in their room. The discussion with Commander Simms, the Minister of Defence, and the head of the space police had gone very well. Permission had been granted for the Saturnians to install the cloaking device on their spacecraft, as well as the speed booster device. Craig held up a glass of champagne and toasted his wife. "To you my darling, I wish us only good health and happiness."

"I love you Craig! May every day be as wonderful as today has been. I hope that we will be together for years to come."

Craig nodded. "While we are toasting, we should give thanks for the Saturnians. Without them we would be lost. They saw the flaws in our spacecrafts and did something about it."

"They certainly did," Constance replied. "We owe them so much and I'm proud to number them amongst our friends."

Craig picked up the tray of refreshments and put it outside the door. He came to sit next to his wife and put his arm around her shoulders. "I wonder how long it'll take the technicians to install those devices in our ship?"

"I don't know. A few hours at least I suppose. What should we do for the rest of today?" asked his wife.

"Well they have some beautiful tourist spots here and I've heard good things about that restaurant by the lake. It is a lovely scenic drive and should take us an hour by road. We can have an early supper and then come back here afterwards. What do you think?"

"It sounds like a good idea. We should get changed then," Constance agreed.

An hour later they began their journey to the restaurant. Their armed escort prepared to come with them, but Craig waved them away. "Thanks very much, but I don't think we need to trouble you. If we get into any danger, which I doubt, we can always contact you. I know your spotter crafts will reach us in a very short time."

Their escort looked at one another and shrugged their shoulders. "All right Craig, but we have to tell Lara where you are going. She's worried about you."

Craig smiled at them. "I understand. We were going to tell her anyway but you can save us the trouble. Thank you; we'll see you later."

The couple waved and their hovercar began gliding slowly away.

Constance grinned at her husband. "Ah! Alone at last! They mean well of course, but frankly I'm starting to feel very claustrophobic with them around. I know they are very discreet and we never really see them but I can always sense them watching us."

"I know what you mean my love, but our hosts would be very offended if we refused their help. I know they are intruding, but they mean well. Our time alone is growing short and soon we'll be back on Earth and there will be no one watching our backs."

"I suppose so," his wife conceded. "We only have a week with Tanus on the white planet when we leave here in two days, and then we'll be going home."

An hour later the couple arrived at the restaurant. By now dusk was falling and a golden haze reflected off the glass buildings. They sat outside nursing their drinks and watched until the sun disappeared. Lights came on around the complex, which housed not only the restaurant but several other small shops. As it was still early the couple went into a curio store and browsed around. They purchased a few trinkets, including a delicate necklace. The beautiful blue charm was shaped like the planet Saturn and it hung on a thin gold chain. When Constance held the necklace up to the light, it sparkled as though there were tiny diamonds set all around it. Craig paid for the necklace and put it around his wife's neck. She looked in a nearby mirror and grasped her husband's hand. "Craig it's beautiful! I love it!"

"You deserve it. It looks as though it was made just for you."

She kissed him and arm in arm they made their way to the restaurant.

While they were waiting for their food, Craig looked at his wife as though it was the first time they had ever met.

"I love you so much, Constance!" he thought happily. *"You could have had any man you wanted but instead you settled for me. I'm so lucky to have you as my wife!"*

After dinner, the honeymooners stayed for the entertainment. A young Saturnian woman sang in a haunting voice and everyone was enthralled by her. Her wings fluttered gently as she sang and as the light caught her wings, prisms of light danced around the large hall.

The time seemed to fly by so quickly and soon it was very late. Constance stifled a yawn as they stood up to leave. They thanked the manager and left to make their way back to the hotel they were staying at.

When they arrived, they went straight to their room and it wasn't long before the ywere fast asleep. They didn't hear the guards take their places close to the door once more.

The following morning, Lara invited the couple to have breakfast with her. She told them that the Saturnian technicians would install the devices in their ship and that it should be ready by lunchtime. Afterwards they would explain to the explorers what had been done and how to operate the devices.

Craig and Constance went back to their hotel.

"Today is our last day here Craig. What do you want to do to pass the time?"

Her husband patted his stomach. "My clothes aren't going to fit me soon if we keep on eating the way we have. I was looking at that large cliff in the distance. How about a hike up one of the trails? We could use the exercise!"

Constance grinned at him. "Well I certainly don't want to get fat, so let's get some things together and do this!"

The couple fetched their rucksacks and filled them with the necessary items they would need for their climb. They went to their hired hovercar, followed by the ever-present security guards. Craig waved them away. "We really appreciate you looking after us so well, but we are going hiking for most of today. I'm sure everything will be fine."

One of the men looked worried. "We were told to watch you all the time. Jorrel will be angry with us if we don't do our duty."

"Really, it'll be fine, I assure you. If we get into trouble, one of us will press the locator beacon installed on our mobile devices. I'm sure the hiking trail we are going on is full of tourists.

We'll walk on the most popular trail, and should be back before it gets dark."

Reluctantly the men let them go and watched until the hover-car was out of sight before turning back to the hotel.

The young couple arrived at the entrance to the trail. There were a number of other beings carrying rucksacks and talking excitedly. Several humans were also waiting to be admitted into the trail park. There was a long line and it took a while before Craig and Constance were admitted.

"Okay, finally we can begin our hike," Craig said. "Which trail should we take, honey?"

Constance looked at the names and was quiet for a while. "Well, we can't go on that one I suppose," she remarked and pointed at a sign which said "Devil's peak".

Craig shook his head. "No way, nor that one over there," which read "Widow Maker's Cove".

Constance pointed to another sign a little further down the path. "Look, that one is called 'Scenic Rambling Route'. Should we try that one?"

"That sounds a good idea," Craig replied. "I see a number of beings ahead so we should have plenty of company on this route."

The couple hurried to join the other tourists and they began their hike. The terrain was rocky as they went along, and some hills were higher than others, but it wasn't a difficult climb. There were plenty of rest stops along the way where hikers could relax and have refreshments. The couple made friends with some of the hikers and they discussed all sorts of things as they walked.

Meanwhile, a few kilometres away, some more experienced hikers were taking a different route. A family was climbing a fairly large cliff. The mother and father were lagging slightly behind, while their teenage daughter and younger son were competing with one another.

"Hey Brian, what's the hurry?!" his sister shouted. "We have lots of time to do this climb."

Brian looked back at his sister and grinned. "Gee slow coach,

I'm younger than you but I bet I can get to the top of this hill before you!"

His sister laughed at him. "Oh no you won't! I was feeling sorry for you so I deliberately hung back, but seeing as you are so cheeky, here I come."

Their mother was concerned and she spoke sharply to her children. "Emma, Brian, take it easy! This is a hike, not a competition! There are a number of loose rocks here and you could trip and hurt yourselves."

Both children slowed down and Brian pulled a face. "Awww Mom, we were just having some fun!"

"Your mother is right you two. Just slow down and enjoy the scenery," their father replied.

The family continued at a slower pace, but the children playfully nudged one another from time to time.

The climb became more difficult as the terrain became steeper and rockier. The higher they climbed though, the more breathtaking the view became. Each time they crested another hill, different things caught their attention. There were beautiful flowers, and exotic little creatures that skittered away when they saw the hikers. A few hours later they reached the highest point of the mountain and sat down on a bench. Emma gasped in wonder and took her smart phone out of her pocket. She walked to the edge of the mountain and stepped onto an outcrop of rock. Her mother was pouring some liquid into plastic tumblers for her family when some instinct made her look up suddenly.

"Emma, what are you doing?!" she exclaimed.

Emma smiled and turned slightly towards her mother. "I just want to take a picture! The view is incredible!"

Suddenly the teenager's smile turned into a grimace of fear as the rock she was standing on suddenly began to quiver and shift. Her mother jumped up, kicking the tumblers over as she realized what was happening. Emma's mouth opened and she screamed in fear as the rock began to move downwards. Her mother grabbed frantically at Emma's ankle, but her hand closed over the girl's shoe and it came off in her hand. There was a blood curdling scream as the teenager plummeted down into the abyss.

"EMMA!! TOM, EMMA'S GONE OVER THE CLIFF!" Mary screamed hysterically.

Her husband was already beside her and they looked over the cliff in dismay. There was no sign of their daughter.

Alerted by the screams, several other hikers rushed to the family's aid.

"What happened?" a man asked.

Mary was hysterical and began to cry uncontrollably. Brian went to comfort his mother as tears ran freely down his face Their father shook his head in disbelief. "She ... she fell! My daughter fell off the cliff!"

The hiker peered carefully over the edge and shook his head.

Meanwhile, back on another trail, Craig and Constance were enjoying something to drink when suddenly their guide jumped up in alarm. There was a whispered conversation between him and a woman. He looked at his smart phone screen and shook his head. Constance nudged her husband. "Craig, something's wrong!"

They went up to the guide and spoke to him. "Is there a problem?" Constance asked curiously.

"There was an accident on Devil's Peak. I'm not sure what happened but I think someone got hurt. I tried to call for help but there is no reception up here."

Craig looked at his device. "He's right. There's no signal."

"Surely you must have some other way to get help?" Constance remarked.

The man held up a satellite phone. "I have this, but unfortunately I dropped it and it broke. The next rest stop is too far away and unless we hurry, it'll be dark and we'll be trapped up here."

"Don't you carry a spare one?" Craig asked incredulously.

"We didn't think that it would be necessary," he replied miserably. "This is our quiet season."

Constance shook her head at the stupidity of the guide, but decided not to berate him. There would be time for that later.

Turning to her husband she asked. "We cannot leave until we know what happened on Devil's Peak. How do we get the help we need?"

Craig thought about it for a moment, and then he smiled. "I know! I'll alert the security forces by switching on the locator beacon installed in our phones!"

His wife nodded vigorously. "Do it!" Turning to the guide, who seemed to be in a state of shock, she shook him. "Can someone take us to the Devil's Peak trail? How far is it from here?"

The man pointed in a northerly direction. "Over there! That path will join up with the one in Devil's Peak. If we hurry, we can be there in twenty microns."

"All right then, let's get started! Do you have anyone who can take these hikers back down this trail?"

The guide pointed to the woman who had spoken to him earlier. "She can take them back. Deana knows this trail."

"Okay then, let's get moving!" Constance instructed, but the man stood still.

"What's the problem now?" she snapped at him. "We still have about 2½ hours of daylight left, but time is moving on."

"How ... how will the security forces find us if we keep moving? Shouldn't we stay here and wait for them?"

"They'll find us. The signal is very clear on my device." Craig remarked. "Let's get going."

The hikers split up with Deana leading the group back down the slope, while Craig, Constance and the guide headed for the trail that would take them to Devil's Peak.

They had almost reached the intersecting path that would place them on the Devil's Peak trail when a hovercar filled with security men appeared above them. Their guns were trained on the party.

Craig put up his hands. "Hey take it easy! You can put your guns away. We are in no danger, but someone else is!"

The security forces holstered their weapons and landed gently near the party. "What happened Craig?" asked one of the guards.

"There's no time to explain right now, but someone is in trouble on this trail. We aren't sure what happened but we're going to find out."

The head of the Saturnian security forces and another woman climbed out of the craft and began walking with them. "I'll send my people up ahead of us so they can find out what the problem is. Let's continue up the path in the meantime."

Five microns passed and the hovercraft returned with only the driver on board. He stepped off the craft and it hovered in place. "Sir, we found them! It's bad! A young girl fell off the cliff about 30 parsecs from here."

Constance wasted no time and turned to the head of the security forces. "Abner, can I go up there with you? I can find out what happened."

"I'll go too," Craig replied.

"Yes, of course!" he replied.

The two Carters climbed aboard the craft together with the driver and the head of security. The guide was also allowed on board and the craft moved up the hill.

When they arrived on the scene, they saw several hikers talking to a man. Nearby a woman was sobbing and her son was holding her hand and crying as well. The security police were standing nearby, talking quietly amongst themselves. Constance went up to the woman and spoke to her. "Hello my name is Constance. Can you tell me what happened?"

The woman blew her nose and fresh tears fell onto her cheeks. "My ... my daughter went over the cliff! One moment she was standing on a rock and the next she was gone."

The young woman saw several cups lying on the ground and a bottle containing some sort of cool drink half full with green liquid. She found a cup in one of the knapsacks and took it out, filling it with the cold liquid. "Here, drink this," she ordered gently.

Obediently the woman did as she was told. Constance put her arms around Mary and held her close. Her touch seemed to calm the woman down a little and she drank the liquid. Mary's eyes were swollen from crying and Constance took pity on her. "Help is coming soon and we'll find your daughter, I promise you."

She moved out of earshot of the woman and took Craig and Abner aside. "We have to do something! Once it gets dark, we have no chance of recovering their daughter ..."

She left the rest of the sentence unsaid, but both men knew what she was thinking. They had peered over the edge of the steep cliff, but could see nothing below but lots of greenery. It was possible that the search would be to recover the girl's body, but no one voiced their concern, for fear of making the situation even worse. While there was hope, there was a chance she could be alive.

CHAPTER 24

Craig spoke quietly to the security policeman. "Abner, can you organize a search party? We'll do whatever we can to help, but we need a decent medical kit. Do you have a smaller hovercraft to lend me? I was hoping to go through those woods and see if I can spot the girl. It'll make things easier if we know exactly where to look for her."

Abner pursed his lips. "I can get you a hover-scooter, but I have to warn you it's dangerous. Some of those trees are barely wide enough to fit a human through and the vegetation is so dense that you'll only see obstacles when you're on top of them You could end up breaking your neck down there. It's too much of a risk!"

Craig pointed to the young couple sitting miserably on a rock. "You want to tell those folks that you can't help their daughter? What would you do if that was your child who needed help? Wouldn't you do everything in your power to see that she was safe? We have to try!"

Constance agreed. "Craig can pilot anything, from the smallest hovercraft to the biggest spaceship. There's no one more qualified to do this. I would offer, but I think it would be better if I climbed down the cliff face and looked for her that way. She could be lying in a thick clump of bushes and no one will find her. I can keep in contact with Craig and in that way, we stand a better chance of locating her."

"I think you are both crazy, but thank you for offering. What do you need?"

He took out his electronic notebook and began typing out the list of equipment they would require. When he had written down everything they asked for, he returned to his men. "I'm leaving two of my staff here with you. I'll be back soon with the things that you need," Abner promised.

When the hovercraft had left, Constance went back to the remainder of the hikers. She knelt down by Mary who had stopped crying, but every now and then her body shook with grief. "What's going to happen now?" she sniffed miserably.

"Everything is going to be fine I promise you. The police are organizing a rescue operation as we speak."

The woman clung to Constance. "I don't know what I'll do without her," she sniffed. "What if she's already dead? What if no one can find her?" she wailed.

Mrs Carter squeezed Mary's hand reassuringly. "I'm sure she'll be fine. We're going to do everything we can to bring her back to you. Can I ask you a few questions about your daughter?"

The woman nodded and Constance continued. "What's her name?"

"Emma … Her name is Emma."

"How old is she?"

"Fifteen," Mary replied.

Constance looked at the young boy sitting miserably a little distance away. "What's your son's name?"

"Brian," she replied, "he's twelve, and my husband's name is Tom."

Craig shook the boy's hand, and then his father's as well. "My name is Craig and that lovely lady over there is my wife Constance. We're newlyweds and are here on honeymoon."

The woman's face brightened momentarily. "That's wonderful! Congratulations!"

Both newlyweds told the couple some things about their own lives in an effort to distract them from the seriousness of the situation. By the time the police returned, accompanied by a doctor, a nurse and a fully equipped ambulance, Tom, Mary and Brian had calmed down a little. They were given medication to help calm them further.

While the medical team asked Tom and Mary some questions, Craig and Constance were conferring with Abner and an experienced rock climber who would talk Constance through the dangerous climb she had offered to undertake. The tour guide was told he could leave but he stubbornly refused to do so. The equipment they had requested was handed over to the newlyweds. This included two satellite phones with fully charged batteries that would last a whole day if necessary. After checking they had everything they needed, both space explorers got ready to begin their dangerous rescue mission. Meanwhile overhead, a spotter craft announced that all the trails were now closed and everyone was requested to make their way down the various paths immediately.

Craig waited anxiously as his wife put on her safety harness and thick hiking gloves. A strong rope was tied to a large tree and she pulled it, testing the strength. Then Constance lowered herself gingerly over the side of the sheer cliff. She knew she should be accompanied by a more experienced climber, but didn't want to endanger anyone else. She had complete faith in her husband and knew he would watch her back. Everyone peered nervously over the cliff as Constance rappelled further and further away. When she was a safe distance away, Craig climbed on the hover-scooter and began searching the surrounding area for any obstacles that could interfere with her climb. Every few minutes he would fly out of her sight, checking the surrounding area, then he would return. As Constance climbed further and further down the steep cliff, Craig widened his sweep of the area.

Craig noticed a ledge further down and he contacted his wife to warn her about it. When she got there, she saw it was quite wide. Some dense bushes grew close to the edge of the ledge and Mrs Carter walked around cautiously, calling the teenager's name, but there was no answer. Something glinted in the sunlight and the woman went to investigate. A smart phone which had been smashed into pieces lay on the ledge. The young woman gathered up the parts and put them in her knapsack. Constance searched the ledge thoroughly, but there was no sign of the missing teenager. When she looked over the edge, her stomach knotted, for there was still a long way to go before she reached the bottom of this enormous cliff. Glancing at her watch she became concerned as an hour had already passed. If they didn't find the young girl soon, they would have to give up the search, because it would be dark in 1½ hours. Already she could feel the temperature dropping and she knew it got very cold during the nights on Saturn.

Once again, she continued down the steep slope, Craig watching her carefully as she went. He risked a quick sweep away from Constance and found the foliage was becoming denser the lower he flew. He too noticed the drop in temperature. Carter watched as Constance balanced deftly on two rocks and added another rope to the one in her hand. The metal coupling slid effortlessly over the two ropes, joining them into one.

Knowing that time was of the essence, he flew away from his wife again and searched the surrounding landscape. The trees were very dense and he peered into the distance with his binoculars and saw a rocky outcrop. He told his wife about it and she promised to look out for it. Agonizing minutes passed and he was surprised to find that another half an hour had passed by. In an hour, it would be dark!

Constance reached the outcrop of rock and was surprised to find that it was larger than the one she had seen before. This section of the cliff was filled with trees and bushes. She walked around, calling the girl's name and willing her to answer. If she wasn't here, then Constance didn't think they would get to her on time. The explorer looked upwards and saw just how far she had climbed down the steep cliff and she shuddered.

The woman walked carefully around, peering into bushes and looking behind trees. She called the girl's name, but received no answer. Even though it seemed impossible that the girl was alive, Constance refused to give up. Somehow, she sensed the girl still lived. Mrs Carter put her head in her hands and rubbed her tired eyes. She pulled off one of the thick gloves and saw the red welts crisscrossing her palm.

Suddenly she sat bolt upright. She thought she heard something and called insistently. *"Emma, Emma, can you hear me????? Answer me please!"*

From somewhere nearby she heard a groan and ran towards the sound. She sighed with relief when she went behind a tree and found the teenager lying there. Her eyes were open but they were dulled with pain. Constance contacted Craig. "Honey I found her! Can you land here and help me please?"

"I'll see you soon," her husband promised.

Constance stroked the girl's hair gently. "It's going to be okay! Help is coming," she promised.

"I … I fell …" she whimpered.

"I know sweetie, but you're going to be fine!"

Constance took water out of her knapsack and placed a straw in a tumbler of water. She lifted the girl's head slightly and helped her drink some of the liquid. When the teenager had finished the water, Constance looked around. There were a number of branches scattered about and it was obvious these had broken the girl's fall, but she had fallen a long way down and Constance had no way of knowing how serious Emma's injuries really were.

Craig landed next to her and hugged her gratefully. "I was so worried about you! How is Emma?"

Constance examined the girl gently. Her hair was tangled and dirty and her clothes were torn. She lay on her side and Constance saw that one of her legs was bent at an unnatural angle. The bone was showing through the skin, which was badly lacerated. There was a large gash on her forehead and a bruise had begun forming on her left elbow. She lifted the tattered t-shirt and noticed a number of bruises on the girl's stomach. There were several cuts on her body as well.

The girl sighed and closed her eyes. "I'm so tired!" she complained.

Constance took some of the cold water and rubbed it on the girl's face. "Emma, stay with me! Don't go to sleep!"

Constance turned to her husband. "It looks as though she has a bad concussion as well. I don't want to move her because there could be more injuries on her back."

Mrs Carter took a tool out of her knapsack and handed it to her husband. "Craig, I don't want to leave her alone. Can you cut some strong branches off one of these trees for me please? I need to splint her leg."

Her husband went to the nearest tree and pressed a button on the tool. Immediately it lit up and hummed as a laser beam appeared. He selected the branches and aimed the tool at them and soon had cut down several, which he brought over to Constance. She rummaged in her bag and brought out some rope, which she cut into sections.

Constance rubbed her arms vigorously. "It's getting colder by the minute Craig. You had better get back topside and organize for someone to come down and fetch us. Time is running out and it'll be dark soon. I'll finish splinting her leg in the meantime."

Craig nodded. "I'll leave right away! Will you be okay?"

"We'll be fine! Just hurry please."

Constance went back to the girl and began talking to her. "Okay sweetie, your leg is broken and I have to put a splint on it. I'm sorry, but it's going to hurt a bit. Just be brave, okay?"

The girl bit her lip and nodded. "I'll try," she whimpered.

Mrs Carter got everything ready and then put her hands on the broken leg. "Take a deep breath honey! I have to straighten your leg first."

She took hold of the injured leg gently and began to straighten it. Emma's screams echoed off the cliffs.

Constance gently pushed the bone back into the lacerated limb and fresh blood oozed from the wound. Deftly she cleaned it with more water and began to bind the leg. As she worked, she spoke to the girl. "How old are you, Emma?"

"Fifteen."

"Do you like hiking? I met your family at the top of the cliff and they seem wonderful. You are really lucky to have them."

The girl smiled wanly. "I know that. Mom and Dad like to take my brother Brian and me on hikes. They want us to exercise, not just play with our phones all day. We hike whenever we get the chance."

"That's great! I can see you are very fit. It's good to exercise. Your parents have the right idea."

The girl grinned. "You should be having this conversation with Brian. He's a couch potato. Usually my parents have to bribe him to come with us."

Constance laughed. "I bet he's clever, not lazy. He just wants a reward. Do you two get on well together?"

Emma considered this. "Yes, we do – I mean I really like him you know, even if he is kinda dorky sometimes. Do you have any brothers or sisters?"

"No, it's just me. I'm an only child. I often wondered what it would be like to have a sibling, but I was never that lucky."

Constance finished splinting the girl's leg and stood up.

A larger hovercraft descended to the ledge and Craig climbed out, carrying a wire structure containing a thin mattress. No sooner had he landed on the ledge, when another hovercraft also alighted on the rocky outcrop. Abner smiled at the couple and watched as Craig brought the cage over to Constance and laid it down near the girl. His wife turned the girl over slightly and they slid the structure under her body. Emma was trying to be brave but fresh tears leaked out of her eyes. The couple tied her into the frame and Constance covered her with a warm blanket. She kissed the girl on her cheek and wiped away the tears. "You are so brave Emma! That man over there is going to take you to your parents and then you'll be taken to a hospital. I'll see you in a short while, okay."

The girl stretched out her hand and Constance squeezed it reassuringly. When the cocoon had been placed in the medical hovercraft, it lifted off. Abner took Constance by her hands and smiled. "You were wonderful! Thank you for going out of your way to help this girl."

The woman shrugged. "Someone had to help her," she replied simply.

The trio climbed into the hovercraft and it alighted at the top of the trail. As they landed, the sun disappeared and darkness descended on the group. Immediately the trail was lit up with solar lighting. The teenager was already in the ambulance and her parents and brother were talking amongst themselves. Someone placed a blanket around Constance's shoulders and she smiled her thanks. Abner took Constance by the arm and led her to his ship. Both she and Craig climbed into the craft and left the scene. The space explorer sighed and put her head on her husband's shoulder, closing her eyes briefly as the adrenaline began to leave her body, replaced by a feeling of extreme tiredness.

When they got back to their hotel, they were met by a number of Saturnians who cheered mightily. Constance yawned expansively. "I'm so tired my darling! I want to have a shower and just climb into bed if that's okay with you?"

"You're the heroine of the day, my angel!" exclaimed Craig proudly. "You go ahead and have your shower and I'll order something for us to eat afterwards."

Constance yawned once more and made her way to their suite. Much later she sat with Craig and ate some food, but her body was bone weary. She climbed into bed and fell asleep immediately.

The next morning when she woke, her body was tired and stiff from climbing. She joined her husband at the table in their suite and ate hungrily. Afterwards, Constance looked at her watch and jumped up hurriedly. "Craig, it's late and we were supposed to be leaving within the hour to go to Tanus's planet!"

Her husband took her by the hand and sat her down again. "Honey, don't stress! You were tired so I let you sleep. I've already contacted Tanus and told her we'll only leave Saturn tomorrow. We still have to meet with Lara and learn how to operate the cloaking and speed devices before we go. Don't you want to go and visit Emma in hospital too? Her parents wanted to thank you for what you did yesterday."

"Oh, of course! How is Emma, do you know?" asked Constance.

"I don't know very much. All I learnt was that the doctors operated on her last night and that she is fine, all things considered. Do you want to go and see her now, or later on today? I have to tell Lara and the others when we'll be available to learn more about those devices that were placed on our ship."

"Let's go and see Emma this morning. I'm worried about her. That was a very steep cliff and she fell a long way down it. It's a miracle she is still alive! Afterwards we can go and speak to those technicians."

"Okay, I'll let the hospital know we are available this morning and I'll see what time is convenient for us to visit."

While Craig went to find out when they could visit Emma, Constance hurried to get ready.

They arrived at the hospital an hour later and were taken to meet the doctor who performed the surgery on the young teenager. He showed them into his consulting room and closed the door. He invited them to sit down opposite him at his desk, after shaking hands with them.

"Mr and Mrs Carter, thank you for coming. I wanted to talk to you before you went to the ward. I have to say that Emma was really lucky. Her injuries are quite severe, but she is a strong young woman and should make a very good recovery. As you know of course, she broke her left leg and suffered many contusions and bruises. She does have a concussion, but we have been monitoring her all through the night and it seems to be okay. Also, her left arm was injured. It isn't broken, but the bone is cracked slightly, so we have put a splint on it as well. She also broke four ribs, but none of her organs were damaged, thank the stars! There's a lot of trauma to her spine, but nothing is broken. She's just going to feel very sore for a while. We have stitched up a number of small gashes on her face where we assume several branches cut her as she fell from the cliff. It's a miracle she isn't paralyzed! She fell from a dreadful height! I can only assume that because she's a very fit young woman, she survived the fall. Also, you managed to get to her before it became dark. If you had not rescued her during the daylight hours, she would have had suffered from hypothermia as well. It gets very cold over here in the evenings, as you know. Mrs Carter, what you did was amazing! That young woman is very lucky to be alive."

Constance waved away the doctor's compliments. "I did what I had to, that's all. I'm glad she's going to be okay. Can we go and see her now?"

The doctor stood up and shook their hands again. "You may go and visit her, but she's still a little drowsy from the pain medication we gave her. Her parents are with her as well."

The couple went to the ward. When Mary saw them, she embraced Constance. "I'm so glad to see you. Things were a little crazy last night and when I looked for you, you had already left. I wanted to thank you for what you and your husband did. Without your help, it would have been a different matter entirely. We could have lost Emma!" Mary exclaimed miserably, wiping fresh tears from her eyes. Constance handed her a tissue and she blew her nose.

"Everything is going to be okay now. We spoke to the doctor and he said Emma will be fine in no time at all," she reassured the woman.

"Can we say hello to Emma?" Craig asked Tom. "The doctor said that she might be a bit drowsy though."

Tom smiled and took them in to see Emma. Brian was sitting on the edge of his sister's bed, talking to her. The teenager looked very tired and Constance held her hand. "I'm glad you're okay Emma. You gave us quite a fright, but everything is going to be fine now. You just need to rest and recuperate."

Emma smiled at her rescuer. "Thank you – for everything you did."

Constance could see the girl was very drowsy. She leaned forward and kissed her on her forehead. "You rest and get better soon Emma. I've never met such a brave young woman before."

The teenager smiled and closed her eyes. Craig and Constance shook hands with the couple and left them to take care of their daughter. When they left the hospital, the couple went to eat lunch at a nearby restaurant and afterwards they made their way to the space centre where Lara, Karnd and Jorrel were waiting for them.

They spent most of the afternoon with the scientists, learning about the devices that had been placed on their ship. The couple also flew around Saturn along with another ship which put them through their paces. All the information was placed on a memory stick and given to them. This included the instructions on how to install the device into other ships on Earth. Craig and Constance were amazed how small the devices actually were. They were given a number of the devices to place on their ships which were currently in use.

That night they packed their belongings and stowed them in their spaceship, ready to depart early the next morning.

The day dawned bright and clear and the three scientists watched their friends lift off vertically. Saturn was soon out of sight and the couple began their journey to the white planet where they would spend a few days with Tanus.

CHAPTER 25

They touched down on the white planet where Tanus met them. She embraced both her friends happily and took them to a spare bedroom in her castle. Craig looked at the winding staircases and was amazed by the size of her home. When Tanus had rescued him from his induced coma, he had been too weak to explore the castle. Tanus had kindly given him his own room and bathroom on the ground floor and he had spent most of his time recuperating there.

The newlyweds were given a complete suite on the second floor of the castle. When they had settled in, Tanus took them on a tour of her home. Constance was already very familiar with the layout of the place, having spent a number of months with Tanus, after escaping from Andocia.

Craig discovered it comprised four levels. The top floor was for her helpers and the third floor was where Tanus lived, while the second floor contained the guest suites. The first floor contained the enormous kitchen and also the lounge which was a large and comfortable room where her guests could relax when they were staying over for a while. Although some of the larger suites, like Craig and Constance's, which were on the second floor, had their own lounge where they could rest quietly and not be disturbed, if they were feeling sociable, they could join any other guests on the first floor, which they did from time to time if Tanus requested it. The ground floor was where she entertained the beings from the various planets. Craig was amazed by the sheer size of the place, but after all, she had lived for centuries and therefore had plenty of time to get everything she wanted.

The grounds were spacious as well and Craig smiled when he saw the two swimming pools. The physiotherapist who had been treating him had spent many hours with him in both swimming pools, helping him to strengthen his weakened muscles. One was located outside the huge structure, while the other pool could be found indoors, next to the gymnasium. There was a heated jacuzzi too. The complex was surrounded by a park, which was used primarily by the children of her staff members. Another smaller place stood on the premises and Tanus informed him that her friend Tarmin lived there. Craig could only gape at the sheer size of Tanus's domain. On Earth where space was very limited, this homestead was the size of a whole city on Earth. Their own little flat was situated on the fortieth floor of a high-rise complex and it would probably have fitted into one of Tanus's guest bedrooms.

There were a number of smaller structures dotted around the area, and he was informed that the security detail lived in one of the buildings. Other buildings housed some shops where the staff could buy their groceries and clothing. Craig and Constance were told there was a large shopping mall not very far away.

Later that same day, when the couple had settled in, they joined Tanus in her private lounge. Refreshments were served and the pair exchanged news with their friend.

Craig looked around the spacious room and smiled at his host. "I'm so sorry we were delayed another day Tanus. We were both looking forward to staying with you a little longer, but it was not to be."

Tanus smiled at her friends. "Is everything okay with the two of you? You didn't really explain why."

"I'm sorry if I worried you, but there had been some drama on Saturn and I left Constance asleep in our room – she was exhausted," Craig replied.

Tanus's eyebrows lifted enquiringly and the couple explained briefly what had happened. Afterwards she shook her head disbelievingly. "Oh, you poor dears! You were on holiday and ended up saving someone's life. Well I would expect nothing less from you two. You seem to get involved in all kinds of situations out in space, but I'm glad it worked out well in the end. There will be other times when I'll invite you over here to visit me."

"Even Andocia left us alone, thank the stars!" Constance exclaimed, relieved.

Tanus nodded. "That's good! Well, what's going to happen when you return to Earth?"

Craig shrugged his shoulders. "We go back to work, as normal I suppose."

"Are you both going to return to space exploration?"

The couple exchanged glances. "Well, that is our jobs you know!" Constance replied.

"I know, but I thought maybe now that you are married, you would find a safer job, especially you Constance. I don't have to tell you how lonely space travel can be."

Constance held her husband's hand. "We've had plenty of time to discuss this, but we both agreed to continue exploring space. I love my job and Craig has wanted to explore space from the time he was a young boy. We are used to being apart, so we should manage fine in the future."

Tanus nodded. "I understand. Well I want you to know that whenever you need me, I'll be there to help you both, no matter what the situation is."

"Thank you!" Craig replied sincerely. "It's good to have friends we can count on. How has Andocia been behaving? Is she causing you any problems?"

Tanus smiled, remembering the conversation she and her arch enemy had a few weeks earlier. "She seems to be behaving herself. I've not heard anything about her and I hope it stays that way."

The friends finished their tea and snacks and Tanus excused herself, explaining that she had another meeting to attend. Craig and Constance got up and went outside the castle.

"What should we do first Craig? This place is amazing! I don't think I'll ever get tired of visiting Tanus."

Craig smiled at his wife. "It is a lovely afternoon. Maybe we should have a swim in one of the incredible pools?"

"Indoors or outdoors?" Constance asked.

"I don't mind. Either is fine by me. What's your preference?"

"I like the outdoor one,"

Craig nodded. "Excellent choice! Let's go and get changed."

The couple put on their swimming costumes and went to the pool. Waiters were always nearby and when either one of the Carters needed something to drink, they were served promptly. They sat and sunbathed on reclining chairs and sipped their cocktails. Constance sighed happily. "I could get used to this! Don't you feel like a king, sitting here, being handed everything you want?"

"It's wonderful my love, and we had better enjoy it while we can. Soon we'll be back at work and this will just seem like a dream."

"I know what you mean!" she agreed.

Craig put his arm around her shoulders. "We've been very lucky you know. Our honeymoon has been wonderful. Not many couples get to spend three months away from work and still get paid for it. Commander Simms is a kind man and we are fortunate to have such a wonderful boss."

Constance clinked glasses with Craig and they toasted one another and their boss. The couple spent the rest of their day relaxing around the pool, enjoying the sunshine. That evening they dined with their hostess and after supper retired to their room.

The next day they had breakfast in their suite and afterwards spent some time working out in the gymnasium. At midday they were greeted affectionately by Tarmin, who had returned from completing an errand for her mistress. "It is good to see you both, especially now that you are both so relaxed. When I first met Craig, it wasn't under the best of circumstances."

Craig smiled at their new friend. "None of it was your fault anyway. It may not have been a very positive experience, but at least I got to meet you. Besides, everything turned out well in the end."

Tarmin's face clouded over for a second as she remembered how she had tried to get him away from Andocia's clutches. A few tears dropped from the bird's eyes and fell to the ground. Craig hugged her compassionately. "It's okay! Put this behind you and let's look to the future instead. There are no hard feelings because you were not responsible for what happened to me."

Tarmin stretched out one of her wings and wrapped it around Craig. "Thank you! I feel much better now."

The bird looked at her two friends. "I was wondering if you would like a quick tour of this planet. The last time Constance was here, she didn't want to go anywhere – she was so worried about you, Craig. You, of course, were too weak to travel."

Craig looked at the two females and shook his head. "Maybe another time Tarmin. I wanted to speak to Tanus about something. Why don't you take Constance on a tour and we can get together later on?"

"That's fine with me honey. I would love a tour. You go and see Tanus in the meantime. I'll catch up with you later," his wife promised.

Craig took his wife in his arms and kissed her tenderly. "See you later. Have fun you two."

Constance turned to her friend. "So, what means of transportation are we going to use?"

Tarmin smiled. "Well we could use a small hovercraft, but it is much more fun if you ride on my back. I usually take Tanus around the planet that way."

The woman stared up at the huge bird, but Tarmin knew what

she was thinking and she shrunk down to the size of a small pony.

"As you can see, I'm able make myself smaller or bigger as the situation demands. Sit up near my neck and hold onto my feathers there. You aren't scared of heights, are you? If you are then we can use a hovercraft."

Constance grinned at her friend. "I'm up for the challenge. If that's how Tanus rides, I'm happy to do the same."

She climbed onto the bird's back and once she was sitting comfortably, the bird grew larger. Constance marvelled at how she seemed to fit comfortably on the bird's back. She held onto a bunch of feathers and the bird flapped her wings and rose slowly into the air. Constance let out a whoop of joy. "Oh, my goodness, this is great!"

The bird soared carefully over the planet, going slowly so that her passenger could see everything around her. It was too big to cover in one day, but Tarmin showed her all the highlights. The young woman was surprised to find that the planet was larger than she had thought at first. They flew for a while and then Tarmin pointed out a large body of water. "I am going to take you down there Constance. This is one of my favourite places. I often come here when I just need some time to myself."

The bird landed and Constance climbed off. They walked towards a small cove and the young woman was entranced by the beautiful blue water. When she peered into the water, she saw many different kinds of fish. Strange birds were also flying around. They sat on a bench near the water's edge and Constance questioned her friend. "So Tarmin, what's it like working for Tanus? Are you very close?"

The bird met her gaze. "We are very close indeed. I would do anything for Tanus. I owe her my life. She has been very good to me and my family."

"How long have you been working for her?"

The bird was quiet for a moment. "We have been together ten years now, but I don't think of this as a job. I love her like I do my family, so she is more like a companion and friend to me."

Constance nodded and looked out into the distance where

several water craft were sailing.

"My family aren't here with me," Tarmin replied. "They are back home on my planet. I made a choice to leave them when Tanus asked me to be her companion and friend, but we still keep in touch."

The woman's head snapped around, for she had not asked the bird for this information, but she had been thinking about it.

"Oh ... you are also telepathic," she smiled.

The bird looked ashamed. "Sorry! Forgive me, I didn't mean to eavesdrop on your thoughts. That was rude of me."

Constance stroked the bird's soft side. "You don't need to ask for forgiveness. I understand completely."

The bird began to move away. "It's getting late now, Constance. I'm feeling a little bit peckish and there is a restaurant here that serves the most delicious food. It's warm today and I could use a snack."

Constance's stomach rumbled. "I think I could use something as well," she agreed. "Let's go and see what they have to offer."

A waitress approached them and took their order. While they waited for it, Constance was thoughtful. "I guess I wasn't much fun to be around the last time I stayed here. I was with you and Tanus for several months and not once did we do anything like this. Even when Tanus gave us the grand tour today, it was like I was seeing her home through different eyes. She showed me around her castle and I never really paid much attention before to just how beautiful it is."

"I know exactly what you mean. Tanus and I just watched you and gave you time to sort out your feelings. It must have been so hard for you to be apart from Craig. No one knew what Andocia was going to do, or even if he would live very long."

"Yes, but what made matters worse was that I left the red planet feeling angry with Craig. I thought he had betrayed me and I was furious!"

"It's all in the past now Constance. You came to your senses and realized that he did it for your sake. He was prepared to sacrifice his life as he knew it, so that you could be free. If that wasn't love then I don't know what is. You two are meant to be together!"

"I know that now my dear friend, but it's hard; especially when someone like Andocia keeps meddling in our lives."

Tarmin stretched out a wing and touched her on the shoulder. "You have to be realistic Constance. It's easy to blame Andocia for everything, but you have other enemies as well. If you want to live a quiet and peaceful life, you are in the wrong profession. Being a space explorer is filled with perils. Either you have to live with danger, or you should retire and find a more sedentary job. Are you prepared to do that?"

Constance shook her head. "I love my job. Most of the time good things happen, but sometimes things go wrong."

"Then you have to learn to deal with it."

"Thank you Tarmin! It makes perfect sense when you put it that way. I must have been so boring to talk to at that time."

"We didn't want to intrude. You needed time to heal and that's exactly what you did."

"I'm so grateful for friends like you and Tanus! Thank you for understanding."

"It was no trouble at all." The bird replied as their waiter put the food on the table. "Let's eat – I'm starving!"

While they were eating, Craig was sitting with Tanus. He was pensive and she knew what was troubling him, but she waited for him to mention it. Craig looked at her, already knowing that she knew what was on his mind.

"Tanus, we have been very blessed to have spent our honeymoon with so many of our good friends. It has been wonderful, but tomorrow we have to head back to Earth and life will continue as normal once again. I have been enjoying our honeymoon, but it has always been in the back of my mind that Andocia could come and spoil everything for us. You know her far better than we do. Do you think she'll leave us alone in the future?"

Tanus looked earnestly at her friend. "I know it has been especially hard for you, having to deal with someone as powerful and dangerous as her, but I cannot answer that question. Yes, she is very interested in you and Constance, but you know that anyway. It doesn't mean however that she is going to come after you every second of your lives. She also has a planet to run and staff to take care of. I doubt that you or Constance are her first priority anymore. I think she has found out all that she needs to know about you and Constance. You know that exploring space is not an easy task and there is great danger out here, but you do it anyway because it is your job and you love doing it. I can see that passion in both you and Constance. It's what makes both of you stand out amongst your companions. If you start living in fear, what kind of a life will you have? You have many other enemies, besides her anyway."

Craig smiled at his friend. "You're absolutely right! I'm just being silly. I love my job as you said and I wouldn't change it for the world. I suppose I thought things would be different because I'm now responsible for someone else as well."

Tanus smiled and took his hand in both of hers. "Craig, you and Constance were together for three years before you even got married. The only difference now is that you share the same surname. Constance can take care of herself, as you very well know. Your situation hasn't worsened since you became a husband."

"Wise words Tanus! I always feel better when I share things with you," remarked Craig.

"Don't underestimate your wife, Craig. She's tougher than you think. Share your thoughts and fears with her and be honest at all times. Constance knows you better than anyone and her female intuition is very good. She probably has the same thoughts and fears you are experiencing, but is also keeping them from you."

"I promise not to keep secrets from her Tanus. I'll never give her cause to doubt how much I love her."

"I'm glad to hear it. I'm proud to call you one of my friends, Craig. Remember I'm here to help you if you need me. I can't watch you every minute, but I have your back and will help wherever and whenever I can."

Craig was still thoughtful and Tanus could tell something was worrying him. "Craig, what's wrong? I can tell you are still unhappy about something. Care to share it with me?"

Carter shrugged his shoulders and sighed. "I am worried about something actually. Tanus, do you know what Andocia did to Constance when she forced her to come to her mother ship? I know we discussed this briefly and you told me that it hadn't been pleasant, but you didn't elaborate."

Tanus frowned. "I also told you that Andocia purged the information from her brain afterwards, so she won't ever find out. Believe me you don't want to go down that road ever! Constance will be scarred for life if she knows everything."

"I understand and I don't want to know all the details, but I have something else to tell you. I need your advice."

"What is it?"

"I haven't told anyone this, but after Andocia had been chased away from Earth when she tried to rule everyone, I had a talk with Constance's mother. Andocia seemed fascinated with Constance and kept her under close guard. It bothered me, because she had not met Constance before, yet she seemed very suspicious of her. By that time of course, Andocia and I had already met, yet I had fewer guards watching me. I got suspicious and I badgered Alexis for answers after the danger was over. She told me about the Gregg family history. Seeing as you two are related, because you are twins but centuries apart in age, you must know what I mean."

Tanus sat up straighter. "Did Alexis tell you everything about the Greggs?"

"Yes. I know Constance's secret. I also know that she takes tablets that inhibit her gifts. She knows nothing about this, but thinks they are vitamin tablets. Why would her mother do that to her? Surely Constance has a right to know what she is capable of?"

Tanus looked around her anxiously. "Craig, Alexis did what she thought was right. I don't know why she chose this course of action, but she must have deemed it necessary. Maybe Elizabeth couldn't come to terms with her powers, so Alexis chose to hide these in Constance. I cannot give you an answer. However, consider what would have happened if Constance knew her capabilities and used these gifts. Andocia can read minds as you know, and she would have found out immediately that your wife was special, and killed her immediately, because she would have been dangerous."

Craig sat up suddenly. "Now I understand! I met Beth and she didn't seem to make any sense when we spoke. I now realize why she was so upset when she gave Constance advice, and her granddaughter didn't grasp what she meant. I suppose she didn't know that Alexis had given Constance medicine to stop these gifts from appearing."

"That's probably what happened. You may not like your mother-in-law's decision, but it probably saved Constance's life."

"If you put it that way, then I suppose it makes sense, but something else occurred to me a while after we had that talk, but I never asked Alexis about it. I meant to try and see her again, but life suddenly became hectic and I never got around to it."

"What were you wondering about? Perhaps I can help."

"Well, when I spoke to Mrs Gregg, she mentioned that these 'gifts' or whatever you would like to call them, occurred in every second generation of the Gregg family, but only in the women. I know that marriage is no longer required in this day and age, but both Elizabeth and Alexis married their spouses and usually this means they take the man's surname. Do the Gregg women just keep their surnames perhaps?"

"Ah! I see your dilemma and there is a simple explanation for this. Elizabeth was also a descendent of the Gregg family, but her name was Elizabeth Lambert. She would have acquired her powers by being a second-generation child descended from the original Greggs. Remember, in the early days, before technology and the population explosion, people would sometimes have up to six or more children. All the women in the second-generation group probably had some type of gifts. Say for example a family had six children, three boys and three girls. The girls would have married and the cycle would have continued. As technology advanced and people travelled on airplanes, ships and trains, they would usually emigrate to other countries and perhaps lose touch with one another, but the pattern would be the same in their families. They would never know that the Gregg legacy was various gifts that varied from person to person."

Craig still looked puzzled and Tanus continued. "Elizabeth's great grandfather was a Gregg. According to the family history, he was one of three brothers, and the youngest son in the family. Going through the existing records I managed to discover that the oldest brother had a disagreement with his family and they disowned him. He left and they never heard from him again. He was 19 years old at the time. Obviously, he must have got married at some time and had children. Many years later, quite by chance, Alexis met the estranged uncle's great grandson. They fell in love and got married."

"You must have done quite a bit of digging to discover all of this Tanus."

"I did Craig, because it was important to me. When I met you and Constance, I was so surprised but also pleased to have the Gregg name back in my life. When I first laid eyes on your lovely wife and saw that she was my exact twin, I realized that even though we were born centuries apart, she is a member of the first Gregg family that ever walked this earth. I come from the original generation as well. It must be true because how else could I have found an exact twin so many centuries later. Obviously, the Greggs have intermarried more than once during their existence. We must have many descendants who once walked this earth, so it is not impossible. Records in the very early days were probably lost, or never recorded. Even though Alexis's surname was Lambert, she was also a descendant of the original Greggs, but wasn't aware of this. The fact that history repeated itself, caused Constance to be extremely powerful. If she had been allowed to use her powers, she would have been a force to be reckoned with. Andocia would never have managed to terrorize planets the way she does now."

Carter rubbed his forehead. "Whew, no wonder Andocia put Constance though all those tests."

"Yes, she certainly had her reasons, but I still don't like the way she tried to find out if Constance was going to be troublesome. However, I'm sure you are aware that there are others who have similar gifts, Craig. Many families don't want to advertise the fact that some people are more special than others. They could be all around you on Earth, but you would never know this. I know about the Gregg family history because I am a Gregg as well. Andocia would also know about this, because my powers are similar to hers, so you can be sure she also did some research. That was why she was so keen on running tests on Constance. You know, I'm embarrassed to admit it, but Andocia and I were friends once. We lived on adjoining farms, until the 'transformation' took place. Right until that moment, we were both fully human. After that, we drifted apart. I know you are curious about our history but now isn't the time to discuss it. One day I'll tell you the whole story, I promise. For now, treat your wife with love and care, and never tell her about her 'gifts' either."

"I won't, I swear. Thank you for explaining this to me. I understand perfectly now!"

Craig hugged her gratefully. When they moved apart, Tanus pointed upwards. "It looks like Tarmin and Constance have returned. I have to go and attend to something, so I'll see you later."

Tarmin landed and Constance climbed off her back. Her face was flushed and her hair was dishevelled. Craig stared at his wife and knew he had never loved her more. His wife was grinning widely. "Oh Craig, that was amazing! I cannot begin to explain what it felt like looking at this planet from a bird's point of view. We had such fun, Tarmin and I!"

Tarmin opened her beak to say something, but the two lovers were kissing passionately. She shook her head and whispered. "Goodbye you two. See you later, I guess."

They never saw the bird leave because they were so wrapped up in one another. They made their way to their suite and locked the door. No one disturbed them.

Much later they joined Tanus and Tarmin for dinner. Afterwards the couple went to a nearby cinema complex and watched a movie. They returned late to the palace and found everyone asleep so they went back to their suite.

In the morning, they had a hurried breakfast with Tanus and then packed their spacecraft with all their belongings and some gifts from Tanus. Husband and wife joined their hostess and her friend for lunch and then headed to the spaceport to begin their journey back to Earth.

Tanus went to see them off and hugged them both in turn. "Good luck you two. I wish you good health and happiness always. Never forget that you have friends here. Anytime you need us, we'll be here to help."

"We appreciate all you have done to help us this far anyway, Tanus," Constance remarked gratefully. "We'll remember, and thank you for your hospitality. I'm sorry that due to unforeseen circumstances, we arrived a day later than expected, but hopefully we can make it up with you next time. I'm sorry Tarmin couldn't be here to see us off, but tell her we are going to miss her."

The couple waved and went through to the departure lounge. When they were out of sight, Tanus returned to her palace.

At the palace, Tanus and Tarmin looked skywards. "Well they must be on their way home now, Tanus. I really like them. They are just so kind and considerate. I'll miss them!"

Tanus smiled at her friend. "Yes, I'll miss them too, but life goes on I suppose. I don't envy them at all. Exploring space is something only very dedicated people can do."

On board their spacecraft, the young couple sat in the observation deck and watched as the planets whizzed by. They were drinking some coffee and holding hands.

"Well Craig, in a few days it'll be back to reality for us. The blue universe is still relatively unexplored. I wonder what other beings live here? Maybe one day we'll find out."

"I have no doubt of that my love," her husband replied. "I must confess that I'm ready to return to work. I was getting bored with all the free time – not with our honeymoon," he interjected hurriedly. "I know we have a wonderful and fulfilling life ahead of us."

Constance put her arms around her husband and snuggled closer. "I agree with you. Here's to our future!"

They bumped their mugs gently together. "To us, forever and ever!"

A few days later, Earth appeared on their scanner and they began their descent to Mission Control Headquarters, where they would continue exploring space for their commander in the future.